The Skipper Goes to War

Book One of 'The Skipper' Series

Mark Tissington

Wandering Tree Publications Limited

Publisher: Wandering Tree Publications Limited

First edition 2023

ISBN Numbers:

Paperback, 978-1-7396384-1-2

eBook, 978-1-7396384-0-5

Cover Design: Andrew Rainnie

Dedicated to my wife Christina.
Centre of my world, queen of kindness, source of support
and top notch copy editor.

Preface

When casting around for the subject of my first novel I was spoiled for choice. I've had a number of ideas bubbling away for years but I am so often drawn to the sea that I felt it ought to have a nautical theme. Researching for suitable areas which have not already been covered in fiction, I came across the Royal Naval Patrol Service, 'Harry Tate's Navy'. The achievements of this collection of fishermen and reservists were truly stunning and, as I read deeper, the humour, irreverence and, to be kind, the 'ad-hoc' nature of their training struck me as incredible. Yet, as they had in World War One, this ragtag group of converted trawlers, drifters, whalers, ferries, and even yachts performed miracles; albeit with terrible losses. Set against one of the most fearsome naval foes in history, these men never flinched. They did their duty with dedication and skill but also, I suspect, a kind of humour; perhaps of the gallows variety but humour nonetheless. Whether minesweeping, patrolling or escorting convoys in all the theatres of that terrible conflict, these men could always be relied on. This is a good place to say that I repeatedly refer to 'men' but the truth is that this was the 1940s so the seagoing element were inevitably male: women did not serve on operational warships until 1990. That said, the WRNS (Wrens or Jennies) did every conceivable job other than serving on warships so their contribution should never be overlooked.

So having read about the exploits of these extraordinary men I decided that I'd take one requisitioned ship, with its crew (as was common) and let them represent the whole service. This being fiction I have added a Boys' Own adventure overlay but I have tried to represent the activities of these heroes, so far as I can imagine it, and will develop this through the rest of the series.

If you'd like to know more about the series, writing, offers, and the world of The Skipper, then please subscribe to my monthly newsletter using the link below. You will receive a free ebook, exclusive to subscribers to my newsletter. I ask only for your first name and email address to add you to the mailing list. We do not collect data to pass on, and you can unsubscribe at any time; at which point your details will be removed.

For your exclusive free eBook novella
'The Skipper's First War'
please go to: https://subscribepage.io/zMC2Ri

Chapter 1

54° 16' 5" N, 00° 23' 25" W

(Scarborough, North Riding)

Friday 19th May 1939

Arthur Stainton slowly strolled along Quay Street with a contented smile. He put aside thoughts of ice, snow, and fog for the time being. Their trip to Bear Island was behind; a few days at home in Scarborough ahead. The old houses and other buildings seemed to lean in protectively over the street. Hazy drizzle wet the cobbles, which reflected the warm glow of streetlights. After fishing the Barents Sea, the damp kiss of Scarborough spring rain was pleasant weather indeed. Arthur was of medium height and slightly rounded in the middle, as his wife Elsie put it. Despite the softening belly, Arthur was made of flint if the situation warranted, and strong with it: useful skills in his job as mate aboard the trawler 'Ganton Lass'.

He spotted the sign that he and the rest of the crew revered above all others: The Mariner's Rest Inn. Nights at sea felt less icy if getting home promised a pint or two of Sturdy Mariner: the finest best bitter in Yorkshire, and therefore, of course, the world.

As Arthur's thirst quickened his pace, the door of the Mariner's Rest flew open, disgorging three loud and angry youths, followed by a tall figure carrying a cricket bat. Arthur sighed as he recognised his friend, neighbour, and employer. The street rang with the Skipper's voice, sharp and angry.

'I'll not have you speak to a lady like that, you ignorant thugs. Now bugger off and sober up!'

The men ran off as Arthur strolled up to the scene of action.

'Now then Skipper.'

'Now then, Arthur. Just a minor lesson in manners,' he nodded toward the retreating figures, 'there's a pint in the barrel for you.' The Skipper was tall and slim, with dark hair, slightly greying at the temples.

Arthur pushed open the door to the taproom and the warmth, tobacco haze, and malty smell washed over him like summer rain. He took in the warm lamplight, crackling fire, and gleaming brass work. Young Tilly, who lived in a house nearly opposite the pub, was walking toward him, clutching a bottle of stout and looking shaken. She often fetched one for her Ma, who swore a bottle of stout twice a week was good for the constitution. He held the door open for Tilly, realising she must be the lady in question.

The Skipper strode through the door. 'I'm sorry about those idiots Tilly, they'll not bother you again.' His brown eyes twinkled down at her.

'Thank you, Mr Hurton,' she said. Her eyes flickered away from him, betraying her shyness. The Skipper patted her arm gently.'You're always welcome Tilly, give my best to your Ma,' the Skipper replied.

Arthur smiled to himself. The Skipper should have been some kind of avenging angel from the Bible. Well, assuming that angels cursed a lot and wielded cricket bats as weapons.

The Skipper waited in the doorway until Tilly got to her front door, then re-entered, strolling to the bar. He smiled at Gerald, their friend and landlord of the establishment.

'I think we're done with Excalibur for tonight, Gerald. Also, I suspect Arthur is ready for his pint if you'd be so kind.'

Gerald smiled his thanks to the Skipper, whose full name, Reginald Gordon Hurton, was unknown to most. In reality, it was most frequently used by his mother in moments of frustration. Close friends such as Arthur called him Reggie in private. His crew and most of the old town knew him simply as 'the Skipper.'

Gerald returned Excalibur to its mount on a large and highly varnished wooden board, topped with a crest and the words 'Mariners Rest Fishermen's Eleven'. The team was fictitious. Their local policeman, Constable Nigel Osgodby, had ticked off Gerald some years earlier about his home-made truncheon: the issue under discussion had been Gerald's over-willingness to use it if customers became over-stimulated. Gerald's solution had been to have the display board made and the Constable, unaware the bat was removable, considered the display harmless. Regulars would often whisper, 'There'll be a test match before long,' if unruliness started. As the Skipper had a low opinion of bad manners and a reputation for tough justice, Gerald would frequently hand Excalibur over the bar. Gerald knew the Skipper's reputation meant the need for actual violence was rare. On the occasions where such action was justified, the Skipper delivered it swiftly, fairly, and with minimum damage to furniture or persons, a great boon from Gerald's point of view.

The Skipper sat down at a nearby table, upon which sat a full glass of beer and a folded copy of the Yorkshire Post. Arthur waited for Gerald to pull his pint before sitting opposite the Skipper. He gazed lovingly at his beer for a few seconds before raising the glass reverently to his lips and sucking in nearly half of it in one thankful draught.

'What's doing then Skipper - is Mother alright?' Much of the town referred to her as Mother.

'Not so bad, Arthur, not so bad. Her lumbago bothers her a bit, but no worse than normal. She misses T'owd Skipper when I'm out. You know how it is. What about your Elsie and young Peter?'

'They're grand Reggie. Elsie is relieved we made good time on this trip.' They flipped between first names and onboard titles without even noticing, but if the crew were present, it was always Skipper. 'I recall T'owd Skipper getting a right earful from Mother when bad weather delayed us in a fjord for 2 weeks,' Arthur continued.

'Well, the thing with Mother is that worry often emerges as fury. She can't help it.' They laughed as they raised their glasses to Mother and Elsie.

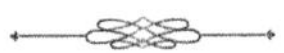

The Skipper and Arthur had started their second pint when their engineer, Svein Bergland, and the rest of the crew strolled in. The Skipper bought his crew their traditional homecoming drink.

'Cheers Skipper!' said George, one of his deckhands.

'Here's to heavy nets - and bugger the Customs and Excise!' called the Skipper. Nearly everyone in the taproom raised their glass in response.

After twenty minutes the crew dispersed: some to wives and families, the younger men to a dancehall. Only the Skipper, Arthur and Svein remained.

The Skipper was puffing contentedly on his pipe, though this simple act led the occupants of the adjacent table to decamp to less noxious seats. Many who endured his pipe-smoke claimed that the 'Pudsey Navy Blend' tobacco, which he ordered in from Leeds, was three parts tree bark, with coal tar, paraffin and something from the compost heap added. The Skipper felt their appreciation of life's finer things was sadly lacking.

The Skipper mused, 'I was thinking Iceland for the next trip but, all things being equal, I'd say returning to Bear Island is the safest bet. It's producing well.'

Arthur nodded agreement. 'Makes sense if the last two trips are a guide.'

Svein prodded the Skipper's newspaper. 'Seems we'd better get in as many trips as we can if they're right about war.' He stubbed out his cigarette.

The three men looked distant, as they considered possible futures. The Skipper was the first to revive.

'Bugger Adolf Hitler, and all the rest! We'll continue as we are, and deal with what comes as it arrives.'

The three men raised their glasses and drank to that.

Just after nine pm Svein passed them their 'nightcap' - a pint of Sturdy Mariner with a large tot of rum as a chaser. Given they had docked at five-thirty am, unloaded their catch and washed down the deck and fish hold before going home for lunch with their families, they scarcely needed anything to help them sleep, but the hand of tradition was on their shoulder.

As Svein sat, 'Tunny' Smith joined them. A grizzled merchant seaman who had cut his teeth under sail, Tunny made a living running well-to-do gentlemen a few miles offshore in his sailing coble to fish for tuna with rod and line.

'Now then, gents.'

'Now then, Tunny,' the Skipper said, sipping the head off his beer.

'I supposed you've heard about yon spy then?' Tunny's eyes crinkled as he scanned their faces.

The Skipper looked hard at him; Tunny had fewer years ahead than astern, but his mind was sound.

'What spy would that be then, Tunny?'

'Nobody has his name, Skipper, but you'll see him skulking around the harbour watching and noting down whatever vessel leaves or enters. It's strange, and quite a few of the lads reckon he's a Nazi spy.'

Svein rolled his eyes. 'Tunny, I've lived here for nine years, got my naturalisation papers and worked for T'owd Skipper, as well as this one. Despite that, depending on who you speak to, I am a Bolshevik spy, a Gypsy king, or part of a white slaving gang. Everyone seemed suspicious until the Skipper here clarified that I was a trusted part of his crew. Then it more or less stopped. Are there any other explanations?'

'I don't know lad, it may just be harbour gossip, but it's odd. We're all keeping an eye out, that's all.'

The Skipper put his hand on the old man's shoulder, 'We'll keep a weather eye open, Tunny. I'll let you know if we learn anything.'

'Fair enough Skipper. Goodnight lads.' Tunny waved as he walked to the door, Arthur and Svein both calling goodnight.

'Can't be much happening if that's top news!' said Arthur with a grin.

'I'm not so sure,' the Skipper stroked his chin, thinking hard, 'I don't believe the spy story for a second, but I am hearing alarm bells. Mind, why they don't just ask him what he's up to is beyond me!'

Chapter 2

54° 16' 5" N, 00° 23' 25" W

Scarborough, North Riding

Saturday 24th June 1939

After their return from the planned trip to Bear Island, the Skipper strolled toward the harbour with his chart portfolio slung across his back. He had picked up some Admiralty Notices to Mariners from the harbour master's office and he liked to make the painstaking amendments to charts undisturbed.

He dressed in his shore going rig; navy blue suit, white shirt, cricket club tie, and flat cap. He liked to dress smartly when ashore, because there was always the chance of meeting Mavis Everley. Mavis was both his heart's desire and the single most frustrating human being he had ever known. As he often thought, 'That lass can bugger up my day, or make it, with a tip of her head.'

Despite walking so slowly he might be taken for a mourner, Mavis did not cross his path, so with a philosophical sigh, he climbed down the harbourside ladder and went aboard his trawler, 'Ganton Lass'. He quickly climbed the ladder and steps to the wheelhouse and unlocked the aft door. The corridor within led to a companionway down to his cabin: a small, wood panelled space, with a bed over some storage drawers, a corner wardrobe and a table. The table had a bench seat behind and drawers underneath because the cabin doubled as a chartroom. Spreading the first chart on the table, he took out his pipe and patted his pockets, looking for his tobacco pouch.

'Bugger it. Where's my baccy?' he groaned. He recalled stowing a packet in the wheelhouse so he retraced his steps. As he opened the wheelhouse door, he could make out a figure standing at the end of the fish sheds. He went inside, grabbing his binoculars from the folding table. He could see the man was middle-aged, dressed in a grey suit and wore a Homburg hat. As he watched, the man pulled out a notebook and pencil.

'Well bugger me, it's Tunny's spy!' Whether it was disappointment over missing Mavis, or the excitement of the chase, in that moment the Skipper was entirely invested in Tunny's version of reality. He reached into the small locker next to the wheelhouse door and pulled out his seagoing cricket bat. This weapon was his security against drunken shore louts, or aggressive patrol boats if he accidentally strayed into foreign territorial waters (as he had occasionally done if the fishing was poor elsewhere). He rushed down to deck level before climbing up to the harbour side, carefully avoiding bladder wrack hanging over lower rungs of the iron ladder. He slowly lifted his head above the weather-bleached wooden beam topping the wall.

The Nazi was still in the same place so the Skipper could stroll undetected, bat held behind him, past the fish sheds. The screeching of gulls hawking around a returning coble effectively covered his approach, and he could get close enough to the man to be confident of stopping him running. At this range, he could make out dark hair and a clipped moustache below the Homburg.

'Now then, Fritz! Turn around and explain what's going on before I turn you in!'

The Skipper's jaw jutted forward, and he held the bat high in the backswing. The man stared ahead, then spoke loudly and with a cultured accent.

'If I *were* a Nazi spy, as you seem to imply, I recommend you don't flag your suspicions by peering at your target through binoculars,' he remarked conversationally, still jotting in his notebook, 'Oh and, for the record, my name is Horace McDonald, not Fritz.'

The Skipper bridled, the bat quivering in anticipation of action.

'Well then Horace, you'll be able to prove who you are with identification, no doubt?'

They heard a pounding of boots and both turned to identify the new combatant. It was a very red-faced Constable Osgodby, approaching at speed. The spy's eyebrows rose when he noticed the Skipper's cricket bat.

'Hold hard Skipper,' huffed the good Constable, 'he's one of ours!'

The cricket bat descended slowly but the Skipper still looked suspicious as the spy pulled an envelope from his pocket while eyeing the red and breathless policeman leaning one-handed against the last fish shed.

'A letter of commission from Sir Warren Fisher, head of His Majesty's Home Civil Service,' he held out the envelope, nodding toward the bat, 'Do you play?'

The Skipper snatched the envelope, leaning his bat against a bollard. It was indeed an official letter, royal crest and all. 'That seems in order, Mr McDonald, and yes, I still get asked by a village team to fill in occasionally if one of the mid-order is unavailable.' he slid the paper into the envelope and handed it back.

McDonald tucked the envelope into his pocket, 'As you may have seen from my commission, I am to carry out a brief survey of long-distance trawlers which may be of utility if war breaks out, as well as determining the number, condition and type of inshore boats to estimate our capacity to feed ourselves should the need arise.'

'I expected we'd hear something about requisitioning. I was deckhand in a requisitioned trawler during the first lot.' The Skipper frowned at the memory.

McDonald smiled sympathetically.

'Unfortunately, we simply can't afford the luxury of maintaining a fleet of minesweepers and patrol ships in peacetime, so we must commission or requisition trawlers if war breaks out. We are starting our preparations now, naturally.'

The Skipper nodded. 'Aye, well, that's what I feared.'

'Well, I'll let you get on, then. You've a bit to do and I'm due in nets,' he glanced sidelong at the Constable, but Osgodby was still too distressed to notice his weapon of choice.

'Actually, I would appreciate some help,' McDonald glanced toward Ganton Lass. 'Might we have a word in private?'

The Skipper nodded and turned toward the ship. As he reached the Constable, he patted his shoulder.

'I should have a word with Tunny if I were you, Nigel. He's got half the town believing the enemy is among us.'

The Skipper and McDonald walked beside the fish sheds, leaving the Constable to recover.

Once aboard, the Skipper led McDonald up the ladders to the wheelhouse. He stowed his bat and collected his tobacco, McDonald frowning and scratching his chin. The Skipper smiled. 'I once had some local louts come aboard in search of the bonded store,' he explained. 'On that occasion, I genuinely was on my way to cricket practice and discovered how a confidently hefted bat makes a fine deterrent.

Since then, my old bat has warned off several wrong-uns and an elk. But that's another story.' He led the way down to his cabin.

Leaning into his tiny wardrobe in the corner the Skipper rummaged for his bottle of Laphroaig. 'I have whisky, the rum is all in bond. It's a good malt, and you're welcome to a drop?'

McDonald nodded, closing his eyes as the soft peat smell filled the small space when the Skipper poured.

'I'm taken to the Highlands and Islands as soon as I smell an Islay malt,' remarked McDonald.

The Skipper smiled. 'I have a pal in Stonehaven who puts a bottle aside if I telephone before we go on a trip. We rarely get to the west coast, so it's helpful. Anyway, how can I help you?'

McDonald put his glass down. 'Of course; thank you for your courtesy. I've spoken to a few of the deep-water skippers since I've been here and your name has come up many times, in a positive sense, I should add.'

'Aye?' the Skipper's eyes narrowed.

'It seems you're familiar with Scandinavia and northern Europe: Iceland, Norway, Holland, Denmark, and France, I'm told?' McDonald's eyebrows lifted.

'True; but so are many others,' the Skipper replied.

McDonald smiled, nodding. 'Yes, but I understand that, as a shipowner yourself, you take time to make acquaintances in those places whereas the others are reliant on their owners to organise bunkering, provisioning, etcetera?'

'Oh, I see. Yes, that's perfectly true, but what of it?' the Skipper stroked his chin, 'and why is it relevant, may I ask?'

McDonald met the Skipper's eyes. 'Skippers who are familiar with continental and Scandinavian ports could be an asset. We believe we understand the route the Nazis would take to reach our shores and we're confident that, with our allies, we would stop their advance, as in the last war. However, we would be remiss if we neglected contingency plans.'

The Skipper stared at him. 'And?' his voice trailed off.

'Well, they asked me to sound out Skippers of trawlers to find out if they will join the Royal Naval Reserve. Especially those with knowledge like yours,' he lifted his hand slightly as the Skipper opened his mouth, 'there are advantages for you. As you know, our navy has no permanent establishment of minesweepers, minelayers or submarine patrol craft and trawlers are just the job. You also know that trawler crews have all the skills needed to both sweep for mines and lay them. You chaps are the best at handling heavy gear from a pitching boat without smashing up the gear or the vessel.' McDonald sipped his whisky before continuing, 'My point is this; if they requisition your vessel, then you and your crew, as reservists, could serve in her. The worst that might happen is that they put a regular junior officer under you. Surely it would be better if you carried on working the ship, rather than a regular officer or conscripted skipper taking over?'

The Skipper's hands were clenching, and McDonald had the uncomfortable feeling that he was gripping an imaginary cricket bat.

In fact, the Skipper was thinking of the 'bowler hatted bugger,' who had addressed Hull fishermen in 1914. Looking across at McDonald under furrowed brows, he said, 'In 1914 owners were told their boats and crews were essential for the war effort, that they would receive adequate compensation if their vessel became damaged or lost. They omitted to say they would assess compensation payable using the date loss occurred, rather than the going rate when payment was due after the war. Food shortages and a rise in fish stocks led to a boom in fishing and a large uplift to ship values after the armistice. As a result, many owners couldn't replace lost vessels, despite their valuable service.' He sat in silence with his memories. McDonald judged it best to let him think.

At last, the Skipper spoke again, 'I understand your reasoning, but the aftermath of the last war was horrific: lost livelihoods, and the hardship our communities went through. It damps down my patriotism, even though I suspect Hitler is a genuine tyrant. I'm not sure I can legally refuse if you want to requisition my ship, and I'll consult my lawyer on that point, but I must warn you, if forced to release her, I would seek an ironclad legal agreement with His Majesty's Government. I'd want it contracted that payment would be for market value on the day of payment, not the day of loss.' His finger stabbed toward McDonald as he spoke.

McDonald met his gaze. 'In fact, your point has already been raised. I am assured the Government discussed this point in the Cabinet and are planning new legislation. The Government intends to negotiate specific terms for requisition with the owner of the vessel. That way, you have a mechanism to include the terms you want. I shall pass on your point to my superiors: they have heard it before, but you expressed it more clearly than most. I'll be here for a couple days. Think about my question and perhaps we can meet before you go to sea?'

The Skipper knit his fingers together, 'I'm afraid I lost my trust in Government honesty in 1918, but I'll speak to my lawyer and perhaps to the crew in the morning. Would you join us in the Mariner's Rest tomorrow evening? I'll treat you to a pint of the best beer you'll ever taste. Then we can speak at leisure.' he reclined a little as he filled his pipe and lit it.

McDonald smiled and nodded agreement, then his eyes bulged, 'Good God man, what are you burning!' He lurched for the companionway as the Skipper slowly followed, puffing contentedly. The Skipper followed McDonald up to the dockside, shaking his hand before returning to his charts. McDonald was still wheezing slightly as they parted, and the Skipper mourned the fragility of the civil servant's constitution.

When McDonald left, the Skipper did his chart corrections, then he sat in his cabin, puffing his pipe. His eyebrows were drawn together, and he repeatedly stood, pacing, as he considered his options.

Later that evening, the Skipper sat with Mother in their parlour, two coloured glass standard lamps and an open fire giving a warm glow to the unseasonably chill evening. He had accepted McDonald's credentials and the Constable's breathless confirmation, but ingrained mistrust of authority still kept him worrying.

Mother sat on the other side of the fire, her knitting needles clicking hypnotically as he sipped his whisky. She paused her knitting, put down her needles, then smoothed down her apron before speaking. Smoothing was a sign she had something important to say.

'Reggie, I don't think you should fret too much about this navy business you mentioned earlier. The fact is, you would probably be called up, anyway. If McDonald said they'll keep the crew together, it seems the best way to go. If the lads are called up individually, they'll go wherever the navy wants them, whereas you'll be able to keep them near you.'

The Skipper nodded as he lit his pipe. 'That's my thinking, Mother. I can look after the crew, and they're led by someone who cares about the ship as well as stopping the Nazis.'

Mother looked over and smiled. 'You're a lot like Father lad.'

A cloud of smoke rose from the pipe. 'Well, I don't know about that, Mother, but thank you.' His smile betrayed his pleasure at such a rare compliment. He went on, 'Mother, would you have a chat with the solicitor, please? You know him better than I do, and he's usually too formal with me. I want to know if I can legally refuse the requisitioning if I feel McDonald isn't being straight with us.' Mother frowned, saying, 'Of course, Reggie. But surely we lose the advantage of keeping the crew together if we did that?' She frowned at the carpet.

'I know Mother. It's just that McDonald felt too good to be true. My gut tells me I can trust him, but my head isn't convinced and so I'd like to know if I have any options, if I feel the ship is at risk.'

'Reggie, you decide what's best for those men and the ship. Father trusted you, I trust you, Arthur and the lads also trust you. So, you stick to your guns lad, and things will turn out.'

For a long time, they were alone in their thoughts. The fire faded to orange and red embers. Occasional jets of flame came from partly unburnt coal at the back of the fire and Mother's art nouveau wallpaper seemed to come alive. Warmth and soft light took effect on the Skipper, so, tapping out his pipe and putting up the fireguard, he ushered Mother toward the stairs.

Next day, the Skipper called the crew for a meeting in the Mariner's Rest while Mother went off to see Mr Blenkinsop. He sat with Arthur and Svein on a corner settee, with two tables pulled in front of them to accommodate the crew. After an initial sip of Sturdy Mariner, the crew sat looking at the Skipper expectantly. He took a last pull on his pipe; the stem making a crackling noise as the smoke billowed upward, then put it carefully on the table.

'Now then, lads. You may have read in the papers that this war is looking more and more likely. I understand Hitler has made speeches saying he's torn up the naval treaty with us and the non-aggression pact with the Poles. So, the Nazis can build as many ships as they want, and Hitler seems intent on attacking Poland. Given we have a good relationship with Poland, I'm thinking war will come soon. When it does, my aim is to hold this crew and ship together. Questions so far?'

Len Egdon, an experienced deckhand, raised a finger, 'How can you hold us together Skipper, won't we be called up?'

The Skipper grunted, nodding, 'That's the thing, Len. I think it might be possible to beat the authorities to the gun. I had a chat with the bloke who Tunny reckons is a spy, and it turns out he's a civil servant surveying for the Admiralty. He says that if we volunteer to join the Royal Naval Reserve, and they requisition Ganton Lass, we can crew her. We'll probably just get a regular officer billeted on us. It seems likely they will requisition the ship in any event, and I'd like to keep us together. I think our pay would drop compared to fishing when on active service, but it'll be a regular income and payment can be split between a man and his family, as I recall. If conscripted, that would happen anyway, so I'm not weighing the pay issue too heavily. Righto; Arthur, Svein and I will have a game of darts, chat amongst yourselves, and let us know what you think.' The crew quietly discussed the idea for fifteen minutes before George, the lead hand, spoke for them.

'We're all agreed Skipper. The reserve is the best of a bad lot. We're with you on this.'

The Skipper and Arthur nursed their pints as they waited for McDonald. Gerald had lit a small fire, and the Skipper watched the flames waving and flaring in the taproom fireplace. Arthur stared at a beer mat in front of him. It seemed to the Skipper that the glowing embers and slowly shrinking flames were a good analogy for their current situation. Mother had confirmed that there would be no way out of the requisitioning process and he preferred more choices than were currently available.

'This war seems powerful close suddenly, Reggie,' Arthur said between sips. The Skipper's gaze lifted, and he nodded. 'It is that, Arthur, it is that. What makes it sting is, twenty years ago, we sat in this room celebrating when the "War to end Wars" was over. So much for that...'

Arthur nodded, 'Aye, well, the thing making it bearable for me is that yonder Hitler is a wrong un through and through. I'll not have my family living under the likes of him!'

As they spoke, the door opened slowly and McDonald entered. He raised his hand to the Skipper and wove his way between tables to reach them.

The Skipper stood, hand extended, 'Nice to see you again, Mr McDonald. Can I introduce Arthur Stainton, my first mate? Arthur, this is Mr Horace McDonald, the man I told you about.'

McDonald smiled, reaching for Arthur's hand. 'A pleasure Mr Stainton.'

'Likewise, Mr McDonald. The Skipper put you a pint in the barrel. I'll ask Gerald to pull it now.'

McDonald laid his homburg and overcoat on the spare chair at their table. 'A pleasant little place. I've been looking forward to the beer you mentioned. I should ask, while Mr Stainton is away, may we speak freely in front of him?'

The Skipper nodded, 'Of course. Arthur is a long-term family friend and has been with the ship as long as I have.'

Arthur returned, carefully placing McDonald's glass in front of him before sliding into his own chair. McDonald took a sip of his beer, his face filling with surprised delight. 'By God, gentlemen, this is indeed a magnificent pint of beer!'

'Well, keep it to yourself or Gerald may get a rush of new customers! We don't want to find he can't keep up with the brewing!' the Skipper grinned at McDonald as he spoke, 'Arthur and I wouldn't fare well if the beer ran out.'

McDonald raised an eyebrow. 'He brews it himself?', the other two nodded. 'It's a hell of an achievement to make ale of this quality!'

They all enjoyed a sip or two before McDonald spoke. 'Well gentlemen, I suppose we should address the business of the evening? Did you give consideration to what we discussed?'

The Skipper looked him in the eyes, saying, 'We did. The crew unanimously agreed after we met this morning. We will join the Royal Naval Reserve on the understanding that my crew will stay with the ship for the duration. I want it in writing that value will be assessed on the date of payment, rather than the date of loss, as I mentioned earlier. We should also be involved with any modifications to her hull or equipment; my engineer has a vast amount of knowledge which no dockyard engineers will possess, so his involvement will make the job faster, but also ensure the safety of the vessel.'

McDonald was scribbling in his notebook, nodding at most of the Skipper's words. As he finished, he looked up, 'Are any of the crew under eighteen?'

Arthur frowned. 'Our apprentice is seventeen. He'll be eighteen in a few weeks. Does it matter?'

McDonald shook his head. 'Nothing I can't deal with. We may accidentally record his birth date wrongly and correct it later if training starts as quickly as I suspect.'

The Skipper frowned, saying nothing.

McDonald flicked through his notebook, sipping at his beer as he did so. He glanced up as Gerald rattled his coal scuttle before swinging it to mend the fire. Sparks fled up the chimney as coal landed on the embers. McDonald flicked back a page. 'Ah yes, there was the matter of compensation for shipowners which you raised yesterday. I made enquiries. An act will be laid before parliament soon. When passed, it will require agreement on terms to be reached with owners of requisitioned vessels, on a case-by-case basis.'

'What's that about starting training quickly?' the Skipper's jaw set and his eyebrows lifted.

McDonald nodded enthusiastically. 'Yes, that's right. The Admiralty think we should get ahead of the game: war could break out quickly.'

The Skipper spoke slowly and carefully, 'So how long do we have before we begin?'

McDonald completely missed the undercurrent of menace in the Skipper's voice and sailed on oblivious. 'I don't know. I should think maybe four weeks?'

The Skipper's voice had increased in volume, and this time McDonald caught the mood, 'So beside asking me to give up my ship, now you're saying we have to forego our livelihood?'

McDonald snapped, 'I did not say that, Mr Hurton! They will pay you at rates set down for Naval reserve officers and ratings, including the time you are in training. Once training is complete, your pay on active service would, I expect, almost match that to be had from fishing. At the very least, it would be a living wage! I shall fetch us another drink while you and Mr Stainton consider what I have said.' With McDonald at the bar, the Skipper turned to Arthur and lowered his voice, 'Listen Arthur, I'm probably being oversensitive, but this feels a bit off. He says he's a surveyor but appears to know an awful lot about policy and training, which I would imagine are well beyond the remit of a requisitions surveyor! I think we'll need to watch this one.' Arthur nodded thoughtfully. When McDonald delivered the drinks, they were sitting upright and looking comfortable. McDonald sat down, and they lifted their glasses to him.

The Skipper was the first to speak, 'Well Mr McDonald, we take your point on pay, but our currently favoured fishing ground is producing well. Given the schedule that you mentioned, we intend making a last trip to Bear Island. After we return, we will present ourselves for training. The three-week round trip should fit very well with your timetable, however please warn whoever is in authority over the training that bad weather is beyond our control and could delay us, though it is unlikely at this time of year.'

McDonald realised the Skipper's tone had changed to 'official business' and it would be unproductive to antagonise him further. He nodded to the Skipper and Arthur, 'Well Gentlemen, I believe your proposal will be acceptable and, as you say, it will fit very well with the likely schedule. I shall warn those concerned that you will enter training quickly and ask them to write to you with full details in the next few days. I assume you won't be putting to sea for a few days?'

'No, I've promised the lads an extra day or two, given we've just done back-to-back trips,' the Skipper stared at the smiling McDonald, 'so I say we finish by enjoying our drinks and talking about something else.'

They chatted amiably for an hour before McDonald excused himself because of an early start the following day. They shook hands as they parted, the Skipper and Arthur heading to their respective homes to pass on the news.

Constable Nigel Osgodby tapped his pencil on the desk. He was aware of the civil servant's activities. In fact, they had instructed him to assist where he could. Despite that, he decided that McDonald strolling into the station at ten pm, demanding a secure line to Whitehall, was beyond the pale. He planned a subtle hint that the station was settling for the night, so he loudly checked the cells. To add emphasis, he made a point of returning via the corridor where McDonald was making his call from an empty office. Not normally a curious man (a trait which had somewhat stalled his career in the constabulary), he clearly heard McDonald speaking.

'Yes sir, I believe this is exactly the team we need. The Skipper and his crew are clearly a close-knit unit and extremely self-reliant. Sorry? Oh yes sir, I'll shall pass that on and will contact you again when I return to Broadway Buildings. Yes sir, good night.'

Constable Osgodby suspected senior civil servants didn't work past six O'clock, but his mind was focussed on the brisket his wife was cooking for supper. Perhaps unsurprisingly, his questions faded from memory in seconds.

Mr McDonald reappeared. ‘Thank you Constable, I’ll be away now.’

‘Goodnight sir, watch your step on the way uphill.’

Chapter 3

55° 30' 15" N 00° 42' 04" W

(Northumberland, Farne Deeps)

Thursday 1st June 1939

The Skipper glared through the Kent clear-view screen, its spinning glass disc flinging off spray, which frequently lashed the wheelhouse windows. They were bound for their usual fishing grounds off Bear Island. He favoured a spot around twenty-four miles northwest of the island where the bottom shelved rapidly and currents gathered bottom-feeding fish against an underwater ridge.

The Skipper's glare was aimed at:

1. The fool who left a wire hawser in the harbour, which tangled around the prop, damaging it;

2. The bigger fool who sold the last standard size and pitch propellor, then compounded the situation by failing to re-order; and

3. The 'mindless bugger' who had caused coal prices to rise by 3%.

On the last point, nobody felt inclined to point out that the said, 'mindless bugger' was probably Adolf Hitler, allied to the threat of an increasingly likely war.

While the Skipper concentrated on glaring, Arthur went quietly about his business: making sure they carried out small repairs, that shelves were ready in the fish room, and Danny had trimmed the bunker. He knew the Skipper would recover his sense of humour quickly, if he just left him to it.

For the last few days, the wind had stayed northerly, blowing at force six, so they ploughed into head seas. The old trawler flung them aside with ease. 'Ganton Lass' was a steam trawler built in 1913 by Hall, Russell & Co. in Aberdeen. At 125ft length and 23' beam, she was smaller and slower than more modern trawlers, though her triple expansion steam engine drove her at 9 ½ knots if needed. Not that the Skipper would drive her hard unless it was very necessary. He was pure Yorkshire and had carefully calculated the revolutions which gave him the most economical coal consumption, so they mostly cruised along at around 7½ knots.

After another hour of fuming, the Skipper found himself able to consider matters other than the architects of his enforced delay, and the cricket bat related solutions he had dreamed up in response.

The news from McDonald had cheered the Skipper after their conversation in the pub. McDonald called at the house, telling the Skipper the Admiralty had recognised the vast sea time and experience which he and his crew possessed. They had decided that prolonging instruction on seamanship was unnecessary, and that they could follow the rules of the supplementary reserve. The result was they would receive a 10 day course in naval discipline and weaponry, followed by five days of practical live firing drills, and could then return to fishing until war started.

The only thing keeping the Skipper awake was thinking of ways he might ensure the safety of ship and crew. He concluded that he and the crew would need to absorb the tactics and training for war, despite their loathing for the formality of Navy life. He knew his crew could turn their hands to anything. Military skills needed to keep them safe were well within their capability.

The noise of Arthur moving snapped the Skipper out of his thoughts. Arthur clumped up the steps with two large mugs of tea.

'If you want the rest of your tea, Skipper, it's on the deck outside,' laughed Arthur.

The Skipper couldn't resist chuckling back at Arthur. At sea, in the company of his crew, he seldom carried worries or negative thoughts for long. He often felt more at peace at sea than ashore. It wasn't about being busy; it was being busy with purpose. Though much of his navigation and seamanship was about preventing disaster, the satisfaction of doing it well gave him that purpose. Pulling his ship through whatever the elements threw at them was a source of pride.

The Skipper looked over his mug toward his First Mate, who was peering out of the starboard wheelhouse window.

'How are the lads taking the plan so far, Arthur?'

'Early days yet, Skipper, but morale seems good. They're happy to be taking a regular wage home, but also there's the fact that we'll still be a crew. That seems to mean a lot.'

'That's it, Arthur. It doesn't make us invincible, but it certainly strengthens us. Did you notice McDonald's reaction? He seemed relieved once we'd sorted out the problem of training. It felt strange.'

Arthur shook his head. 'Can't say I did, Skipper. A couple of pints of Sturdy Mariner is enough to make the world drift by without me worrying about it.'

The Skipper grinned. 'Arthur, I might read too much into McDonald's face for the same reason!'

Toward evening, the ship was rolling hard as she dug her bows into the green walls ahead. Tons of foaming water crashed over the whaleback which covered the foredeck, the spray splattering against the wheelhouse windows. The weir plates on top of the whaleback guided most of the water over the side, avoiding swamping the ship's waist. As her stem rose toward the iron-grey clouds, she crested the wave, rolling back in the opposite direction. The impression below decks was of a violent, twisting, corkscrew motion.

Arthur made his way from his cabin below the wireless telegraphy shack, through the galley passage, and out on deck. Billy was coming aft with some mugs. Arthur frowned. 'Billy, you know better than this! One hand for the ship, one for yourself.' Making sure that he had a hold on the grab rail at all times, Billy worked his way aft.

In the wheelhouse, the Skipper glanced round as Arthur came in. 'Now then Arthur.'

'Now then Skipper, what's doing?' Arthur hung his oilskin and sou'wester over the small teak grating in the wheelhouse's corner.

The Skipper slowly eased the wheel over to counter the push of the next wave. 'Not much Arthur. As the low clears away, this weather should improve. The seas are mainly leftovers from the last few days. As a precaution, I've come up a bit more northerly to give us a good offing as we pass the Norwegian fjords.'

'Thanks Skipper, what's my heading now?'

'013° compass. Thanks Arthur and I'll see you in three or four hours.'

Arthur shrugged. 'If the motion has eased when you wake, have an extra hour. We'll need you sharp when we shoot the trawl.'

'Aye, well I'll see. Thanks Arthur,' the Skipper turned and headed down the companionway to his cabin.

Just under four hours later, the seas had indeed moderated. Earlier, it had been impossible to tell sea from sky, but visibility was now improved. The remaining seas were a slate grey, capped by white horses when an occasional wave broke. Arthur was tidying, religiously looking up to check the view out of the wheelhouse windows as he worked. They all knew of trawlers run down by merchantmen through lack of proper watch keeping. Once everything was to his satisfaction, he resumed his position behind the wheel. A few minutes later, he heard the Skipper coming up the companionway.

'How's she doing, Arthur?' the Skipper said, glancing out through the windows.

'Champion Skipper, champion. The seas started settling an hour after you left, and it's virtually flat now. She's going well and holding her course perfectly. The wind is only force three now I'd say. I've marked up the deck log for dead-reckoning, but you might get a star-sight before it gets light.'

'Grand Arthur, you get away to your bunk now. I've got her.'

The next few days alternated between pleasant sun and misty rain. On the fifth day, they arrived at the fishing grounds. The sun shone on a hazy sea, the water glassy and moving uneasily as the energy in waves dissipated. The crew took the trawls from the net room and thoroughly inspected them. They laid the main trawl by the starboard rail with the spare lashed to port. All lines and shackles were secure and Arthur checked the cod-end knot which was tied by George Sneaton, the lead hand. George had never tied a poor knot, but as the Skipper said, good seamanship is all about checking, regardless.

Arthur traced the rest of the gear and, after a last inspection of shackles on the otter boards, Arthur nodded up to the wheelhouse. The Skipper then yelled, 'Shoot the trawl lads,' and rang the engine-room telegraph to slow ahead. When the trawl was on the bottom, Doug applied the winch brake and Mike clipped the two warps together at the towing block - they were fishing!

There was a three-hour break during which Billy served lunch and mugs of tea in the forecastle and wheelhouse. When he judged the time right, the Skipper yelled down to haul the net. The crew unclipped the towing block and hauled in the warps using the steam winch. With the otter boards surfaced and shackled to the gallows, they hauled the ground rope in on the winch and stowed it. The crew hand-hauled the body of the net to preserve it. As the catch neared surface, they passed a bight of rope around the net and winched in to get the cod-end up. The crew swung the derrick inboard, the net dripping water over them and the deck, then undid the cod-line to release the flopping, wriggling catch. Once empty, George re-tied the cod-line, and they shot the net after Arthur's checks. When back on bottom, they began sorting, gutting, and washing. They then lowered the fish into the fish room, where they shelved them, covered in ice to keep fresh.

This gruelling process continued for hours until the catch on each haul declined or the Skipper called it a day. This was why the crew stayed with the Skipper, whatever the circumstances. A skipper paid by shares of the catch (as in larger companies) would continue shooting and hauling regardless of fatigue. Sometimes they fetched food and hot drinks, even rum, on deck to keep the deckhands on their feet until a skipper felt they had enough fish. The accident and fatality records (such as they were) reflected the levels of exhaustion. The Skipper, like his father before him, recognised one benefit of owning his own boat was that he could look after the crew. Their record showed this made them many times more efficient than other crews. This worked because the Skipper had no ambition to develop into a fleet owner. As long as they all lived comfortably, with enough profit saved to enable him to replace the ship eventually, he was happy.

After five days of fishing, the shelves were full, and the Skipper called time. They stowed and secured gear and, as they readied for the passage home, the Skipper called Arthur up to the wheelhouse. 'We can't hang around, but I'd like to speak to Lars on the way home. I've asked Billy to keep some beef and taters for tonight, which the lads can eat on board while you and I chat with Lars. We won't sleep ashore. After we finish, we'll get underway and give the lads a rest overnight before they check and repair nets. The weather looks settled. Does that sound right to you?'

'No problem Skipper, but what are we discussing?'

'A backup plan, Arthur, just a backup plan. Oh, can you let Svein know where we are going? He may want to slip ashore himself.'

It took four days to reach Slyngøya Island, north-west of Bud. There was a harbour at Talga, the island's largest settlement, but Lars lived in Friyatoft Inlet, a bay west of a hilly promontory which separated the inlet from Talga. There were some crofters' cottages surviving in the inlet, which had a serviceable jetty, usable in calm weather. Lars believed whalers had built the jetty far in the past.

The Skipper had met Lars many years before when seeking shelter from a nasty south-westerly blow. Lars and his wife Anna were a model of hospitality and the Skipper had given them malt whisky in return for the excellent local akvavit Lars had pressed on them. Over time, they returned often, and it was here the Skipper met Svein.

They tied up to the jetty and walked up-slope in the evening light, passing herring boats hauled to the top of a shingle beach, with a small boat store to their left. They walked along a path worn into the grass, reinforced in places with stones. The cottages spread to the right of a wide strip of sheep cropped grass, with trees at the base of the hill to the left. In the centre of the grassy area, a worn path meandered, avoiding dips and boulders as it picked a way past the crofts. Arthur picked out the grassy, damp smell of the sheep as they walked. After a time they turned, walking toward a low croft surrounded by outbuildings and jumbles of farm machinery. The door flew open as they approached, Anna and Lars spilling out. As ever, the welcome was wonderful: all friendship and warmth. Before long, they were sitting around Lars' dinner table and handing over a bottle of scotch.

'Is Svein not with you today, Skipper?' Lars asked.

'Yes, and no Lars. The second engineer was having difficulty after twisting his knee. He needed a cold compress and some rest, so Svein has been standing in for him since yesterday morning. He's snoring in his bunk as we speak.'

That is typical of Svein. He sleeps and misses the party. Was he down there the whole time?

The Skipper nodded. 'When he got exhausted, we sent the apprentice down below to wield the oil can for him. It seemed to work. The young lad understood oiling, so Svein let him do routine work, staying in case of problems. The boy said Svein's head nodded more than his engine!'

Lars smiled, shaking his head slightly. 'Well, this is a pleasant surprise. It's always good to see you; even if Svein won't wake up for his cousin! We weren't expecting you, though. What brings you to us, my friends?'

There was a pause while Anna served up plates of Kjøttkaker, homemade meatballs with potatoes and cabbage.

The Skipper shoved a mouthful of food in and chewed happily, 'Thank you Anna, so delicious!' he smiled up at her, 'As for why we're here Lars, well that's a tough question. In England, the talk is of war and my crew and I must do our bit, as you might expect. We don't object, because we are agreed that we must defeat Nazi aggression. The problem only arises if Britain falls. If that happens, I want to live in a free country. We know Norway will remain neutral, so I wanted your view: would Norway welcome people who are effectively refugees from tyranny?'

'Interesting question, Skipper. As Svein will have told you, we had our own problems with the Norwegian fascist party and antisemitism, although I think they are now well in decline. I hope, considering your friendships here, we could make a case to the authorities for you to stay. Problems could start if floods of people arrive. It's likely, if Britain had fallen, that people would also be fleeing from the rest of Europe. As a country, even if Sweden helped, I doubt we could cope with such a volume of refugees. Also, I suspect that, if the Nazis were winning, our own fascists might reappear. I can make this promise, though: if we can help, you must come to us and we will deal with whatever happens together.'

The Skipper reached to pat the back of Lars' hand. 'Thank you Lars, decent; as always.'

Arthur smiled at Lars, then studied the tabletop for a few minutes.

Lars clapped the Skipper on his back, 'Let's toast!'

The Skipper glanced at Arthur before replying, 'Just one quick toast, Lars. We need to go soon. We have lots of fish for market. You'd be welcome to some if you can use them.' He winked.

Lars belly laughed, 'Fish is the one thing we have plenty of!'

Lars sloshed akvavit into four glasses, then raised his own, 'To peace and friendship!'

They all stood to drink, 'Peace and friendship!'

The Skipper licked his lips, the sweet, herby spirit was wonderful. 'Well now. We have to leave, sadly. Thank you both for your hospitality and especially you, Anna. It was a fine meal.' They both hugged Anna and shook Lars' hand.

As the Skipper and Arthur reached for their coats, Lars opened a cupboard and pulled out his own and Anna's oiled canvas jackets. 'We'll go with you and see if Svein has joined the waking world!'

As they strolled downhill, Lars looked serious. 'A storm is coming to Europe and I pray our lives can return to normal when it dies away.'

The Skipper clapped him on the back, 'If they stick a gun on our ship, we'll have the Nazis sailing home in no time!' Lars raised his eyebrows and smiled.

'Hoy!' a voice bellowed from the jetty.

'Svein!' Lars dashed downhill to bearhug his cousin. 'I hear you have been in bed all day!'

'Ah well cousin, you know how easy it is being a fisherman!'

They switched to Norwegian and the Skipper and Arthur went on board to call the crew and start preparations to leave. They waved Svein away so he could chat with his cousin for a while.

As they hopped over the rail, Archie Lythe, the second engineer, was waiting for them, cigarette drooping from the corner of his mouth. 'I'm as right as ninepence now, Skipper. Your cold compress worked like a treat. I'm fit enough if I go steady on the engine room ladder.'

'Good man, Archie,' said the Skipper, 'If you need help, I'll let you borrow Alf. Oh, and watch your step in the future!'

Archie smiled and limped off. The Skipper couldn't help but compare Archie's attitude with that of some seamen he had met during his apprenticeship.

He smiled at Arthur. 'No backup plan then, Arthur. When war comes, we'll just have to win the bugger!' They both nodded silently.

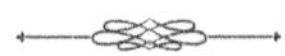

They clambered up to the wheelhouse, making sure everything was ready. The Skipper had already jotted down the course for home once they cleared Norwegian waters.

Arthur detailed a couple of deckhands for casting off and climbed up onto the whaleback to call Svein back.

Once everyone was aboard and the engine room was ready, the Skipper gave a nod, and Arthur told the deckhands to cast off.

Going slow astern in the fading light, they could see Lars and Anna waving before they turned back toward their Croft. They raised their arms in return as the couple merged with the haze.

Once in open water, the skipper rang half ahead and headed north-north-west to clear the Gorseklakken shallow ground. Arthur appeared in the wheelhouse door and the Skipper beckoned him in. 'Can you hold her on 327° for a few minutes, Arthur? I need the heads, so I'll bring up a brew.'

He reappeared five minutes later with two enormous tin mugs steaming in the cooling air.

'Here you go.'

'Thanks Skipper.' The two men sipped at their tea in companionable silence. They could see the light of the buoy marking the Gorseklakken shallows, so the Skipper altered course to the north-west as it came abeam on the port side. After steaming for a further ten minutes, he swung her to port, steadied her on 245° and lashed the wheel.

'There we are, Arthur, homeward bound. When you've finished your tea, would you give the lads a double tot of rum and tell them to get their heads down? We can shake them in the morning: it's open water between us and home now, so they can put their feet up. I checked the fish room, and it looks like we've had an excellent trip. I reckon they deserve a rest.'

Arthur nodded, and The Skipper looked at him with a crease on his forehead. 'Are you alright, Arthur? You seem quiet.'

'I am not so bad, Skipper, just talking to Lars about Britain being overrun, well it knocked me back, that's all.'

'I should have spoken to you first, Arthur. It's been on my mind since we spoke with McDonald and you know what I'm like; make a plan but have a backup. I realised if I'm committing to look after the ship and the lads, then I can't just rely on optimism and patriotism because it looks like Hitler has a powerful and modern army so, while instinct says the British Army can hold their own, I can't help thinking a lot of things have moved on since the first war. There are so many imponderables that I planned for the worst case. Lars' answers suggest I'll just have to do everything within my power to avoid the worst case!'

Arthur nodded, 'I understand Skipper, and I know you wouldn't speak like that in front of the crew, or anyone at home but it was hard to hear, especially given that two or three weeks ago I was still hoping we might avoid war - whatever the papers said.'

'I was the same Arthur, to be honest,' the Skipper smiled wryly, 'but listening to McDonald, I'm more than ever convinced that war is inevitable.'

'We're agreed on that Skipper, anyway there's no point in me fretting. I'll get on down and give the lads their rum. If you're nice to me, I might even bring us one up!'

Half an hour later, Arthur reappeared holding two tiny measures of rum. They downed them in one gulp, toasting victory as they drank.

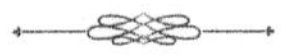

Three days later, Ganton Lass steamed into Scarborough to offload her catch. The Skipper had been right; it was a marvellous trip, and prices were high too. They had done well.

Once offloaded, they moved the ship to her berth and tidied up. Arthur checked the fish room, and the Skipper made sure the logbook was legible. He was cleaning and polishing the binnacle when he spotted McDonald standing on the quay. He opened the port side door and called. 'Would do you like to come on board or shall I step ashore?'

'I'll come to you. It looks like you're busy but it won't take long.' McDonald swung his legs over the edge and came down the harbour ladder to deck level. The Skipper met him with extended hand, and after formalities, they went to his cabin.

'Sorry about the mess,' the Skipper said, pointing at the scattered charts, parallel rule and dividers on the chart table. 'We just got back.'

'I know,' McDonald replied, 'how did it go?'

'Very well,' the Skipper replied, 'prices are strong, and we had a reasonable haul.'

McDonald nodded, 'That's good news Skipper, and I have more good news to come. You're in good time for your training as you predicted. They say you and your crew are to report to HMS Rosebery near Sutton-on-Sea in Lincolnshire on the first of August. You will be subject to ten days' training for entry to the Royal Naval Reserve. On passing out of the course, yourself and your crew will receive ranks with commissions or warrants as required, and will then undertake a five day naval gunnery course.'

The Skipper smiled tersely. 'Capital, Mr McDonald. Thank you. I'll impress the importance of absorbing the training on the crew. I know from my experience that they will probably kick back against authority at first, but the training, especially gunnery, might save lives once war is upon us.'

'Good to hear, Skipper. Thanks. They asked me to give you this,' McDonald said, handed over a bulky manila envelope. 'it contains the rail travel warrants, and various letters with joining instructions for both yourself and your crew. You may notice I made a slight error with young Cloughton's birthday. I'd be grateful if you could brief him so that he can answer that question without thinking.'

'I'll do that. One thing, why did they land you with this? I understood you were surveying.'

McDonald paused. 'Do you know Skipper? I don't have the first clue! I simply do as I'm told habitually. It must be a civil service thing. You're quite right though, this is actually outside my remit, but I doubt any complaint would go far!'

The Skipper laughed, 'Well now you know how I feel when the Ministry of food ask me to fill out damn-fool paperwork. Silly buggers to a man if you ask me!'

McDonald coughed into his hand. 'One would not want to be disloyal to one's masters, Skipper, as I'm sure you would agree, so I shall gloss over that one.' He winked broadly as he checked his wristwatch. 'Thanks for your time, Skipper. You'll be wanting to finish tidying up, so I'll be off. All the best to the crew.'

'Good Day to you Mr McDonald.'

As McDonald left, the Skipper felt an emptiness, perhaps even foreboding; but they had agreed, so he would follow it through to the best of his ability.

Chapter 4

53° 17' 3" N, 00° 17' 30" E

(Shore Base HMS Rosebery)

Tuesday 1st August 1939

The Skipper and his crew huddled in the drizzle before an impressive gold crested sign marked 'HMS Rosebery'. Once past the sign, the word impressive seemed a bit of a stretch. The blue-grey painted bus which had brought them from Mablethorpe railway station drove away, and they felt abandoned as the bus whined away into the mist, its gears clashing.

The Skipper scratched his head. 'Bugger me lads, this "ship" is a holiday camp. Somebody is having us on!' he looked disconsolately at some grey-painted huts behind a peeling swimming pool building. 'Well, the sign can't lie, so come on, let's find out the worst.' They shouldered their kit bags and walked through the gate. They expected some sort of guard, barbed wire perhaps, at least some sign the military was in residence, but there was nothing. As they passed through the gate, shaking their heads, there was no sign or notice, so they took aim for the double doors of the swimming pool. The only thing looking cared for was the lawn, which they strolled across. They jumped, startled, as they heard a furious voice bellowing, 'MAN OVERBOARD! MAN OVERBOARD!'

The Skipper held his head in his hands. 'Who's this silly bugger? We're a quarter of a mile inland!'

The deluded individual arrived, red faced and sweating. 'Who the HELL do you think you are walking across the GRASS?'

'I'm Reginald Gordon Hurton, owner and skipper of the trawler "Ganton Lass, SH.423" are you the groundsman? It's just that I didn't see the crease, so I never guessed...'

'SHUT UP! I am Chief Petty Officer Rose of HMS ROSE BLOODY BERY!'

The Skipper held his gaze and replied in a low voice, 'Now hold hard old lad, they sent here us because we volunteered but much more of this and we can always un-volunteer.' Muffled snorts sounded behind the Skipper.

Chief Petty Officer Rose seemed about to burst. Veins stood out on his neck and his right eye seemed to bulge out, seemingly in danger of leaving the socket altogether. Fortunately, a fresh voice entered the fray.

'I say, Mr Rose, would you bring those chaps over please?' The speaker was tall and slightly stooped, dressed in a naval uniform.

Mr Rose snapped to attention, bellowing 'SIR, RIGHT AWAY,' his gaze tracked over the crew, 'You heard the officer, MOVE YOURSELVES!'

George, the Lead Hand, chose this moment to ask the apparently burning question, 'Skipper, shouldn't he be wearing a hat when he's outside? I mean, in the movies...'

'I SAID SHUT UP!' Mr Rose's sense of humour seemed once again to be rapidly ebbing.

The Skipper turned and glared at George, but his eyes twinkled.

Mr Rose led them to the swimming pool entrance, and they heard him muttering something to the officer about 'apologies' and 'without my headgear.'

The officer beamed at Mr Rose. 'Not at all, dear boy, fear not. You might do me a favour, though. The chap you detailed to "man the brow" I think you called it, well, he seems to have sauntered off and left his rifle in the guard post.'

Mr Rose quivered, the veins once again in evidence. He dashed inside and returned wearing a dark naval cap, before sprinting off toward a small hut resembling a privy which stood near the entrance gates. The Skipper sighed with relief, realising his crew had missed what would have been the unguarded souvenir of a lifetime. He paled at the idea of Gerald armed with a Lee Enfield, even unloaded.

The officer spoke again, 'Come on in chaps, let's leave Mr Rose to what he does best.' They filed in by twos through the double doors. It surprised them to find what was clearly a hotel lobby rather than a municipal bathing facility. 'Now, I'm Commander Vincent and I'd like to welcome you all to HMS Rosebery. It was called "The Excelsior" before the Navy took it over. I'm not sure either name really fits. What!'

The Skipper strode forward, hand extended, 'Commander Vincent. I'm Skipper Hurton of the trawler "Ganton Lass, SH.423." Good to meet you.'

'Ah yes, I was told to expect you with this intake. Welcome Mr Hurton and welcome to you all,' he beamed at the rows of faces in front of him, 'I'll take this opportunity to reveal my thoughts to you, if I may. Your seamanship and expertise are beyond anything that most naval officers could ever aspire to, so, as you'll be aware, you gentlemen are on a drastically shortened induction to the reserve. The downside of that situation is that the remaining syllabus is all about tactics, gunnery and, I'm sorry to report, naval discipline and tradition. Now I worked with trawlermen in the first war so I know that naval discipline is pretty low on your list. They sent Mr Rose to us because the top brass want some level of, well, uniformity I suppose is the right word. Anyway, Mr Rose and his marching, saluting and the rest, well, it's a necessary evil. To spread the pain, we've organised the syllabus so that foot drill is first thing in the morning, with a brief lecture on naval tradition and discipline afterward. From ten a.m. onwards you'll be doing gunnery and some small arms range practice every two or three days. This is important for any vessels who may become involved in minesweeping because rifles are used to crack the mine casing and sink it. I'll pass you on to the paymaster and purser who will organise uniforms, gear and billets for everyone.'

Two hours later, they stood holding piles of blankets, sheets, uniforms, and boots. They topped off the whole wedding cake with a cap. The Skipper and Arthur got peaked caps, the rest of the crew got standard ratings caps. Everyone had white ribbon to put around their hatband, denoting they were trainees.

They gave the Skipper and Arthur single rooms, while the rest of the crew bunked in an eighteen man barrack room. The barrack was clearly one half of a dance floor: the dividing wall sat on a thick pine plank, presumably there to protect the floor beneath. Leaving the barrack room via the rear door gave access to a corridor leading into the other half of the dance floor. This half formed a lecture theatre. They had put rows of chairs in front of the low stage and the back of the lecture theatre contained several tables with chairs around them.

There followed an afternoon of complete torture for all hands. They got a haircut, regardless of whether they needed it, then learned the right way to wash and iron the uniforms, polish their boots or shoes, and wear their caps. The instructor ignored the Skipper's wry comment 'On their heads would be my guess.' Finally, they were all required to sign the Official Secrets Act and given a ten-minute talk about the dire consequences of 'loose talk.'

That evening, the Skipper and Arthur were told to read a booklet containing guidance on standards of dress, etiquette, dealing with defaulters, and leadership. They sat in the Skipper's room reading, alternating between shocked disbelief and uncontrolled laughter.

The Skipper had remarked on the Tannoy speakers in corridors and the barrack room. Arthur suggested they allowed Mr Rose to warn everyone if they spotted a submarine in the field next door, while the Skipper, in a moment of rare optimism, suggested they would play relaxing piped music. Next morning, however, they learned the awful purpose of the speakers: 'Reveille, Reveille! the time is 05:45. Reveille, Reveille!' The broadcast was bad enough, but then came an appalling ditty on a bugle.

They had been told to square away their bed spaces when they woke, prior to an inspection being made. When comparing notes afterwards, the Skipper and Arthur got the best of it when an unseen voice shouted 'Officer on Deck!' and a relaxed but slightly bleary Commander Vincent strolled in. He glanced around their rooms muttering, 'Good, very good, capital' with minor variations, and rounding off with 'first class!'. After offering some gentle suggestions on correcting their dress, he told them he didn't see the necessity to repeat this exercise every morning, then strolled off for breakfast.

Things were different in the barrack room. Mr Rose announced his presence by screaming, 'STAND BY YOUR BEDS!' from the doorway before conducting his inspection. The only sounds were the crash of lockers being flung open, thuds as Rose flung around inadequately polished boots and a constant stream of words such as FILTH! DISGUSTING! REVOLTING! and UNBELIEVABLE! He rounded off by turning smartly around in the doorway and remarking, 'You lot should have joined the bloody AIR FORCE!' before storming out.

They ate breakfast in a communal mess-hall, which still bore the legend, 'Sunshine Restaurant' over the entrance door. To their surprise, it was very palatable.

After breakfast, things deteriorated rapidly. Mr Rose was at full volume and began by teaching how to sort themselves in order of size, then form up in three ranks such that the tallest were on the ends, with the smallest in the middle. He began marching them back-and-forth across the parade square, which appeared to be tennis courts with nets removed. Mr Rose called the cadence. It seemed remarkably important to him they should march at the right speed. They hit a glitch when they tried turning to prepare for marching: young Alf understood port and starboard, but apparently left and right proved challenging.

After a tea break in the NAAFI (which looked like it was an ice cream kiosk with small tables and dining chairs placed outside), they attended their first lecture, an overview of the role of trawlers in World War One. The Skipper and Arthur felt it was slightly dramatised, but the roles were correct.

Another lecture followed lunch: a PT session, which was mostly on-the-spot exercises. They had tea-break, then a last lecture on the mechanics of minesweeping. At the end, Commander Vincent entered, his presence announced by Mr Rose with, 'ROOM, AH-TEN-SHUN!' at roughly the volume of a foghorn. Commander Vincent was more serious than they had seen him before.

'I wanted you to get into the routine before I spoke. You now know how the day goes; aside from Sunday, when there is a church parade instead of drill.' Mr Rose visibly flinched at this announcement. The Commander continued, with a glance toward him, 'You gentlemen represent your industry: intelligent, independent, hardworking and tough. As a retired naval officer who was only recently reinstated because I had pursued a career in teaching after my service ended, I respect those qualities. However, there is one thing that I wish to highlight. Civilian vessels requisitioned by a Government are in a somewhat precarious position. If the crew are in uniform and subject to military law, then they are legally a combatant vessel. Otherwise, they would be classed as merchant vessels, and therefore not at liberty to attack warships of other nations. Gentlemen, this is important: the Nazis, or any sovereign nation, could apprehend you and the best you might expect would be internment. The worst could be a firing squad. So whatever your views, and I know from experience that they will often not completely align with the traditions of the Royal Navy; yes, THANK YOU Mr Rose, your protest is noted! Even though some of this course may slip from memory, I implore you to wear a uniform at all times when in active service. If you are more comfortable in your own oilskins, then so be it, but please ensure that you have service dress underneath and wear your naval cap. I witnessed the bravery and achievements of the reserve in the first war. It would be a shame if your efforts, which I am certain will be equal to theirs, were to end in a shabby death. Thank you all.'

Despite themselves, there was a ripple of applause as he left, the thunderous face of Mr Rose following behind. As they left for dinner in their mess later, they saw a bunch of lads putting a striped barrier pole across the entrance. They had also erected a flagpole on the grass, which now flew the white ensign.

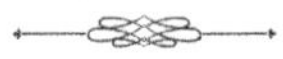

And so they fell into their routine. The man they saw as a wet blanket on first meeting had emerged as a thoughtful and intelligent leader (though the absent minded schoolmaster occasionally swamped the naval officer). Mr Rose was, well, he was what he was. To his credit, though, once he started small arms instruction, he mellowed slightly, at least when off the parade ground. On the second evening, the Skipper had to ask them not to wind Rose up deliberately, otherwise they would be likely to lose the small amount of leisure time at their disposal to peeling spuds or painting kerbs. The days rolled on, mostly in routine dullness.

Other intakes arrived, trainee numbers growing, but they realised they had been the first.

With two days left on the course, they sat for a brief examination on what they had learned. In addition, they went to the rifle range where, firing from a prone position, they aimed for the bullseye and tried to achieve the tightest grouping possible. The star of the show was Arthur. He made a hole about the size of a shilling right in the centre of the target. It impressed even Mr Rose. After they had cleaned their weapons, the Petty Officer running the range gave the Skipper a list arranged in order of their groupings. He suggested the Skipper could use this list to decide who was most suited to shooting at mines, if they ended up minesweeping.

On the last day, the morning drill session comprised performing the evolutions they had learned; culminating with marching past and saluting Commander Vincent, who stood on a dais in front of the flagpole. This, according to Mr Rose's first attempt at humour, was their passing out parade, even if nobody fainted. In the afternoon, Commander Vincent gave them a recap on the course, and they received travel warrants for the following morning to take them to Southend-on-Sea, where they were to practise using two-pounder, nine-pounder, and twelve-pounder guns on practice buoys.

They 'fell in' in front of the flagpole as they waited for the bus to the railway station next morning. Commander Vincent shook every man by the hand and wished them good luck before they left. When he came to the Skipper, he looked him in the eyes, saying, 'I can see you have their best interest at heart, Skipper. I don't have to tell you to look after them; so I'll wish the very best of luck, both to you and to your ship.'

'Thank you Sir, much appreciated, and I have every confidence my crew will do their part.'

Vincent nodded, 'Well said Skipper. Here's the transport now. Enjoy the fizz bangs!'

As he watched the crew climb onboard, the Skipper could see a real spring in their step. Perhaps military life had some benefit after all. Alternatively, maybe it was just easier than hauling nets in bad weather! He spent much of the journey studying the pack of papers the paymaster had given him before they left. Much of it was routine admin and confirmed that they would designate him as 'Skipper RNR' and Arthur as 'Chief Petty Officer, RNR.'

The weather brightened as they travelled and the entire crew was in good spirits when they arrived at Southend-on-Sea station where, once again, they boarded a bus for transfer to Shoeburyness range.

Shortly after passing the garrison church, they disembarked on a parade square where a naval lieutenant waited for them. The young officer showed them where to go to present themselves at the barracks and pointed them toward the essential places, like their accommodation block and messes. He instructed them to report to a Lieutenant Matheson at 0900 the following morning. This Royal Artillery officer would supervise their live practice firing.

After stowing their gear and changing, the Skipper suggested they explore the local area and find some decent grub. They found a little inn nearby, which served pie and peas until eight. After sampling the local beer, they switched to bottled stout: the local bitter did not compare well to Sturdy Mariner. The pie and minted mushy peas with creamy mash were a triumph, however. The Skipper suggested they turn in relatively early, as they would handle live ammunition the next day.

On returning to their room, the Skipper and Arthur indulged themselves in a tot of rum. They chatted for a while about home, making tentative plans for fishing: it was hard to be precise without feedback from returning boats. The Skipper leafed through his gunnery notes to make sure that it was fresh in his mind, while Arthur wrote a letter to Elsie, making sure he asked her to tell Mother the Skipper was well. He knew the Skipper wasn't much of a letter writer himself. Despite the unfamiliar surroundings, they both fell asleep quickly that evening.

They woke feeling refreshed the following morning and made their way to the mess. After breakfast, they rounded up the rest of the crew and walked around the parade square to where they had met Lieutenant Matheson. The young officer duly arrived just as a green bus pulled onto the parade square. 'Bugger me lads, we've spent more time in buses than in boats since we joined the Navy!' grinned the Skipper. During the journey, Lieutenant Matheson explained some of the history of the range and told them that their first task would be to master the Lewis gun, which they would clamp to the bridge rail, to provide some level of anti-aircraft protection. After that, they would work up through two, six, and twelve-pounder guns until they were proficient in loading, aiming, and firing them all. The entire crew would fire the guns live, but they would give the deckhands most of the practice time on the larger guns. The lieutenant turned to the Skipper and Arthur, 'You gentlemen will get extra time on the Lewis guns as, I'm told, your position is closest to them.' He advised everyone to make sure they stuffed cotton waste into their ears when firing.

They memorised the range rules in a well-used Nissen hut. After that, they learned about deflection shooting by sitting on a kind of bicycle seat attached to a model gun mount. A metal frame with paper stretched upon it moved around in front of them and when they pulled the trigger, it fired a ball bearing like an air gun. They quickly learned the art of aiming in front of the dot in the middle of the sheet of paper in order to get closer to their target. At a dummy six pounder breech, the teamwork needed to load the dummy round and remove it after firing was ground into them by repetition.

When they mastered the routines, they found themselves in a concrete emplacement with a plinth, on top of which was mounted a Lewis gun. They practised changing the drum before each man fired the weapon at a nearby buoy. The instructors then took the deck hands to the two-pounder installation. As the days went by, they alternated between classroom instruction and drills with two more days when they practiced live firing. By the end of the course, their confidence was much improved, but the Skipper knew they would need frequent practice to keep them sharp.

After packing up their kit bags, they were told to wait in an empty room inside the administrative block until a bus arrived for transfer to the station. The Skipper was filling his pipe when an orderly popped his head round the door, asking, 'Mr Hurton?' the Skipper stood as the man continued, 'Could you spare a moment please, sir?'

The Skipper followed the young soldier, who escorted him to an office along the corridor. As the door opened, the Skipper froze in mid-step. Behind the desk was McDonald, dressed in an army officer's uniform! Recovering his wits, the Skipper strolled into the room and sat down on the chair opposite McDonald. 'Either you're the fastest bugger ever to be commissioned, or you've got some explaining to do.'

McDonald's face betrayed nothing. He met the Skipper's gaze, 'Sometimes Skipper, it is necessary to take extraordinary precautions in the national interest. The truth is very simple. During the last lot, I was a young subaltern within army intelligence. They asked me to work with the Foreign Intelligence Service, which eventually became known as the Secret Intelligence Service. I remained within that organisation for years, so I really was a civil servant, but more recently, they reinstated my commission. I am now one of a team who liaise between my organisation and military intelligence. We try to share information and avoid buggering up each other's operations.'

The clock on the wall sounded very loud as he paused. 'I can tell you this now you have signed the Official Secrets Act. War is coming, almost certainly. As in the first war, trawlers will be needed. All this you know. What you will not know is this: beside the demand for suitable craft within the Admiralty, we in intelligence have very specific needs. We will need extremely trustworthy and self-reliant men to help transfer people and supplies to or from operational theatres. I can't give you a detailed picture at the moment, partly because the situation is fluid, but also because I am restricted to giving you an overview. As things stand, you won't need more until you become operational.'

The Skipper blew out a slow lungful of air, shaking his head as he did so. 'Well, I'll be buggered. Tunny was right: you are a spy!'

They both remained silent for a full two minutes as the Skipper processed what he had just learned. The ticking clock threw away the seconds with hollow clunks. 'I suppose my ship and crew will be in harm's way more than we would've been?'

'Not really, Skipper. You know yourself that minesweeping can be a very nasty business. We lost a lot of trawlers in the first war trying to cut the cables of mines. Submarine patrols or convoy escort can be equally difficult. I know you have the wellbeing of your crew and their families in mind, however, I don't believe the work we give you will be any more dangerous than that which the patrol service undertakes. Given that, and the fact you will perform routine patrol service duties in between our operations, I'm only really asking you to accept a level of risk that you were taking on already.'

The Skipper's hard stare softened somewhat. 'I can see your point, but if we're involved in espionage, surely my lads would just get lined up and shot?'

'Well, Skipper, I asked Commander Vincent to underline the importance of wearing uniform,' the Skipper's eyebrows shot up, 'and of course you will have enough military equipment on board so there would be no suggestion of involvement with espionage.'

The Skipper rubbed his eyes. 'Well, if that's the job, then so be it, but I want an agreement between the two of us. I know you can't share all your secrets, but I need to know that we're finished with me and my crew being puppets. You give me a job, you tell me what outcomes you need, what the dangers or threats are, and when you need it finished; then let me get on with it. I've agreed to serve during hostilities, and that's what I'll do, but I can't work for somebody who manipulates, rather than leads. We're all human beings and deserve some basic respect, even while working in a situation as grave as the one we are likely to face,' he glared at McDonald, 'we don't expect to be privy to the whole picture, just the points that apply to our part in the plan and the safety of the ship.'

McDonald tapped his teeth with a pencil, 'Skipper, I understand your feelings, but please understand that I had to be sure of your character and abilities in training before I could reveal more, and until you signed the Official Secrets Act I could say nothing. I can make this promise: I will always give you as much information as you will need to do your job, and as much background as is safe for you to know. Agreed?'

The Skipper nodded, his lips tight, 'Agreed.'

'Good show,' McDonald smiled, his shoulders relaxing. 'Now, I was particularly interested in you because of your knowledge of countries bordering the North Sea and the Barents Sea. As you know, it will be hard to make predictions, but the Nazis will advance in much the same way as they did in 1914, and indeed, we should stop them in the same way. In that case, we will need intelligence related people and equipment moving to France and the Low Countries without fanfare. There is also a suspicion the Nazis might have some interest in attacking Scandinavia. I must insist that this information remains strictly between us. I know your Chief Engineer originated from Norway and I assume that possession of this knowledge would put him in a difficult position regarding warnings to friends or family, but frankly, we don't consider it the most likely of scenarios. Until we know more, I'd like it kept between us.'

The Skipper nodded. 'So, will we be involved immediately? I was hoping for some workup time initially.'

'Definitely not Skipper. You'll need time to get used to the new roles and I imagine there will be more training. There is another thing. We spoke with the Admiralty, intending to reduce the number of regular naval officers on these special duties vessels, but they were adamant that at least one officer and one signals rating would be required on every special-duties trawler. We resisted initially, but they pointed out that the Navy has very specific rules and procedures for signals, both visual by Aldis lamp, and using wireless telegraphy. They said that a signals rating to use the equipment and an officer in charge are the bare minimum they will accept.'

'Fair enough,' the Skipper smiled, 'it's what we were expecting. Although I hadn't thought of the signals bloke. It's probably a good thing, mind: neither Arthur nor myself would ever win a morse code competition.'

McDonald laughed, handing over a piece of paper. 'Your transport will arrive soon, so we had better wrap this up. This is a telephone number where you can reach me, or leave a message. Just ask for Captain McDonald. I'll be in touch when I have anything to report. Finally, I'd like to thank you for your understanding Skipper. We agents of the state often dwell too much in secrecy and mistrust. I knew you were sound but rules and prudence meant I had to hold back. I suspect your world is much cleaner than mine.'

As the Skipper turned, he took in the shelves of beautifully bound books on the walls. He realised, with sadness, there were more books dealing with ways to kill people, than there were about living together amicably.

Chapter 5

54° 16' 59" N, 00° 23' 25" W

(Scarborough, North Riding)

Sunday 20th August 1939

The Skipper awoke to the sound of his alarm clock at 6 a.m. He stretched, feeling lazy; a real contented Sunday morning feeling.

He had enjoyed a slow Saturday after their late arrival on Friday evening: there had been changes and delays at Kings Cross and Doncaster. He'd allowed himself a lay-in until 7a.m on Saturday morning and after a good long chat with Mother and a read of the newspaper, he had taken a slow walk down to the harbour to check over the boat. His stroll became much more enjoyable when he bumped into Mavis.

'Hello, it's Reggie Hurton. I thought that you'd joined the Foreign Legion!'

As usual, the Skipper's brain went to mush when Mavis spoke, 'Well, in a manner of speaking Mavis. We joined the Navy, well, sort of: it's the reserve. Anyway, we've been away doing some training.' Her auburn hair and greenish eyes gave her a striking beauty.

Mavis giggled like a teenager. In the Skipper's estimation, this was a move calculated to find out whether she could get his legs to buckle, and she damn near succeeded. He resolved to have some stern words with himself later. Mavis went on, 'Aye, there'll be a lot of that soon, I expect. Oh, will you be in church tomorrow? The Vicar asked as many of his flock to attend as possible. I'm going early with my Ma to do the flowers: shall we save seats for you and Mother?'

'Oh, that'd be champion Mavis, champion. We'll be there, definitely,' the width of his grin would have caught herring if he'd been swimming.

She tutted, 'Listen to you Reggie, a service to pray for our country and you say Champion!'

He reddened, 'I was talking about the company Mavis, as well you know.'

'Well, I'll have to leave you to your ungodly thoughts Reggie Hurton, this lamb's liver won't buy itself and I must get back to the Post Office!' she spun away and clicked off up the hill in her weekend high heels. Later, the butcher remarked to his lad that he couldn't recall having seen Mavis smile so much.

Saturday ended well with Sturdy Mariner and a good chat near the fire with Arthur and Svein.

The Skipper was careful with his ablutions, making sure he was well shaved and applying a small quantity of hair oil as he combed. He also made sure that his shoes were spotlessly clean and shiny, as well as checking the creases on his best trousers. Once satisfied he would pass an inspection from Mavis, he thumped downstairs for breakfast.

Mother was in fine form, with two rashers of the finest bacon, two Yorkshire pork and herb sausages, a slice of fried bread, and a fried egg.

As they ate, the Skipper thought about Mavis and their patchwork history. They had been sweet on each other at school but, what with his need to learn fishing and his apprenticeship in Hull, not to mention the first war, well he simply hadn't been attentive enough. The result was that she had a long engagement to another school friend, David, who had drowned at sea three months before their planned wedding. He had stayed clear of Mavis out of respect to David and fear of annoying Mavis, but in his heart he felt he should have been more of a friend to Mavis in her grief.

The clock advanced achingly slowly toward nine-forty until at last it was time to leave. With Mother on his arm, he strolled up the hill, turning left and heading for Saint

Mary's. They left in plenty of time, but the church was already busy when they arrived. Fortunately, Mavis had been as good as her word and stood waving from the fourth row back when they entered the church. Once inside, the Skipper's plans went rapidly south. First, he realised he had to allow Mother to enter the pew before him, but also Mavis had put herself on the opposite side of her parents. His dream of sharing a hymn book evaporated in a cloud of Mother's lavender perfume and the slightly damp smell of the church. To top it all, every time he leaned forward to sneak a quick smile to Mavis, her mother grinned back at him like an insane cat. His Sunday was plummeting from the heights he had imagined on Saturday evening. The service itself was very moving and in places, even stirring. The Vicar had excelled himself and the congregation had sung energetically.

Outside, they finally had a chat with Mavis and her parents. After a few minutes devoted to the vicar's performance and the rising costs of living, Mother remarked that, since Reggie might be on active service soon, it might be nice if the Everleys could come round for tea. The Skipper's spirit soared, as though he were cresting one of those giant waves off Iceland. His eyes met those of Mavis and he felt the hand of fate on his shoulder. This was it, Mavis would come to tea! Unfortunately the hand of fate, having steadied him to present a sitting target, delivered a resounding slap. Mrs Everley struck the fatal blow, 'I'm so sorry Beatrice, Mavis has already invited her cousins to our house for tea. We would invite the two of you, but with my sister and her husband, we'll be like sardines. Maybe we could meet next Sunday if both of you are around?'

'Yes, champion,' said the Skipper rather too loudly, 'we'll look forward to that, won't we, Mother?' Mother nodded brightly and began chatting to Mrs Everley about her sister and family. Mavis moved to the Skipper's side.

'Are you alright Reggie? You seem tense,' she gave him an up from under look which had his heart thumping about inside his ribcage, 'at least we can look forward to next weekend, I suppose.'

'Absolutely Mavis, it'll be grand.' Mavis pivoted away as the Skipper reached to touch her arm.

'Come on parents, there's lunch to eat and a haslet to be sliced for later.'

Mavis left the Skipper as she so often did. Confused.

'Well, Reggie, I tried,' mother rasped as she took his arm. 'Better luck next week.'

'What do you mean, Mother?' he gasped.

'What... good grief lad! You were rocking back and forth like a swing, trying to peek at Mavis. I thought you were going to faint!'

'Mother! Don't be daft!' he said, trying to look offended.

'Ee, you're a soft ha'porth you are,' she whispered as she tugged his arm for home.

Monday dawned warm and bright. The Skipper felt positive, but needed to be busy to avoid brooding about Mavis.

He headed for the Harbourmaster to check if there were any chart corrections and to get a weather forecast, having missed it on the BBC National Programme.

As he entered the office, with the slight disinfectant, floor polish and cigarette smell of most public spaces. The duty officer looked up. 'Ah, just the man we wanted. There's a gentleman next door wanting a word,' he pointed to a scuffed door, 'through there Skipper, if you've got a minute.'

The Skipper creaked open the door and entered. A greying, short man with wire-rimmed glasses looked up. 'May I help?' he said in an East Yorkshire accent.

'I'm Hurton, Skipper of Ganton Lass. I'm told you wanted a word?'

'Ah, yes. Good morning Skipper. My name is Davis. I understand you've been away with the reserve? Good to meet you at last.' He stood with his hand extended.

'Likewise, Mr Davis and, yes, we've been doing some training.'

'Well done, Mr Hurton. Well, to business then. I understand that there have been some preliminary discussions about requisitioning your vessel already. I should probably say, the Foreign Office has specified some requirements, which I believe are to your benefit. You seem to have friends in high places, Mr Hurton!'

'Well, I'm not so sure about that, Mr Davis, but thank you.'

Davis continued, 'There are two options open to you Mr Hurton, the Government can buy her from you and you would have an automatic right to buy her back at the end of hostilities, or the Government can rent her from you at £61 15s per month. In both cases, you would recover the full replacement value of the ship *on the day of payment* should the ship sink or become irreparably damaged (I understand this requirement came from the foreign office). In the event of battle damage, the Government will be responsible for repairs naturally and at the end of the rental agreement or before selling her back to you, she would return to her current specification, and her original equipment refitted.' He looked enquiringly at the Skipper over his glasses.

'Well, this is happening much quicker than I imagined, Mr Davis, but I can tell you I would prefer the rental option. I'd like the hire rate to be £66 per month because an acquaintance of mine got the £61 rate for a smaller boat than mine. Also, where will the refit be done? I'd like to store any removed fittings myself because a lot of the gear is nearly new.'

Davis scratched his head. 'I'll check the rate for you, though I suspect it's standard. As regards the modifications, it's likely the winch and gallows will be required if you end up minesweeping but you can remove all your fishing gear, obviously. I can ask the role intended for your vessel and, if the winch and gallows are superfluous, you could remove them here if you can store them. As for the question of where the refit will take place, I'd need to inquire at the Admiralty, but I know that the yards in the Humber, including Cook, Welton and Gemmell in Beverley will be engaged on building new Admiralty Trawlers. Cochrane's at Selby are flat out with orders, so I suspect possibly Lowestoft?'

The Skipper nodded. 'That'll be fine, Mr Davis. If you can check those things, we can sign the agreement after our next trip, perhaps?'

Davis looked up sharply, 'I'm sorry Skipper, but I'm afraid that we'll need the modifications done immediately. I'm not sure there'll be time for another fishing trip.'

'Bugger me, this is a bit of a landslide!' the Skipper's face reddened.

Mr Davis looked nonplussed. 'But surely other skippers have told you about the requisitioning programme? Three fishing vessels were requisitioned here in the last fortnight!'

The Skipper leaned back in his chair. 'We've been in training for the last two weeks. We only got back late on Friday. I assumed the other lads I know were fishing. I should've asked in the Mariner's Rest, I suppose!'

'No matter Skipper. Look, I will telephone the Admiralty requisitions officer, the chap I report to, and put your points to him shortly. I'll amend the rental agreement based on his answers and if you call in this afternoon, I'll let you have the draft so that you can go over it. I assume you'll want your solicitor to look at it, too. If possible, we'd like it signed tomorrow, Wednesday morning latest, because they want the modifications done so soon. I won't forget to confirm where you will need to take her. Fair enough?'

'It'll have to be, I suppose,' the Skipper sighed. He then straightened his back and stood. 'Right, no point in moping. I'll tell the lads and make preparations. I'll be back at two p.m.'

'Thank you, Mr Hurton. I know this isn't a simple transition for you to make. See you at two.'

The Skipper let the door close behind him, waving to the Duty Officer as he left. He set off for the harbour to find Arthur.***

As he climbed down the ladder to deck level, he heard voices from above. He thumped up the ladder, heading for the open wheelhouse door. As he was about to open it, he heard Arthur saying, 'Calm yourself, lad. The Skipper will be here directly, I'm sure.'

He entered to see Arthur, looking slightly red, staring at a young man in a white naval officer's cap. The young man was facing Arthur and snarling.

'Directly is not what it said on the signal, Mr Stainton. What it said was I'd arrive at 10:30!'

'How do gentlemen, what's doing?' the young man turned sharply. He was slightly smaller than the Skipper, well built, with sandy hair, and wore a naval uniform.

'Who the devil are you, may I ask?' the young man snorted.

The Skipper's eyes flashed to the locker which hid the cricket bat, but he saw Arthur shaking his head.

'I,' said the Skipper slowly, 'am the skipper of this vessel.' His eyebrow raised in challenge.

Unaware of what he had unleashed, the young man pressed on. 'I think you mean to say, "I am the skipper of this vessel; sir!" is that clear?' The young man tapped a cigarette against his silver case and raised his eyebrows.

Before the Skipper could say anything, Arthur piped up. 'Skipper, there's an urgent telegram from Mr McDonald in your cabin which I think you should read before we go on.' The young man's mouth opened, so the Skipper held up his index finger.

'Hold hard young un, I'll be back directly.' He clattered off down the companionway.

The Skipper heard a scuff of boots behind him. The young man's voice saying, 'Get out of my way, man!' He didn't hear Arthur's reply as he turned into his cabin. On the table was a large buff envelope and a paler dun coloured telegram. He read the telegram first.

R.G. HURTON , A GIFT FOR YOU AND THE MATE . YOU HAD TO OUTRANK THE FOOL , THE FATHER HAD MORE PULL THAN ME . THANK ME AFTER WAR = H McD +.

Tearing open the envelope, there were two certificates. He read the first;

By the Commissioners for Executing the Office of Lord High Admiral of the United Kingdom of Great Britain and Northern Ireland. To Mr Reginald Gordon Hurton: Here-by appointed Lieutenant Commander in His Majesty's Royal Naval Reserve... He read no further, his mouth open. Flipping it to read the next certificate, he saw they had commissioned Arthur as a Sub-Lieutenant.

The Skipper re-read the telegram and thought for a second. He could guess who the fool was. Which meant the fool had a relative in high places, but top marks to McDonald for finding a way round the problem. How big a problem was it, though? He thundered up the stairs.

'Now then, young man, what were you saying? I should also ask who I'm speaking to?' somehow he kept his face deadpan.

'I am Lieutenant Fortescue-Smythe, and the thrust of my conversation is that you are required to address me as sir!' the Skipper was relieved, two stripes meant Lieutenant.

The Lieutenant's eyes flashed with shock as the Skipper replied, 'I'm new to all this Lieutenant, but I think you may be wrong,' he handed the commission over to the young man, who froze as he read. The Skipper passed the other paper over to Arthur and waited for a second. 'This gentleman is Sub-Lieutenant Stainton, who actually should call you Sir.' Arthur's eyes speared the Skipper, whose humour was now very much restored.

'I, I'm terribly sorry sir, they led me to believe that you were a Warrant Officer. I apologise Sir, I meant no offence.' He switched to Arthur. 'Nor to you, subby, if I'd known I was addressing a fellow officer, well...'

The Skipper saw his chance. 'On this vessel, we respect the knowledge, skill and work-ethic of a man. Stripy arms are fine onshore but unless we're being inspected formally, I am called the Skipper and Mr Stainton is called the Mate. You, I suppose, will be the First Lieutenant. So Number One, as we will call you onboard, we can leave "Sir" for onshore, where we can be as formal as you like in front of the public.'

The young man's eyes boggled, 'Y, yes sir, as you wish.'

The Skipper overlooked the stray Sir. 'Good man. Now, why don't we start again? Are you drafted to us already?'

'Erm, no, sir. They ordered me to join at Dover in a few weeks. I was in the area and wanted to look at the ship and introduce myself informally.'

The Skipper raised an eyebrow 'Informally you say; you seem quite keen on formality so far...'

Number one glowed with embarrassment until the Skipper laughed, saying, 'That'll be the last time. Don't worry.' He cocked his head at Arthur. 'Right gentlemen. We have work to do. Pending signature of a contract for hire of our ship, the Admiralty will order us to sail south in the next day or two. We will deliver her to a shipyard for a refit. I'll learn the exact destination this afternoon but from what Number One just said, Dover will be involved at some point,' he looked at the Lieutenant, 'Now, this is an informal visit you say but, given the schedule we just learned about, we'd appreciate your help. I'm sure I'll be able to get your leave reimbursed if so?'

'Happy to help, sir.' Number One gazed around, looking slightly dazed.

The Skipper went on, 'Arthur, we need to get the lads here sharpish so we can let them know we're on the move and break the news that there won't be a trip before we're requisitioned after all.'

Number One looked confused. 'A trip, sir? Sorry: Skipper, I meant to say. Where on earth were you going?'

Arthur answered, 'Well sir, we go out of the harbour mouth, swing around the Castle Rock, then steam for just over 1300 miles to a place near Bear Island in the Barents Sea where we shoot and haul nets until the fish room is full. Lovely this time of year. Much less sea ice around.'

Number One's eyebrows disappeared up under his cap. 'Barents Sea! In this?' he realised he'd said it out loud when both heads snapped toward him.

Arthur said gently, 'I expect you're surprised such a fine ship would be wasted on so menial a task, sir. Am I right?'

Number One's eyes flicked toward the Skipper. 'I, er, yes, I suppose so, something like that.'

The Skipper shook his head. 'Pack it in now, lads. You will quickly learn, Number One, that this vessel, properly handled, can take anything the sea throws at her. Also, do you know what she has in common with The Ritz?'

'No Sir.'

'Absolutely bugger all. Now let's get on.'

They put word around that the crew were needed in the Mariner's Rest at lunchtime. A couple of local lads without a ship found them for Arthur.

The Skipper introduced the crew to Number One, stressing that he was 'Sir' from now on, while privately thinking they'd tear the poor sop apart. He explained their trip was off, but they would be on the Admiralty's payroll, so things should work out. He clarified that if any of their families experienced hardship, they were to speak to him, or their wives to Mother, and they'd do what they could. Number One was gaping like a fish by this time. The Skipper asked if anyone had received any paperwork by post yet. None had, so he added a check of their status to his job-list.

After sending the lads off to their wives or families, he introduced Svein to Fortescue-Smith. Number One politely corrected him to say Smythe. He smiled inwardly. The lad had got the message. He then stood and waved to Gerald, who pulled pints. 'What are you drinking, Number One? I'd like to welcome you to the good ship Ganton Lass properly.'

'Thank you, Sir. Pink gin would be lovely.' The Skipper strolled to the bar, leaning in toward Gerald.

'Four pints, please, Gerald. Oh, and I'll settle my tab if you please. We might be away for a while.'

Number One stayed silent when the Skipper placed a foaming pint of Sturdy Mariner in front of him, but after two sips, he whispered, 'I say.' A few minutes later, the Skipper lit his pipe and Number One could only manage a croaked, 'Dear God!'

After a brief lunch of pork scratchings with their pint, the Skipper and Arthur nipped up the street to let Mother and Elsie know the score before setting off to meet Number One at the Harbourmaster's office. Svein had escorted Number One there while they had been briefing the ladies.

They were early, so the Skipper asked the other three to wait on-board while he met Davis. Svein took Number One to a nearby phone box to report in. The Skipper mounted the stairs and asked if Mr Davis was in his office. The Duty Officer waved him through with a wave of his hand. 'Go ahead Skipper, he's on his own.'

'Now then, Mr Davis, I'm a few minutes early. Are you ready for me yet?'

Davis smiled, 'I am Skipper, yes. I contacted the requisitions officer as promised. Bad news first. He can't budge on the rate, but he says the winch can stay on board. If anything changes, you can have it brought here for storage by all means. We planned for the modifications in Dover. Apparently, every yard on the Humber and at Lowestoft is already flat out but I found out today that a slot has come free at Fellows' yard in Great Yarmouth. You'll get a twelve-pounder on the foredeck and a Lewis gun on each side of the bridge, plus some depth charge launchers – looks like you're earmarked for submarine hunting or convoy escort Skipper,' his eyes flicked up but the Skipper was impassive, 'I've got the document here and you are welcome to take it away, as I mentioned earlier. If your advisor is happy, then simply pop back here, and we can both sign. Now, have I missed anything?'

'No, Mr Davis, that's all very clear. Thank you.'

Mr Davis smiled, 'Good luck Skipper.'

The Skipper called his thanks to the Duty Officer before strolling off up the hill to the family solicitor's office. He hadn't felt the need to telephone ahead because, in all the years that he'd known Mr Blenkinsop, he had never actually seen anybody waiting. Sure enough, they showed him straight in. He explained the situation and waited for 10 minutes while the bespectacled sage read the document.

The old chap finally nodded, saying, 'Well, you seem to have struck a good deal, Skipper. You've got two pounds a month more than anyone else I've spoken to. You seem to have tied down all the lessons we learned with your father at the end of the last war, so if you're happy, I'd say you can sign it.'

The Skipper thanked him and hurried back down to the Harbourmaster's office. When he got there, Mr Davies was still alone, so they both signed the document, each keeping a copy and shaking hands before parting. In the fresh air the Skipper felt dazed. The paper he'd signed had potential to turn their world to ash.

The Skipper walked down the steps outside the office and a thought whispered: make the most of this time. He slowed his pace, looking over toward the beach and four towers of the Grand Hotel, drinking in the view under summer sunshine. Time passed as he stared at the heat haze shimmering above Sandside, the perfect reflection of the sky in the wet sand left behind as wavelets broke and slid back into the sea's edge. He walked around the fish sheds to the quay-side and stopped, hearing kittiwakes calling as they circled from the cliffs. The old place looked wonderful. The water in the harbour was calm, occasional dark patches appearing as whispers of breeze found their way past Castle Rock. It all seemed emptier than usual, but the sun glinted off fittings and made the grubby seem clean. This was home. With a small sigh, he told himself to get moving.

The others were in the wheelhouse when he arrived onboard. 'I have news, gentlemen. We are now going to Great Yarmouth, where the fine craftsmen of Fellows & Co will chop my ship about unmercifully unless I set my Chief Engineer on them.' He winked at Svein.

Number One looked ashen, 'Oh Lord, I just told my f, I mean my boss, that I was going to ask if I could take passage with you gentlemen.'

The Skipper looked at him with a furrowed brow. 'If you could travel to our old destination, then the answer will be the same for the new I'd expect?'

The young man smiled. 'Oh yes, of course. Well, that's settled then.'

The Skipper shook his head. 'We wouldn't want you to miss out on our luxurious accommodation, now would we? Also, we do a preferential rate for serving officers.'

Arthur's eyes lit up. 'Can I have a discount, Skipper?'

'Do try to bugger off, Arthur, there's a good chap. Anyway, I don't think we're on the payroll until tomorrow!'

The Skipper continued, 'Right then. We're only a day past neap tides, so we won't be able to get out until about 11 a.m. tomorrow. Sixteen hours to Yarmouth, so we should arrive,' he squinted, 'two or three hours after high water. No problem getting in, it's a dredged channel, anyway. The lads will be here first thing. We can offload the nets before we go, plus anything else we're unlikely to need. Svein, can you inventory the machinery spares, both onboard and in the lockup, before we go? I want to be sure we can bill the Admiralty for any of our spares they use once we've won this war for them!'

Svein nodded and Arthur chipped in, 'Don't forget I did an inventory of all the deck gear and machinery spares Skipper. It was just before the last trip, so it'll be current. We need a lifejacket for Number One, though. I'll sort that.'

The Skipper nodded to Arthur. Turning, he said, 'Number One, will they provide us with charts, do you think?'

'Yes sir. They'll issue current charts and then one of my jobs will be to organise corrections. They'd also issue charts if they ordered us to other theatres.'

'Thanks Number One, I shall leave a passage planner of the East Coast for tomorrow and take my chart portfolio home then, and my fishing log, of course.'

Number One looked blank. 'Fishing log, sir? Why is that confidential?'

Arthur smiled, 'It's the key to years of information the Skipper has gathered. Our Skipper is one of the best. He can sniff out a cod from any distance, because he's methodically recorded positions, catch rates, weather, temperature, pressure, tidal flows; you name it. Many people would lop off their arm for that information.'

'Righto. Got it.' Number One beamed at them.

The Skipper had a feeling of despair nearly every time his first officer spoke, 'Right chaps. Let's have a few hours with family before we set off. Svein, will you have tea with us?' Svein nodded. 'Number One, what about you?'

'Bed, breakfast and evening meal, sir. I'll be fine.'

The Skipper nodded, 'Right, gentlemen. Rendezvous at the Mariner's Rest at eight O'clock this evening for a farewell pint, we must make hay because, pretty soon, we'll be marooned in Great Yarmouth!'

Svein walked with the Skipper, looking up at the old castle, standing guard over the harbour as it had for centuries. 'Thanks for thinking of me Skipper, it would have been very grey sitting in my flat alone. Although we both know I'd have surrendered and gone to the pub.' He grinned ruefully.

The Skipper clapped him on the back, 'You're always welcome Svein, you know that.' He halted abruptly. 'Do me a favour Svein, would you go on to my house and let Mother know that I've invited you for tea? I have an errand to run.'

'Ya, sure Skipper. Take your time.' His eyes twinkled knowingly.

The Skipper opened his mouth to reply, then smiled and turned away. Striding off towards the other end of Quay Street purposefully, he cut off up the steps toward Mavis' house. She would not be working at the post office today. Mondays were her day off because she worked on Saturday. He strode up to the front door and knocked firmly straight away. Experience taught that any hesitation would cause him to turn tail and go back down. Mrs Everley answered the door and smiled with delight when she saw him. Without a word she said, 'I'll fetch our Mavis.'

Mavis appeared at the door and leaned on the jamb, arms folded. She looked at him curiously. 'Now then Reggie, what brings you to these dizzy heights?'

He smiled, hoping he didn't look like a lunatic. 'I just wanted a word, Mavis. The boat is going to be refitted for Navy work tomorrow. We might return quickly, but there's a chance we won't be back for a while. We're no longer in charge of our time, you see.'

Mavis stared at him flatly, 'Oh aye, well, what of it?'

He could feel his heart sinking but for the first time since she kissed his cheek at school he was undeterred, 'Well, no tea next weekend for a start, and I, I was wondering if you'd object, if I...' her eyes widened as he hesitated, 'Oh damn it Mavis, I'd really like it if I could write to you.'

Mavis tried, she tried really hard, but it was too much. She burst out laughing, but seeing the pain in his eyes, she put her hand on his shoulder. 'Reggie Hurton, it would be wonderful if you'd write to me. It would please me to write back too.'

She had expected some romantic gesture after that build up; but Reggie was Reggie, so what she got was 'Champion Mavis, absolutely first-class. Righto, I'll be off then.' She would never regret her relationship with David, but Reggie had been her first love and she understood that his apprenticeship and new working life had been important to him, but why oh why had he never spoken to her?

As he turned, she felt like kicking him but, unusually, she resisted the urge, 'Tarra Reggie. Look after yourself and the lads. I know you always do but, well...'

'I will Mavis,' he beamed as he looked back, 'and I will write as soon as I can.' This time she let him walk away, then reached a decision.

'Reggie, stop!' Mavis ran to him, raised on her heels and kissed him on the cheek. She then turned, ran inside, and slammed the door behind her.

Ordinarily, that door slam would have sent him packing, probably for the pub, but today he just wandered home in a daze, repeatedly touching his cheek.

As he entered his own place, he could hear mother chattering away happily to Svein and, as he put on his slippers, he felt taller than he usually did. Mother turned as he entered the parlour and gave him a wide smile. 'Good lad Reggie, I'm glad you brought Svein back.' He smiled at Mother, walked forward, and gave her a hug.

'Get off, you daft ha'porth. You'll have me over.' Suddenly, her face froze. 'Where have you been, Reggie? What have you been doing?'

Her face looked like she was waiting for the last number at bingo. 'Well mother, I have good news.' He hooked his hands into his waistcoat like an orator, 'Mavis Enderby and I,'

'Yes?' said mother, holding her breath.

'Well, Mavis and I,'

'For God's sake Reggie, get on with it!'

The Skipper looked totally nonplussed. 'We are now corresponding!' he beamed expectantly.

'Corresponding,' Mother looked glazed over, 'corresponding he says.' She lifted her face to the ceiling, 'Don't strike him down Lord, he's too simpleminded to be taken yet.' She then strode off into the kitchen, where she resolutely clattered. To clatter effectively is a tricky thing, but Mother did it. In fact, she delivered a virtuoso clattering.

The Skipper put his hands on his hips, 'Well I'll be a... what's her problem Svein?' He noticed Svein had turned away, looking out of the window at their Anderson shelter, and his shoulders were shaking.

'Skipper, you are... well, ya, you are first rate. I think Mother was expecting something more, well, matrimonial than "corresponding".'

The Skipper's eyes boggled, 'Hold Hard Chief! Matrimonial? We're a good way off that!'

From the kitchen, they heard Mother's voice. 'Forgive him Lord? He hasn't the eyes to see or the sense he was born with!'

The Skipper and Svein set the table and laid the cutlery while mother worked in the kitchen. Slowly, the clattering subsided and they could hear her humming so the Skipper felt reasonably safe.

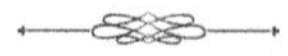

Mother eventually came in bearing an enormous dish of beef stew and dumplings. She smiled sweetly at the Skipper.

'Would you write a letter to the vegetables and ask them to come through?'

The Skipper rose, 'Not funny, Mother, not remotely funny.'

He returned quickly with an enormous bowl of mashed potatoes and cabbage.

The Skipper turned to Svein, 'Would you like to say grace Svein?' He was trying to deny Mother another target. He knew that, if he spoke, she'd have a spiky reply ready.

Svein thought for a second, 'Lord, we thank you for this food and this chance to be together. We pray for fair winds and the strength to climb any mountains in front of us. Amen.'

Mother glared at the Skipper, thinking of mountains unclimbed, but relented. 'That was lovely, Svein. Now let's put this afternoon behind us and enjoy our meal.'

They chatted about the ship, the hire agreement, and terms of the contract. The Skipper was careful to be reassuring, for Mother's sake. He told Mother they would stay near the ship during the modifications if possible, but he was unsure what the Navy would want.

After they had eaten, they had tea while listening to the news on the wireless. Afterward, Mother said she was tired and would go to bed early. She encouraged them to enjoy a drink at the Mariners' Rest while they had the chance. As they put on their jackets, she hugged Svein. She told them that, whatever else they did, they should look after each other.

Once in the taproom, they nursed a pint until the others drifted in. The Skipper felt subdued, but kept the conversation going and as light as possible. Number One arrived saying that after the dinner he'd just had, he would struggle to drink anything but changed his mind when a pint of Sturdy Mariner landed in front of him.

At the end of the evening, the crew drifted away, leaving only the Skipper and Arthur finishing their drinks. Gerald came round from behind the bar and shook their hands. His big ham fists thumped them both on their backs as he said, 'You fellows get back safe, and that's an order.' They promised they would, and after asking him to make sure he kept the brew going whatever happened, they walked off up Quay Street, wishing each other good night as they reach their doors.

When the Skipper got home, Mother was downstairs with a cup of cocoa. Her voice thick, she said, 'I won't get up in the morning. You don't want your old mother going on as you leave. I'll leave some food for you in the pantry. But most important, Reggie; be careful, please.'

She started for the stairs but turned at the parlour door, her eyes brimming. Reggie smiled at her. 'Don't fret, Mother. I'll write to you as well.' She smiled at him and disappeared, shaking her head.

He heard her as she climbed the stairs. 'Ee, just like his dad.'

He smoked a pipe as he sipped a small whisky. He was looking into the fire, but seeing Mavis.

The weather was bright, as they congregated on the following morning. The Skipper had taken tea up for Mother and hugged her tight, telling her not to worry. He knew she wanted a farewell but also realised she was avoiding the parting because worry would make her unintentionally say something sharp, so he ignored her 'no goodbye' ruling from last evening.

The Skipper was bright, 'Right lads, let's get after it! Number One, would you help the Mate in the lockup please?' he flicked a shilling to the cook, 'Billy; nip to the butcher's and see if you can get something for tonight, would you? Svein and Archie, can you give all the machinery a last check, please? Mike, would you check the bunkers and confirm we've plenty to get to Dover in case they change their minds again? The rest of you, we need to get the nets on deck and moved to the lockup. If we've got any dan-buoys or floats below, just leave them: they might come in handy. All of you, check for any personal effects left onboard in bunks or cupboards. We don't know how much they'll strip out, and I don't want any of your gear disappearing. I think that's it. Pipe up if anyone thinks of anything else. I'll be with the Harbourmaster for about twenty minutes, then onboard.'

They all dispersed to their tasks. At the lock-up, Number One's eyes boggled. 'Good Lord, look at all this!' The store was tidy, with racks for spare parts and fittings. The morning sun slanted in through grubby roof lights, highlighting long spider webs, heavy with dust. There were two nets on the floor, neatly bundled. Two more hung over a pole suspended under roof trusses. Number One's nose wrinkled: the whole place smelled of tar. What he had imagined as a shed was actually a small warehouse.

Arthur smiled, 'Most fishermen around the coast, especially in the Humber, work for a ship owning company. Each company has a core of trusted skippers, who often have preferred crews, especially mates, engineers and cooks. The rest get hired in as needed. They make trusted skippers shareholders of the company, plus skippers and mates get a share of the profit from a trip. The crew gets a standard wage, topped up with a small share of the profit split between them. The Skipper's father, we call him T'owd Skipper,' Number One looked confused, so he explained; 'it means the old skipper. Anyway, T'owd Skipper realised those ports were losing out by not keeping hold of good crews, so he made up a crew from folk he trusted and who were grafters. He paid the crew a better standard wage and everyone got a fair profit related bonus. It worked. The best men wanted to work for him and he was selective. He knew that working well together was the most important thing, so he turned away some cracking men who he knew wouldn't fit in. By doing so, he built a really efficient working team. I joined in 1920 when my last ship ran aground and sank. Luckily, all hands survived and got ashore in the boat. Our Skipper carried on with that kind of thinking, and he worked his way up to mate by ability. T'owd Skipper had apprenticed him with a friend, sailing out of Hull. He learned every job on board and did them all well. He stayed with that ship in the last war (Mother didn't want both her men in one ship) and came back to Ganton Lass in 1920, so we both joined at the same time in effect. When T'owd Skipper wanted to make him mate, he worried about the effect on the crew, especially me, so he sent us on an errand, then asked the crew if they thought his lad would make the best mate. They all said yes. T'owd Skipper called me in before he made it formal, and I told him I would have said yes too if he'd asked me. But fair warning to you sir, the Skipper is big on truth, fairness and behaving decently, but he can get himself into a lot of trouble. Usually by reacting to someone who doesn't live up to those standards! What all this means is the Skipper isn't just making the big decisions at sea, he's running a shipping company at the same time. Mother helps with paperwork and financial matters, but he's still got a lot on his plate. So you see the sort of man he is. Anyway, enough chat, we must get on.'

They set to, collecting the few things that Arthur knew were required. They took them on a flat barrow back to the quayside. Arthur noticed Number One stood back when it was time to pull the barrow. He realised the lad had much to learn about life in a trawler.

When they got back, the nets were ashore, so the lads loaded them on the flat barrow, baled using lengths of rope, and Arthur led them back to the lockup, helping to balance the huge precarious bale. He reassured the Skipper that he'd double lock it and drop the keys with Mother before he came back. George, the Lead Hand, was sweeping the deck clear of bits of dry weed and shells which had dropped from the nets, and Billy had lit the stove and was getting a brew on. The Skipper asked Number One to grab his kitbag and told him he'd show him to his quarters.

When Number One returned, the Skipper descended the ladder, then showed him the way aft, telling him to watch his step on the chafe irons at the aft end of the deckhouse, which were raised about half an inch above the deck planking. He explained they kept the liver barrels there after hauling and it was easy to slip on them if unaware. He led around the aft end of the deckhouse, turning under the boat deck. As they ducked under the boat deck support beams, he pointed out a large grating over the rudder head, a storeroom, and heads at the stern (many trawlers did not have this facility, he explained). Opening a door into the galley passage, he pointed out the wireless cabin and galley (Billy always left some cold snacks for the end of night watches on the table; he explained). He then backed down the aft companionway, telling Number One to lower his bag down.

When Number One joined him, the Skipper showed him the mess room at the bottom of the companionway ladder. 'This room is used by the Mate, the Chief and Second Engineers and now, yourself. In really foul weather if the lads aren't gutting, we let them eat here, after they've had a wash, so that the cook doesn't have to carry hot food the full length of the ship. I usually eat in the chartroom, which is my cabin, or in the wheelhouse if the weather is fit.'

They moved into the aft cabin. The Skipper explained, 'On the forward bulkhead there are two small cabins, port and starboard, so once you're officially aboard, and we know what the shipyard plan, then I'll move you into one cabin and the mate will take the other. The Chief and the Second Engineers will be in the bunks.' He waved toward the oval slots cut into the woodwork above a bench seat, which curved around the aft end of the cabin. Forward of the seat was a table, shaped at the aft end to follow the curve of the bench seat. Padding matching the seat upholstery covered the panelling behind the seat, and above that were small cupboards under each bunk. 'For this brief trip, I'd like you to bed down in a bunk: the other two will stand watches tonight. Is all this clear and are there questions?' He tilted his head slightly.

'No Sir, I don't think so. I wonder if we'll get a steward on board once the refit is complete?'

The Skipper paused. 'I can guarantee there won't be a steward on board Number one. Billy, the cook, will prepare the food and deliver it to the mess room I've just shown you, and to the foc'sl'le. There is a strong likelihood that the fish room will also be a mess room, and by the time we're fitted out for our new roles, we simply won't have spare room for hands who don't contribute to the running of the ship and its weapons. Come with me and I'll show you.'

The Skipper led the young officer back up to the galley passage. 'The forward companionway leads to the engine room and boiler. I'll let the Chief show you around down there.' He then stepped back out on deck, turning forward along the port side. He pointed out the aft gallows and the ports for loading coal. 'Number One, I need to be clear on this. I won't tolerate any man on deck in heavy weather, not holding the rails.' He pointed to the hand railing along the deckhouse. 'One hand for the ship, the other for yourself, is the rule. On top of the deckhouse or wheelhouse, you must clip a safety lanyard on to the jackstays unless railings or canvas screens are fitted.'

'Got it, sir. I'll police that.'

'Good man,' the Skipper nodded then moved forward past the wheelhouse ladders and steam winch before stopping, 'these deck ponds where we sort fish are pretty good at stopping anyone going over the wall, but if they're removed, as I suspect they will be, then we'll rig jackstays in the ship's well deck because that's going to be where most movement will take place.' Stepping over each deck pond coaming, he lifted the fish room hatch just aft of the mast. 'This will be the other mess room, I suspect. It's currently the fish room. We'll not go in or your uniform will get scaly; but if you look down, you'll see that space will be at a premium.'

Number One peered into the gloom. 'Oh I see sir, yes.'

The Skipper led on to the storage area, hand windlass (for warping her in port he explained), hawse pipes and foc'sl'le companionway cover under the whaleback, he also pointed out the water closet next to the foc'sl'le companionway screen, 'A lot of owners won't provide these and the amount of lads who go for a swim is shocking: just to be clear, a swim in the Barents Sea will usually be the end of you.' Turning, he backed down the ladder into the foc'sl'le, Number One following. The Skipper flicked on a light switch. 'This is the foc'sl'le. There were originally eighteen berths in here. My father took out three to add storage space for the lads and a vented locker. Never forget, Number One, that any motion we feel further aft is worse in here. I mention this because I know from experience that naval discipline can degrade the performance of these lads, so exercise judgement. You're not in a battleship.'

They left the foc'sl'le and climbed up to the whaleback, which had a small steam winch and fairleads for tying up, as well as the chain pipe for the anchor.

The Skipper glanced at his watch. 'Let's get to the wheelhouse. The lads will be back soon.'

They walked aft and climbed the ladders to the bridge deck around the wheelhouse. Svein was inside and handed them the tea that Billy had left. 'Brews gentlemen. Skipper, another quarter of an hour and we'll have steam up. Mike says we've plenty of coal and it's well trimmed; considering he trimmed it, I can't imagine he'd say anything else mind,' he winked, 'we're all squared up below and I've made a list of spares onboard as you asked.' He handed over a grubby piece of paper.

The Skipper thanked him and asked if he had a spare pair of dungarees. Svein nodded, and he turned to Number One. 'Once we're in open water, perhaps you could go to the engine room and ask the Chief or Second to show you around the machinery?'

'Of course, sir.'

The Skipper nodded thoughtfully, 'When they begin the refit, I'd like you and I, along with the Mate, Chief and Second, to be involved at all stages of the work. It's really important that we know every inch of the ship and her equipment so that we identify any weak points. I doubt we'll all be needed constantly, so if we meet as frequently as we can and have a list of current work and any concerns we may have, then we can talk things through.' As they murmured agreement, the crew arrived on board. There was a lot of bustle and noise, but their gear disappeared down the various companionways in short order. Arthur had come onboard. He reported all's well to the Skipper, then bustled about, making sure everything got squared away.

At last, they were ready to sail. Arthur and Svein appeared in the wheelhouse, reported their readiness, and went to their posts. Arthur to the well deck and Svein to the engine room. The deckhands were at the lines and had already removed the springs . The Skipper sang out of the open window, 'Let her go forward, Arthur!', then rang down for slow astern. As the shortened stern line tightened, he eased over the wheel and her bow swung out slowly, 'let her go aft' he called, ringing down for dead slow ahead. The answering ring confirmed, and she crept forward as the Skipper spun the wheel to starboard.

'Fenders in lads.' They heard Arthur shout as the water chuckled under the bow. Number One had watched the entire process with great respect. He had rarely seen a vessel leave her mooring with so little fuss and wished he'd paid more attention to his father's boat handling tips when he had spent summer Sundays in a slipper launch on the Thames. The Skipper opened the port side window in the wheelhouse as he spun to starboard to line up the harbour entrance. He glanced up toward the watch-keeper at the lighthouse and noticed three figures on the pier side. 'Bugger me! It's Mother, Elsie and... Good God! Mavis!' All three were waving, so he dropped a loop over the top two wheel spokes and leaned out of the window, calling to Arthur. When the Mate's head turned, he nodded at the pier. Arthur looked as amazed as he felt. Never in all their years had Mother or Elsie waved them off. Of course, the Skipper's eyes were fast on Mavis, but all too soon, the ladies slipped astern and the Skipper faced reluctantly forward. Flamborough Head normally felt familiar, friendly even (barring a strong northerly), but today it seemed to have a different cast.

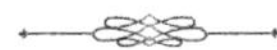

Number One came in and the Skipper spent a few minutes pointing out landmarks before asking him to take the wheel, 'Your course is 122° compass and I'll see you in about ten minutes.'

'No problem, sir, I have her.'

As the Skipper climbed down the wheelhouse ladder holding the tea mugs, he could feel the heel changing. He decided not to react; the steam assisted steering sometimes made newcomers over-steer, so he'd give the lad quarter of an hour and see how he'd held his course. Even a novice should have the feel of steering by then. He slipped off to the galley and made tea from the urn of hot water (one advantage of a steamship, he always thought, was hot water on tap). After a chat with Billy, who promised sausage and mash for tea, he went back to the wheelhouse ladder. Whistled at Arthur to show him a brew was up, he climbed up to the wheelhouse.

He put the mugs in cutouts on the shelf behind the wheel and glanced at the binnacle. She was on 136° and Filey Brigg, a promontory with large shelves of rock which got progressively deeper as they speared out to seaward, was dead ahead. 'Number One, what was the course?'

'122° sir, I'm afraid I found the helm a little twitchy at first, but I'm sure I've got her now.'

The Skipper grimaced, 'Oh you think so?' the Skipper kept his body between Number One and the binnacle, 'what is the ship's head now, Number One?'

The young man hung his head. 'I can't be sure sir, but she was on about 125° I believe.'

'You're not sure. You believe. Words I never want to hear from my helmsman Number One! You are heading 136°, no 138° now. In forty minutes, we would be on the rocks which extend beyond that headland up ahead. Turn to port and steer 115° NOW!'

Number One reddened as the Skipper stepped sideways to allow him sight of the binnacle. He over-steered again but brought her on track and steady.

'Number One, I dropped you in with no warning and you're unfamiliar with her handling. But even allowing for that, you weren't certain of your heading and that's unforgivable,' he raised his hand to stem the protest he felt was coming, 'this is a beautiful piece of coastline but, like all coastlines it has its dangers. I would expect better seamanship than this from a Royal Navy Lieutenant. You must know that kind of error on a calm sea is not acceptable. Did you log any course changes?'

'No sir.'

'So if we were offshore now, there would be additional uncertainty in our dead-reckoning position, because I wouldn't have access to course changes, times and speed!'

Number One was mute with embarrassment.

'Number One, help me understand why you seem so inexperienced. Have you not served as a deck officer? Tell me more about yourself.'

Number One seemed utterly dejected. 'Well sir, first HMS Dartmouth, the Britannia Naval College at Dartmouth, then a short time with HMS Cochrane, a shore establishment at Rosyth, before joining the battleship HMS Resolution. Last year, they promoted me to lieutenant and drafted me to HMS Copra, another shore base at Largs in Scotland. Then my father insisted I do something more becoming if war was to come and moved me here.'

The Skipper looked perplexed. 'Becoming? Whatever is "becoming" about serving in one of His Majesty's Trawlers?'

'It's a great opportunity for action, sir. My father felt that, with our family history, the paymaster branch was not a suitable occupation. My father is Admiral Sir Nigel Fortesque-Smythe, and he feels that the only way I can get away from what he calls "the stigma of the paymaster branch" is to excel in battle. His exact words were "the smaller the ship, the greater the glory" and so here I am.'

The Skipper couldn't help wondering if they chose him for the paymaster branch because he was unsuitable for anything more practical, or whether some drafting officer had felt he was doing the Admiral a favour by putting his son out of harm's way. He considered for a few moments before answering.

'Now I wanted to test you a little this morning, but I can see that I should've asked you about your previous service first. You initially seemed to be a bit of a stickler, so I simply assumed that you were a deck officer, which is completely my fault. I suppose the first thing we should establish is what you actually want to do. Do you have ambition to be a deck officer or should we move you back into your previous occupation?'

Number One looked at the deck before jerking his eyes back to the binnacle and sweeping across the horizon in case he was being tested again. 'If you'd asked me on the train from Edinburgh, then I would've asked for my previous occupation. In the short time I've been with you and the mate, however, it somehow feels as though I belong, or at least I could belong. That's something new for me sir, it's something I'd like to try.'

The Skipper nodded, 'We all find a fit Number One, or sometimes life finds one for us. I'll speak to the mate and get his opinion, but my guess is that with some training from us and hard work from you, then yes, we may find you belong. But know this Number One; if I feel that your level of experience or your conduct is endangering this vessel or the crew, then I will only have one option, however regretfully, do you understand?'

Number One glowed ' Thank you sir, I'll try not to let you down.'

'It's all we can do, Number One, try our best. I need to nip below for a couple of minutes. Are you confident if I leave you at the wheel?' Number One nodded as the skipper turned, 'Oh, and by the way, you're drifting off course again.'

'With the greatest of respect sir, I am steady on 115° as ordered.'

The Skipper smiled, 'Well done, Number One. This time, you were certain of your course. You may now resume on 122°. Carry on.'

The young man's shoulders straightened. 'Aye-aye sir 122°'.

The Skipper went below to lay-off their course after rounding Flamborough, then went to find Arthur. He explained what he had learned about the first officer and asked Arthur's opinion on the best course of action. Arthur had doubts about the young man, but the Skipper's point about the benefits of a friend in high places carried some weight. They both felt that, so long as he could stand watches as supernumerary, Number One could take at least some load from them until they developed him further.

The Skipper also clarified that, while the young officer was supernumerary, the watch leaders were himself and Arthur. He had hopes that Number One would look after gunnery and organising the ship as his contribution, but decided to give his deck officer skills some honing, regardless.On ce he and Arthur had agreed, the Skipper returned to the wheelhouse, where he began finding out the current level of knowledge that Number One possessed, as well as giving some short and easily digestible pieces of advice. After a time, the Skipper took the helm, telling Number One to go below into his cabin, where he would find some exercise books in the cupboard. The Skipper suggested that Number One take notes as they developed his skills.

By the time that Billy appeared with some ham sandwiches, Number One was studying. The Skipper had told him about magnetic variation and deviation. Number One didn't even see Billy as he stooped over a chart, muttering, 'Error West, compass best. Error East, compass least.'

When Arthur appeared for his watch, the Skipper suggested Number One might nip down to the engine room for a change of scenery. The young officer obeyed with a wide grin. Arthur raised his eyebrows. 'Someone has a spring in his step, Skipper!'

'Well, Arthur, I'm still not convinced he'll shape up, but it would be a poor skipper who didn't at least try to move the lad on. It's going to be tough mind but at least he's easily led. Anyway, how are the lads doing?'

Arthur nodded, 'Not so bad, Skipper. It's all a novelty at the moment. You know how it is. We'll need to put more work into them once they're grinding away at the same things every day.'

'True enough, Arthur.'

The day passed slowly for them all. The lads were tidying the foc'sl'le, oiling small fittings and greasing the gallows blocks before Arthur stowed all the blocks, shackles and various other small parts away. After that, he let them sunbathe on the boat deck and whaleback. No sense in cooping them up, he reasoned.

Number One had quite a shock when he returned from the engine room. The Skipper noticed him glaring at the lads as he walked around the bridge deck.

'Everything alright Number One?'

'Oh, er, yes, sir. I was just wondering whether there's anything we could usefully get the crew doing?'

The Skipper sighed, 'Well ordinarily I'd set them on painting, but as the Admiralty is about to paint her grey, I think that would be wasteful. The Mate and Engineers are on top of the routine maintenance. But the clincher for me is this. Those lads have been doing frequent trips to Iceland and also Bear Island once the sea-ice cleared. That was followed by training, then we interrupted their rest days with this delivery. So I don't mind them recharging their batteries, not one bit.'

The Skipper studied Number One's bearing as he took off his cap and fanned himself, the heat in the wheelhouse had become ferocious. The Skipper asked him to open both doors and clip them back to let some air in.

'I hope your trip into the noisy guts of the ship was helpful, Number One?'

'It was indeed, sir. I learned a lot from the Chief and Second. With your permission, I'm going to sit down and make some notes while it's fresh in my mind? I'm afraid that I couldn't write it down as the Chief spoke: it was pretty greasy down there.'

'Certainly Number One, yes. You're obviously keen enough to learn, and that bodes well. I certainly hope so.'

'Thank you sir, I'll park myself on the bridge deck while the weather is nice if you've no objection. Yell if I can help with anything.'

'I will, Number One. If there is anything you're uncertain of, just pop in and ask.'

And so the voyage went on. They had sailed at 11:00 and by 16:00 they were around halfway down the Holderness coast. From 17:00 onward the Skipper, Arthur and Number One took one and a half hour tricks at the wheel, but aside from eating, visiting the heads and brewing up, they remained in the wheelhouse. They were past the Humber by 06:30 as the Skipper had planned, but slowed as the tide went against them. After a little difficulty finding the North Docking buoy, they finally picked it up and began their run around the East Anglian coast, following the channel to landward of the various shoals and sandbanks which run around the coast. Number One had spent a good deal of time taking bearings of landmarks and plotting their position on the chart as practice. He leaned on the bridge deck rail, brew in hand, and watched the shimmering sun transform the land on the starboard side to red, gold, orange and yellow, all bubbling in the heat haze. The Skipper smiled, saying, 'Lovely sunsets on this coast, Number One, but very grey and boring dawns as a rule.'

They finally arrived off Yarmouth around 04:00 and Arthur turned out two lads to put out fenders and handle the shore lines. They tied up by the quay once inside the port. The Skipper went off in search of a duty officer, whom he met walking along from the other direction. He told them where to tie up for Fellows' Yard and where to get breakfast in the morning (the Skipper realised the man was sadly ignorant of Billy's skills). He'd been told to ask them to pop into the yard at around 9:30 a.m. and make themselves known. They eventually rang 'finished with engine' at 04:35 and quickly got their heads down for a few hours of sleep.

Chapter 6

52° 35' 58" N, 01° 43' 28" E

(Fellow's Yard, Great Yarmouth)

Wednesday 23rd August 1939

The Skipper was in the wheelhouse at 08:30 to make sure he would have ample time for breakfast. He strolled around the deck with his tea and he could smell welding and oil, even though they were about 200 yards from the shipyard. The breeze sent catspaws along the River Yare and he looked across the water at the low quay with brick-built workshops and industrial buildings on the opposite bank.

Back in the wheelhouse, he was just tucking into a doorstep of bread filled with bacon and an egg when Arthur and Number One arrived.

'Tea in the pot,' said the Skipper through a half chewed mouthful, nodding aft. Arthur strolled off and returned with two more brews and two sandwiches wrapped in brown paper. Once they finished eating, the Skipper said, 'Right lads, I think it's nearly time.'

Number One hesitated, tapping his cigarette on his case, but felt he must raise his point. 'Err... I think we're going to have to get you both the proper uniforms and rank badges while we're here. In the meantime, we can't have our skipper seeming to be outranked. Here sir, put my jacket on and I'll take yours.'

'I appreciate that, Number One, but the rank would still be wrong. I'll wear my hat and my best gansey, that'll do. They'll be expecting a motley crew!'

The bustle and noise of a port was gaining intensity as they walked along a narrow roadway between large workshops, turning right along Southtown Road and finding the yard entrance gates. Huge sheds and workshops stretched away behind, and the noises of serious engineering echoed from within them. As they entered, a man in a brown overall coat approached them. 'Yes Gentlemen, can I help?' He had to raise his voice over the clank of metal and the machine-gun sound of riveting.

The Skipper stepped forward. 'Good morning, I'm Hurton, skipper of Ganton Lass. We're moored just downstream of your yard and were told to make ourselves known this morning.'

'Yes, I think the Superintendent mentioned you. I'll fetch him if you can wait here, gents?' The man had a strong East Anglian accent, and oil ingrained into his hands.

'Absolutely.' The Skipper turned toward Arthur and reached for his pipe. Number One took a full pace backward and checked he wasn't downwind as the match scraped along the box.

Arthur frowned. 'Didn't I hear you or T'owd Skipper say once that they beefed her up for a gun in the first lot?'

'That's right Arthur. They put doublers on some frames and fitted extra beams. Also, there was some steel plate fitted to the deck-head in the fish and store rooms to strengthen the deck. I'm guessing they'd only need to refit the plate because the frames and beams are unaltered.'

As they spoke, a tall man approached with an outstretched hand. 'Gentlemen, nice to meet you. I am Harry Dennison, the Works Superintendent here at Fellows'.'

They made introductions, and Mr Dennison took them to his office. He had a large partner desk with a leather top, clamshell reading lamp and an ornate desk tidy containing a fountain pen and lots of pencils. The office was stuffed with bookshelves, drawing racks, shelves full of ledgers, and on the smallest wall, where the door was, framed pictures of ships, many of them.

Dennison smiled, 'Righto. First things first. I'm to give this envelope to Mr Hurton and,' he consulted a notepad, 'ask Lieutenant Fortescue-Smythe to telephone the Admiralty on the usual number. Beyond that, it's a survey of the trawler "Ganton Lass" and a refit to bring her in line with the Admiralty Specification for Armed Trawlers AD -T.38/29 (spec). They normally fit out either for anti-submarine patrols or for minesweeping, but your specification seems like a hybrid, so I suppose the "spec" on the end means special. I should mention, there will be a great deal of additional wiring needed to accommodate the specified equipment. Anyway, I just wanted to check you're aware of what's happening, and to ask if I can get you to show me around her yourselves. I find it makes the surveying more effective if we understand why things are as they are.'

The Skipper nodded. 'I agree, Mr Dennison. In fact, we're hoping that at least one of us, and our chief engineer, can be around during the modifications, so we understand what has changed and why. Would that be a problem for you?'

'Not at all. The reverse probably: you fellows will be a mine of information. I'm sure we can point you to a guest-house, unless the Navy can put you up anywhere. I heard they're evacuating the Naval Hospital to a safer location, so there might be berths available there.'

Number One chipped in, 'I can find out, sir, if you like?'

'I suspect these are our orders, Number One,' said the Skipper, holding up the envelope. 'I'll read these first, but if we can remain, then yes, I'd appreciate it if you could arrange lodgings for us.'

The Skipper turned, 'Mr Dennison, when would you like your tour? We're moored downstream. It only took us five minutes to walk here.'

'Well, it's a quarter before ten now. Would eleven suit you?'

The Skipper nodded, 'Definitely. We'll get out of your way now. We'll be onboard, then we'll see if we can find out what the Admiralty expects of us!'

The Skipper felt heartened that the Superintendent seemed a sensible and approachable man. Number One went to find a telephone box to call the Admiralty, and as they went on board, Arthur disappeared to make a brew.

Sitting alone in the wheelhouse, the Skipper opened his envelope. He, Number One and Arthur were to report to McDonald in London next Monday, while the crew were going to Sparrows Nest in Lowestoft to attend training courses, starting on Friday. The ship's Officers would remain at the yard. The Skipper smiled to himself and hoped that they would be exempt from a repeat of the square bashing training. He then began composing his first letter to Mavis.

Arthur reappeared clutching three mugs of tea and put them in the rack. The Skipper quickly pocketed his note and explained their orders, asking him to brief the lads.

Number One hurried up the wheelhouse ladder. 'No problems, Skipper. Apparently there is some accommodation available at the military hospital but very little, and none until the weekend. We'll have to play it by ear. I have a name and telephone number noted down, so I'll ring and tell them when we need accommodation.' The Skipper briefly ran through the orders with Number One and passed him his mug of tea.

Arthur asked Alfie Cloughton, the apprentice, to slip off to the railway station and get a train timetable for Lowestoft. Arthur based his choice on the youth of the lad, making him the least likely to disappear into a pub on the way back.

In due course, Mr Dennison arrived and the four ships-officers showed him round. Before they started, the Skipper filled Dennison in on the history of the ship and the fact that she was refitted as an armed trawler in the First World War. He described the gun on a platform which was mounted over the whaleback, with its aft support legs standing on pads in the well deck. They showed him the doubler frames and extra beams fitted under the deck-head in the fish room and foc'sl'le.

After they finished the tour, Mr Dennison was of the opinion that the refit would be much quicker than he had expected. There was no record of the ship serving in the First World War. He mentioned he would fit a 'flying bridge,' an extra platform above the wheelhouse so that they could keep watch from a higher vantage point. The Skipper immediately pointed out that, depending on what they were carrying, the top-hamper aloft could cause them problems. His father had mentioned this precise issue in World War I. When ice formed on the top decking and rails of the flying bridge, she would lie over for too long when she rolled in bad weather. The Skipper suggested an open framework with removable canvas dodgers, if possible. Dennison was happy with that suggestion and delighted the officers would stay on because they obviously had useful information. He confirmed there were two dry docks, each holding two ships, and that Ganton Lass would be last in the next day, probably mid-morning. He told them not to raise steam in the morning. They could pull her into the dock with warps and their windlass: he'd get a few of his men to help.

The Skipper saw him off and found Arthur and Number One leaning against the front of the wheelhouse. 'Sandwiches are up, sir,' Number One piped up breezily.

'Thanks Number One. Arthur, would you pop round and see Mr Dennison after we've eaten and ask if we can sleep on board until Saturday, please? I forgot to mention it. Number One, once we get the answer to that, I may ask you to either telephone the hospital for lodgings, or find us a guest house.'

'Absolutely Skipper.'

They enjoyed a cheese and pickle sandwich for lunch. Billy had a fine stock of preserves, and secreted away a good cheese (otherwise, it would get eaten in two night watches). Alfie, their apprentice, popped up with a railway timetable he'd got from the harbour master, and Arthur fetched them another brew while Number One studied the London trains. The Skipper preferred a return within the day if possible and, depending upon the outcome of

McDonald's meeting, to begin work with the yard staff, making sure that he and his officers understood the refit. After a few minutes with the timetable, they worked out they could catch the early train via Ipswich on Monday, and be in London in time for their meeting. They would be back in Great Yarmouth late, but they could grab something to eat before they left.

They had all the information that they needed before 17:00. The hospital had rooms for them on Saturday, and the yard was also very helpful. Mr Dennison said that he would connect a shore electricity supply to the ship's system on Thursday and Friday nights so they didn't need to run the oil fired donkey engine for lights. The yard would examine the strengthening already in place so their marine engineer could certify that part of the work was complete. They could then start with the flying bridge so the ship's utilities would be useable until the weekend. Things went smoothly the following morning. With plenty of people to help and with lines run ashore in appropriate positions, they warped the ship into the dock using the yard's windlass and a lot of heaving on their manual windlass. They lined her up using shorelines and kept her vertical with chains as the tide ebbed. When she settled, they levelled her on the chains before inserting props to the edge of the dock. Mr Dennison explained they had already positioned wooden support beams on the dock bottom so that her keel could safely take the ground and his men would further support her with more props under and around the hull once the dock was properly dry. Dennison said they'd shut the dock gates at low water and pump residual water out of the sump at the base of the dock.

With the ship safe, the Skipper walked to the railway station with the crew to stretch his legs. At the entrance, he gave them a wave and called, 'Don't forget lads. Toe the line and learn everything you can from them. It might just be important.' They waved back and joined the throng boarding the train.

They shifted their dunnage to the Royal Navy Hospital on Saturday and allowed themselves a meal in a local inn that evening, happy that things were going well onboard the ship. They couldn't help contrast the sombre looks and subdued conversation in the bar. The fear and threat of war hung heavy in the air.

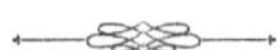

The train fogged the air with escaping steam as they stepped onto the Liverpool Street platform on Monday morning. They walked over to the underground station to get them to St James' Park, from where it was a short walk to 54 Broadway, where McDonald had his office.

Arriving a little early, they had a cup of tea in a nearby cafe. When the bill arrived, the Skipper scandalised the clientele by loudly asking, 'How much? I don't want to buy the crockery, just what was in it!' Number One hurriedly paid the bill and apologised to the waitress, being careful to keep his voice low so that the Skipper couldn't hear. Arthur was so amused by the pandemonium the Skipper created he was wiping tears from his eyes as they left.

Captain McDonald met them outside the building, shaking their hands before they entered. 'I'm afraid the security here is quite high, so they'll search you before you can enter.' As they entered, they signed in at a reception desk, passing through a turnstile which let them into a typing pool. On the other side of the turnstile, McDonald ushered them into an anteroom, where officers patted and squeezed their clothing until content they were harmless. There were wooden cubby holes along one wall where the Skipper presumed visitors had to leave bags, etc. Walking through the room, which was painted an institution pastel-green, they passed into a foyer with lifts and stairs. As they waited for the lift, McDonald exchanged pleasantries about their journey.

Inside McDonald's office, the Skipper noticed the bland utilitarianism compared to the oak panelled warmth of their last meeting. Once seated, McDonald began the meeting.

'Well, Gentlemen, things are going ahead with the ship I imagine?' they all nodded. 'Good news. While I remember, we will rename the ship for the duration of the requisition period; it keeps her identity as a warship separate from her civilian purpose. I've persuaded the brass to call her "His Majesty's Trawler White Nab." I recall the feature close to Scarborough and thought you might like it.'

The Skipper smiled, 'It'll do, captain, thank you.'

McDonald continued, 'Not at all Skipper. Anyway, the main purpose of our meeting is to set out our plans to get you fully operational. Unfortunately, we are not hopeful about the situation in Poland so, unless Herr Hitler changes his stance, then we believe they will declare war sooner rather than later. This puts us under some considerable time pressure. I will come to the details shortly, but briefly, we intend to ask you to conduct a short sea-trial after the refit, then make a passage to the West coast of Scotland to take part in some training. The training will involve practice rendezvous with submarines and surface vessels, as well as practise landings of people and materials at night, and in such a way that your activity doesn't draw attention to the operation. Also, we need to get you familiar with convoy escort duties and anti-submarine measures. Skipper I would like you to travel up to Lowestoft in about a week with your officers, Sparrow's Nest are doing the anti-submarine element of the course for the current intake and the introduction takes three or four days so I think it's important that you don't have to play catch up on that later on. I'll also arrange for some manuals and other training materials to be issued to you so that we make sure that your understanding is adequate.'

McDonald looked around their faces seeking questions, but there were none. 'We have specified White Nab as an intelligence support vessel, though you will not find this designation on any documents aside from the original Admiralty specification. Even the version that the shipyard is using had the designation, indeed the whole introduction, removed. We will equip her with a 12 pound gun forward, Lewis guns either side of the wheelhouse and two Oerlikon rapid-firing guns aft of the funnel. The yard will move your derrick crutches slightly to accommodate these weapons. In addition, there will be a small armoury on board equipped with Lee-Enfield .303 rifles which we will issue to each user as personal weapons so they can accurately zero them. In that way, they can provide accurate beach support fire where needed. For anti-submarine work, we are fitting AS-DIC for detection and location, and depth charge throwers for destruction. With the armament that you have, you will out-gun any surfaced U-boat you may encounter. This is a very capable armament for a vessel drawing only just over 14 feet. We plan to equip you with two rubber inflatable boats, one between the boats and another over the stern grating, these of course, are for beach landings or extractions. Questions so far?'

The Skipper nodded. 'Yes, about those rubber boats. They might be safer if we store them against the bulwarks on either side of the stern grating. They'll be more secure, easier to launch, and won't prevent her freeing herself if we take a green one over the stern.'

'Brilliant! Would you mention that to the shipyard, please? Thank you. Anything else? No? In that case, I'll go on. Depending on events in the near-future which, as you'll appreciate, are difficult to predict, we may have to make you operational earlier than we had hoped. If hostilities proceed as predicted, that shouldn't arise, but I wanted to make you aware of all eventualities.'

The Skipper met his eyes. 'Thank you again, Captain. I appreciate your candour.'

'As we agreed Skipper, I will give you as much information as I can without prejudice to the national interest.' Their eyes met, and both nodded understanding.

McDonald turned to Number One. 'Lieutenant, I wanted to clarify that, as a Royal Navy Officer, you will be in charge of any shore parties which arise. In Scotland, we will train you to secure an area and extract or insert an asset without alerting the enemy. Questions?'

'That's perfectly clear, sir. Thank you.' Number One smiled uncertainly.

The Skipper spoke quickly, 'Ah well Number One, looks like I'll be hunting submarines and you'll be invading foreign soil before we know it eh? Amazing the things that war, or even the threat of it, bring out in us.' Number one grinned at the Skipper, who winked back at him. McDonald glanced over at the Skipper and smiled briefly. He knew leadership when he saw it.

McDonald asked Arthur to think about the relative strengths of the crew and assign the lads to whichever job most suited them. He asked Number One to ease the lads toward naval discipline so he could temper their independence and their reliance on Arthur and the Skipper for leadership. The Skipper bridled a little at that point.

'Hold hard Captain. The reason my crew is so effective is our bond of absolute trust, which goes both ways. My father split with convention and created a tight-knit and very effective crew who responded to more than just fists. I don't want parade-ground automatons. I want competent men who make the right decisions!'

McDonald nodded, 'And those skills are why I chose you and your crew Skipper, but some of your men may well need to respond to the Lieutenant here, and he won't be able to debate with them when he's on an enemy held beach in the dark. They must accept him as one of their leaders, at least for the duration. I'm sure that we can trust the Lieutenant to apply only enough discipline to achieve that end?'

The Skipper glowered at McDonald for a second or two before replying, 'Aye, well, you might have a point there. But hear this Number One,' he began, turning his head, 'always remember that these lads have seen more hardship and hurricanes than you would believe. Respect them and they'll respect you.'

Number One looked slightly shocked, but nodded vigorously. 'Absolutely sir. No question about it.'

The Skipper's eyes flicked between Number One and McDonald. 'Well, I suppose that's agreed, then. The proof will be in the pudding, but I have every confidence in my officers.'

The discussion then moved on to their role in times in which McDonald had no need for the ship. They would carry out convoy escort and anti-submarine duties in between SIS duties. McDonald said he had spoken with the senior officers in the Royal Naval Patrol Service and they understood that flexibility would be essential because the

SIS might need to call on HMT White Nab and her crew at unusual times and short notice.

McDonald then rounded off the meeting. He checked they were all clear on their individual actions arising from the meeting, at least for the near future. Once satisfied, he closed the meeting and wished them a safe trip back. The Skipper mentioned they would eat before they returned to great Yarmouth and that McDonald was welcome to join them, but McDonald politely declined as he had other duties.

As they descended in the lift McDonald coughed, saying, 'I know that you gentlemen are not stupid, however I must tell you that everything we discuss here is sensitive and very secret, so please don't discuss it in public. If the Nazis were sure we had a fishing vessel doing this work, they'd be alert and make our job infinitely more difficult. I'd also recommend that the crew know only what they need to do their job, but I'll let you manage that aspect of things.'

'Aye, well, we will do our best. I'll report back to you on the timetable for our refit after I've had a sit down with Mr Dennison. I assume it's alright to use the phone if I keep the language nondescript?'

McDonald nodded, 'That will be fine Skipper.'

On the ground floor, the doors opened and McDonald shook their hands, asking them to sign out as they left. A few minutes later, they returned to the street, which felt a little strange somehow given the world of secrets they just left. After consulting the timetable, they decided they would get the next train and have an early dinner in Great Yarmouth.

The following morning they set about their normal routine and after breakfast the Skipper went off to see Mr Dennison. They had a long and fruitful discussion, eventually deciding that the refit would be complete by the 22nd of September. On his way back the Skipper telephoned McDonald and updated him.

That afternoon the Skipper treated himself to an Emerson "Little Miracle" wireless for his cabin. The Chief Engineer made a small shelf to hold the wireless securely, and fitted a power outlet, three volt transformer and a wire aerial. The Skipper reasoned that if they were in coastal waters, he may as well listen to the news when off watch. It was in this way, five days later, that the three ship's officers, sitting in the Skippers cabin to avoid workmen in the wheelhouse, listened to a subdued Neville Chamberlain announce that, as Hitler had not responded to the ultimatum delivered that morning to leave Poland, '... this country is at war with Germany.'

The Skipper turned to his officers and grimly said, 'God help the Nazis when they come up against us, lads!' As he poured them each a tot of his single malt, he thought, '*and God help us and keep our families safe.*' They raised their glasses, saying as one, 'To Victory!'

The Skipper wrote a letter to Mavis asking her to please keep herself safe but, as Mavis later remarked to Mother, 'he then killed the moment by telling me in great detail what they are doing to his blessed boat!'

The day after the declaration of war, the Skipper reported at Sparrow's Nest and joined an intake which was just starting training on ASDIC. He became frustrated at the introductory section. The instructor had just explained that ASDIC stood for the 'Anti-Submarine Detection Investigation Committee' who had done research work. This was too much for the Skipper. 'I don't need to know who invented it, young man. I need to know how to work the damn thing. Can you cut to the useful bit please?' The instructor only contained himself when he saw the rank badges on the Skipper's new uniform.

The Skipper had his first officer to thank for his rig. Number One had ordered uniforms for the Skipper and Arthur from his own tailor, for which the Skipper had reimbursed him, planning to claim the expense back from the Admiralty (who dashed his hopes when he found out that part of their salary was a payment for uniform and upkeep). Because his uncle was a tailor, and because he had helped him occasionally, they gave young Alfie Cloughton the job of measuring the Skipper and Arthur. When Arthur broke the news to him, Alfie declared he would not measure the Skipper's inside leg until he was absolutely certain that someone had locked the cricket bat away.

The rest of the course went smoothly, and the Skipper proved remarkably adept at responding to bearings and distance given to him by the ASDIC operator, probably because he was used to juggling bearings and courses to steer in his head. The operators in real life were incredibly skilled because the ASDIC echo-sounder itself only gave a bearing and range to the target, not a depth. Because of a dead zone around the ship, it gave nothing once the ship was within 200 yards of the target. The unit sent a sound wave 'ping' into the water and the hydrophones detected an echo which bounced back. Echoes came from the hull of a submarine and many other things. The sea teemed with misleading echoes. The operators used the hydrophones (underwater microphones) as a passive way to get more information on the contact.

The Skipper learned about tactics and the strengths and weaknesses of their systems and weapons. He also heard disquieting news from the operators. In a convoy, the equipment would often be too insensitive to locate a submarine. This meant that, as well as protecting ships, convoys could provide a convenient hiding place for their attacker. The escort's best hope was to detect a submarine as it approached a convoy and attack it immediately.

At the end, they gave the Skipper a glowing report, and he returned to Great Yarmouth in good spirits on the Friday night. As he arrived at the Royal Navy Hospital to drop his dunnage, the Skipper bumped into Arthur and Number One, also returning. It pleased him to learn that the refit was going very well. The crew from the boatyard were working on the mountings for the Oerlikon guns. Arthur said the shipyard was now working seven days a week and there was talk of implementing a night shift, so they could finish the refit slightly early. Mr Dennison said it could be as early as 18th of September. The problem was a shortage of Lewis guns because of the number of trawlers being requisitioned. It was possible they might have to sail with only one Lewis gun and two mountings because, while the yard had two guns remaining and without one of them, the other ship in the dry dock would be completely defenceless against air attack.

The Skipper filed this away for another day, wondering whether McDonald could help with the Lewis gun problem, or maybe even number One's father. He was starving, and suggested a pint after they had been to the Hospital canteen for dinner. As they ate, they discussed in hushed tones the sinking of SS *Athenia* with such a terrible loss of life. They agreed that the outcome of this war could well hinge around controlling submarines. Number One said the Admiralty had given an order to adopt the convoy system for all ship movements. As well as SS *Athenia,* there had been at least one merchantman torpedoed and sunk, so the idea was to maximise the defences available to the merchant marine by bringing them together under a protective group of escorts.

The following morning, they arrived early at the boatyard and the Skipper went off to find Mr Dennison. Dennison confirmed he had still not received another Lewis gun, so the Skipper said he would try to pull some strings. Dennison was grateful for his effort, but confided to the Skipper that he believed it to be a shortage over the entire country. He said that many of the guns were World War I vintage and indeed the one fitted to White Nab came from an SE5a aircraft's gun mounting and had a 1916 date stamp on it. He was told they had refurbished the guns and re-proofed them before being reissued, but the age of this weapon made him wonder.

He confirmed the dates given to the Skipper by his officers, and also that he hoped to be finished on the 18th, barring any problems. He thanked the Skipper for allowing the Chief and the Mate to stay with him, commenting how invaluable they were. Dennison said Svein had been involved in a conversation with the importer of the Oerlikon Guns, primarily because Dennison did not want to over engineer any strengthening for them, because he was avoiding top-hamper after the Skipper's comments about the flying bridge.

When the Skipper walked to the edge of the dock, he had a shock. A team of painters had been working to paint her hull and upper works grey, and to the Skipper's eye she looked a right old mess. The Skipper climbed up to the wheelhouse and saw Arthur inside. Arthur nodded to some equipment in the wheelhouse's corner, commenting, 'They've only gone and fitted a tannoy system so that we can call the hands to action stations!'

'Good God Arthur! Whatever's next? Let's just hope we don't have to announce abandon ship, eh?' As an attempt at gallows humour, it fell flat with Arthur. His old friend had been brooding somewhat while the Skipper was away. The Skipper asked if Arthur was worrying for his family and Arthur nodded. He patted Arthur's back. 'Scarborough isn't a strategic target, Arthur. They'll be more interested in Hull.' He then went to the engine room to thank Svein for his efforts. The Chief was speaking with two men about labelling some wiring. He grinned as he saw the Skipper.

'Yah, she may never sail under steam again, but other than that we've done a fine job!' The Skipper laughed and clapped him on the back.

'I've heard nothing but excellent reports about your efforts on board Svein, well done.'

Svein frowned. 'Just don't blame me for the paint job, eh?'

The Skipper nodded. 'Well, when we keel-haul the culprits in a dry dock, we'll hear their suffering. Every cloud has a silver lining, I'd say. If you're finished here, shall we get a brew and you can give me the detail?'

'Yah, give me five minutes and I'll join you up there. Wheelhouse or your cabin?'

The Skipper considered, 'My cabin, I can't bear to look at the paintwork. I'll get your brew Svein, go straight in.'

On deck, he quickly rounded up Arthur and Number One, 'Council of war in my cabin Gentlemen, I'll just pop and get a brew and I'll meet you in there.'

Ten minutes later, they were all sitting in the Skipper's cabin sipping at their tea. The Skipper brought them up to speed with what he had learned on his course. He said that, once they'd got things shipshape, he would try to pass on as much of this knowledge to Arthur and Number One as he could. He thought deck officers should be able to cover for each other as far as possible. Svein reported the Skipper had scored a goal for the home team. The two guys in the engine room had heard his comments about the paint job and had promised they would ask if a few of the painters could come back and do some remediation.

The Skipper turned to Arthur. 'Do we know when we get the crew back, Arthur? Everything seems to move around since they declared war and I'm just worried that we will have a ship before we've got a crew!'

Arthur clapped his forehead. 'What is wrong with my memory, Skipper? Yes, the adjutant at Swallow's Nest asked the yard for me to telephone him, and they will formally complete their training syllabus on the 13th; given what we were told, I asked him to hold them until the 20th but earlier today I amended that again to ask for them back on the 18th because Mr Dennison expects us to sail on the 19th.'

They spent a quarter of an hour making a list of things they would need to do before they put to sea, with another list of things to check before their next stage of training. The Skipper said that when they sailed, he'd get the lads to don life preservers because he wanted to throw her around before they left Yarmouth Roads as a rough-and-ready test of seaworthiness.

On the 16th, they re-flooded the dock and warped the ship back to the River Yare, after confirming she remained dry. Once the crew returned and were aboard, Arthur showed them around the new accommodation arrangements. The

Skipper then asked for everyone to gather on the well deck, now cleared of the fishponds, for a briefing.

'Right lads. As you can see, the old lass has had a good deal of work done on her. The First Lieutenant and the mate will take you through the details over the next day or so. We can sleep onboard tonight, but the yard is doing acceptance checks with the Chief tomorrow. The rest of us will go to a room I've organised at the RN Hospital. We can discuss what you've learned and what the plan is. In brief, we will receive some specialist training for our new job up in sunny Scotland before going on operations.'

There was a loud grown from the crew and Billy, the cook, step forward.

'Skipper, we're just about trained out. A lot of the lads we were training with at Sparrow's Nest got drafted to ships straight away and are taking part now. Are we going to spend the war just training?'

The Skipper clenched his fists. 'No Cook, we are not. They selected us for a mix of special operations and escort anti-submarine duties. Am I right in thinking that you've been doing an awful lot of gunnery drills and such?'

'Well; yes Skipper, and the instructor was a right bas—'

'Enough Cook,' the Skipper sounded more angry than most of them had ever seen him, 'that training equipped you for what comes next; and what comes next will be much more of a bastard than your instructor was. If we force a sub to surface, you will need to load, lay and train your gun faster and more accurately than a Kriegsmarine team who have been practising for years and whose lives are in peril.

If you miss, they might have a free shot and finish us, so only the most disciplined and determined will survive in this war.' his eyes scanned them, 'In all the time we spent in the arctic, I've never seen my crew make the wrong decision, and you do that without a mate persuading people with a belaying pin or a skipper breaking jaws with his fists. We are the best because every man knows his job, as well as the job of the lad next to him; which enables us to work as a team. We do it without thinking, and that, gentlemen, is called self-discipline. Now military discipline's purpose is to promote self-discipline, so we are a step ahead of them already. What we now need is the regulars to teach us *what the job is,* step-by-step, so we all know what everyone else is do*ing, and why*. Then we apply our teamwork approach, at which point we'll be as good or better than they are, and that's saying something. Know this lads, we'll never be good at marching, we'll forget to salute, we don't wear the uniform right, but we already have the self-discipline that we need. So that sub's gun crew won't stand a chance. Now, let's stop buggering about and get on with what needs doing. Agreed?'

There was a ragged shout of 'Aye Skipper!' and much nodding as the lads dispersed. The Skipper beckoned Billy over. 'I know you were only sounding off, Billy. We all need a safety valve. But I needed to make that speech, and you handed me the chance. You alright?'

Billy looked down at the deck. 'Aye Skipper, I think I've learned to complain too much while we were ashore, sorry.'

The Skipper clapped him on his back, 'Get on with you, no need to be sorry. But we will need some provisions. If you make a list, the Naval Hospital promised to let us have enough supplies to get us to Scotland.' He handed over some coins. 'This is for some decent bacon and sausage. I suspect we'll need a substantial breakfast or two in the next few days!'

When Billy returned, he had the new hands with him. Pickering was a recently qualified RNR signaller and ASDIC operator and Yorke was a Royal Navy signals rating and very experienced ASDIC Operator. They also had another trawler man, Bert Ryton RNR, who was an extra hand for the Oerlikon guns. Arthur introduced them and showed them their bunks in the converted fish room.

The morning of the 19th dawned bright but with a cool breeze from the north-east. They had worked late into the evening to get the ship ready for sea. They had a good night's rest before bidding the lads in the boatyard farewell in the early morning and thanking them for their work.

Formations of wavelets shivered across the water in the breeze as they crept downriver. A sharp turn to port at Gorleston Pier, putting the leading light and the brick lighthouse dead astern, and they were in the open sea. A light swell gently rolled her as the Skipper rang half ahead. He was steering southeast, through the channel marker buoys and into deeper water outside the harbour limits. Here he rang full ahead and, when speed had built up, they streamed the patent log to determine revolutions at maximum speed. Arthur and the Skipper smiled at each other when they realised that the new screw that Dennison's team had specified and fitted was giving her almost an extra knot of speed.

The Skipper had everyone don life preservers when he spun the wheel hard to starboard and hard to port, gauging roll during full circles port and starboard. According to his brass inclinometer mounted in the wheelhouse, it was not much worse than she was before conversion. Dennison had added a small amount of pig iron ballast in the bilge and two small water ballast tanks, which seemed to have done the trick.

Next, the Skipper headed northeast, and they measured the revolutions for half ahead, slow ahead and dead slow ahead in the same way as before. Number One made a diagram on graph paper of speed against revolutions and copied it for the Chief. They asked the chief to make revolutions for various speeds in-between, streaming the log to check. After a couple of adjustments to the graph, they were happy, and marked up speed and revolutions on a white painted board that Dennison had installed in the engine room. The Skipper swung inshore north of Middle Cross Sands and began checking his speed, using landmarks and a hand-bearing compass. He steamed for fifteen minutes, then reversed course and steamed for 15 minutes back and averaged for a speed through the water. The log was accurate, so he was content with that part. At slack water, he rang for dead slow ahead and used transits of various landmarks, with correction for magnetic variation, to 'swing the compass.' He made adjustments to minimise the deviation of the compass caused by the iron or steel components of the ship. He did this to make their passage safe, but Dennison had arranged for him to call in to Aberdeen for a professional compass-swing and adjustment. That evening they checked all the steaming lights and pronounced the ship seaworthy.

In the early hours of the following morning, they passed Scarborough. It took all the Skipper's self-control to resist running in for the harbour. He had written to Mavis before leaving, but would have given a lot to see her that night. However, he had orders to proceed to a place in northwest Scotland called 'Patrol Base 8'. It was near Badcaul on Little Loch Broom, the entrance to which was about seven nautical miles south of the Summer Isles. Loch Broom, leading up to Ullapool and beyond, was just to the north of Little Loch Broom. Their orders specified the stop in Aberdeen for the compass swing, which went without a hitch, and it gratified the Skipper to see how little needed changing from their rough-and-ready swing off the Norfolk coast. Apparently, the lads doing the adjustments had been seeing a lot of trawler conversions in the past few weeks!

Chapter 7

57° 51' 42" N, 05° 18' 35" W

('Patrol Base 8' near Badcaul)

Thursday 21st September 1939

In the early evening of the next day, they slid into Little Loch Broom after negotiating Cape Wrath and entering The Minch between the mainland and the Isle of Lewis. They went dead slow down the deep-water channel marked on the chart, with Arthur periodically shooting the lead line to confirm depths. To both sides were beautiful heather topped hills with browning bracken at their feet. Nearer the water, strips of green with the odd whitewashed house marked out crofting communities.

The Skipper pressed the button for the radio cabin and asked Pickering to contact Patrol Base 8 on the frequency they had been given, to announce their imminent arrival using their callsign, GTWTK. The yard had left the wireless cabin where it was, in the aft end of the deckhouse, and had fitted an intercom system with telephone handsets serving the wheelhouse, flying bridge, Skipper's cabin, aft cabin, engine room and wireless cabin.

They crawled up Loch Broom until young Boulby sang out they were being hailed. A lamp flashed from a jetty, sticking out into a small bay with a rock and boulder foreshore. He proved he was no slouch at morse-code, by reading out, 'ANCHOR OFF AND TAKE BOAT INTO JETTY - STOP'. They dropped the hook, lowered a boat, and the Skipper, with Number One, went ashore.

An earnest young sub lieutenant met them on the jetty and escorted them up to what they could only describe as a shack. It was large, with a slightly sagging moss-covered roof, and almost hidden on three sides by bracken and clumps of heather. The entrance faced the jetty and an obviously new door contrasted with the aged wood, lichen, and green algae of the wall. They had inserted wooden planks to support gravel steps going back up the hill.

Inside the hut sat a captain of the Royal Navy, smoking a small cigar, who rose and greeted them cheerfully. 'Hello gentlemen. I am Captain Stevenson and have the dubious honour of being in command of this patrol station. I use the term lightly because at the moment the so-called station comprises this shed and a Nissen hut further up the hill which houses the radio equipment. We are awaiting a team from Scapa Flow who are to erect several other huts. Apparently, they plan to make us resemble some sort of Croft rather than a military establishment. Lord knows why when the area is so damned isolated!'

The Skipper and Number One saluted and introduced themselves. Captain Stevenson told them they were his first customers and that he looked forward to working with them. He advised them to sleep on board the ship because the nearest guesthouse had only two rooms which were now occupied by himself and his sub lieutenant.

Captain Stevenson continued, 'It's not as bad as you might think. They connected us to the local telephone system with the help of the post office and we have wireless, as you know. Our role at this station is mainly coordinating but, in a few days when we have more huts, we will run shore-based instruction for you. We are going to throw you into the deep end tomorrow, however. A friendly submarine is conducting an exercise in the Minch and we are going to ask you to run a search pattern to protect Loch Broom from simulated attack. Whatever you do, don't fire any depth charges, though. It may set you off on the wrong foot with the Admiralty!'

The Skipper smiled. 'I can only imagine their reaction, sir. And don't fret about the setup. We once had to shelter for nearly a week at an abandoned whaling station on Bear Island, stormbound. I doubt my lads would lift an eye at the facilities here! What time will the exercise begin tomorrow?'

'10:00. The sub is up to something or other tonight but will simulate evading a harbour patrol in Loch Broom starting then. If they can surface off Ullapool, then will have entered the protected anchorage, but if you locate and pass over them, we class them as detected, and the sub will surface immediately. I can give you only one piece of advice; think like a submarine commander.'

The Skipper and Number One glanced at each other. 'We'll try sir,' the Skipper replied, 'so if that's all we'll get back onboard and start planning?'

'Of course. Make your way back here for debrief after the exercise is complete, and the submarine is caught, or her commander having a pint in Ullapool, would you? Erm, oh look here, do I call you Captain?'

The Skipper grinned, 'No sir, "Skipper" will do just fine.'

Captain Stevenson grimaced and Number One piped up, 'I'm told that "Skipper, RNR" is now a rank in a supplement to the Navy List sir, if that helps.'

Stevenson relaxed, 'Well "Skipper" it is then. Good luck for tomorrow Skipper, and to you too, Lieutenant.'

They saluted and opened the door. Descending toward the jetty, they turned up their collars to wait for the boat.

The next day dawned grey and blustery, but dry. Number One had begun his militarisation of the crew by setting a harbour watch, and Arthur had drawn up the watch list. It was fortunate they had, because at 06:45 they saw a boat heading their way from the jetty. The watch alerted the Skipper; then heaved the rope ladder over the side of the well deck. As the boat approached, it surprised the Skipper to see McDonald huddled in an army greatcoat on a thwart. The Skipper nodded to his deckhands, who were standing by with boathooks to hold her in, and grabbed McDonald's gloved hand to help him over the bulwark.

'Welcome back Captain McDonald. Good to see you... I think?'

McDonald laughed, 'No bad news, Skipper. I was in Inverness and was told about your exercise, so I drove over to witness at first hand what you chaps are doing. I could have saved some time finding out because, after all that driving, I learn that they've tapped themselves into the GPO telephone system!'

The Skipper shook his head and smiled, 'You've nothing to fear Captain, you're welcome along. Pop down to my cabin for a warm and a brew.'

They clambered up to the bridge deck and down the companionway into the Skipper's cabin.

'Have you had breakfast Captain?' asked the Skipper. 'Billy has some bacon left, I think?'

'I'm fine thanks Skipper. They gave me some doorsteps of bread filled with local cheese, which I ate while waiting for the boat. Tea would be grand, though.'

The Skipper pressed the Intercom button for the aft cabin and Svein answered, promising that he would nip up and ask Billy to deliver a brew for the Skipper and his guest.

McDonald smiled to himself. The constant flow of tea was a hallmark of the many trawlers he visited while searching for this crew. 'Skipper, what's the plan today?'

'We had a council of war yesterday evening and took advice from Captain Stevenson: think like the submarine skipper. It's possible to patrol his likely routes into Loch Broom, but we would have to cover a great deal of water, giving him more time to pass through between each sweep. We decided we will sweep back and forth over the entrance to Loch Broom. The entrance is only about three quarters of a nautical mile across, and there's a much better chance of being in the right place. We will sweep fairly slowly because the ASDIC Operator can turn on his hydrophones without pinging and we should be able to hear the sub approaching at a reasonable distance. If that works, then we can ping away and do our dummy attack. There is a dead zone of about two hundred yards around the target where we lose contact. Our submarine skippers apparently say the best thing to do is to turn hard as the attacker goes overhead and once he has dropped charges, he is unlikely to re-locate you straight away. We came up with an idea based upon that information: once we get a bearing we'll charge down on it and once we hit the dead zone, we'll go hard around a wide circle or zig zag up the loch so that we can pick him up again. In that narrow strip of water we think we're in with a chance: his options are more limited than in the open sea.'

'Bloody hell, Skipper, that sounds fantastic!' They both thanked Billy as he came in with two steaming mugs.

'Well, we'll find out today, Captain, that's for sure. Before you get too excited, remember this is the first time for everyone on board, except the ASDIC Operator.'

'True, Skipper. But the operator and you are the two men that will be most vital, so I have some hope of success.'

The Skipper shrugged. 'It's 07:20, so let's get up to the bridge after our tea and make sure we're nearly ready. We're sailing at 08:30 to be on station by 09:30. If I were the sub skipper, I'd nip in before the enemy were expecting me, so I want to look sharp.' He winked at Captain McDonald as he turned.

As McDonald followed him up, he marvelled at how tactical the Skipper's thinking was. He had privately worried that the Skipper had not done enough training, but he now realised that the Skipper's mind was agile and his style of leadership brought out, and trusted, the expertise of his crew, which added to the ship's potential efficiency.

At 08:10, they weighed anchor and headed seaward through Little Loch Broom. As they rounded Cailleach Head, the breeze was whipping up a few whitecaps, and the Skipper hoped that Isle Martin and the Northern shore of the loch would give them a lee. Flat water would make use of his periscope more risky for the submarine skipper, he reasoned, and he wanted his opponent as blind as possible.

By 09:10, they were on station and were doing a practice sweep. The Skipper's wish came true, and the island and shore were giving a good lee. They adjusted speed to determine the speed at which the ship's own machinery and wake made the hydrophones less effective and found that they saw the best results at under six knots and the limiting speed was about eight. They then began a curved track across the mouth of the loch, which swept a large arc out to seaward. Travelling at four knots, they hoped they would hear their target in good time to plan and execute their 'attack'.

The Skipper told the lookouts to keep sharp eyes on the water and scan regularly with binoculars, they would look for a tube sticking out of the water, which would have a small bow wave. He also explained they should be especially vigilant at the start of the exercise, around 10:00, and two hours after the start. His logic was that the submarine would expect them to be disorganised at the start, and complacent after an hour or two of finding nothing.

McDonald looked over at the Skipper. Dressed in Fisherman's oiled thigh boots, his own 'Gansey' pullover, and a navy issue dark duffel coat with, of all things, a paisley scarf around his neck, he did not resemble the seaborne leader of McDonald's imagination. Yet here he was. Straight out of the traps, doing what, to all appearances, was a fine job. McDonald was relieved that the Skipper at least wore his navy issue hat.

At 10:15, they had a moment of excitement until the lookout refocused to discover the periscope was in fact a puffin landing on a wave. At 11, however, the speaking tube whistled and Yorke's voice from the wheelhouse said calmly, 'Contact bearing dead ahead skipper. Propellor noise and wake with possible machinery. Permission to ping him?'

The Skipper checked their heading on the compass repeater and told him to go ahead. He blew into the other speaking-tube whistle, asking the helm to ring for full ahead and alter to 120°, there being no telegraph on the flying bridge. He announced to the flying bridge 'Contact on 092° magnetic gentlemen. Lookouts, you must continue sweeping. This may be a small boat or decoy.' The tube blew again and Yorke reported a very firm echo, bearing red 015°. The Skipper told Yorke to keep pinging, and expect the sub to turn to starboard to get away from the shallows. He blew into the whistle on the other speaking tube and ordered the helm to steer 135°. To the bridge he announced, 'The submarine is following the edge of the shallows on the north shore. Probably trying to sneak in. I'm guessing he'll come into the middle of the loch shortly, so he has more room to manoeuvre.' Once again, the tube whistled and Yorke reported he believed the sub was now astern of them. The Skipper ordered hard to port and, as the ship heeled, clung to the rail. He stared at the water astern as though he could see the sub. Sliding across to the tubes, he whistled the wheelhouse and ordered half ahead and hard to starboard, to steady on 385°. As they hit 370°, Yorke yelled, 'Dead ahead sir, range 800 yards!' The Skipper ordered the helm to be centred and called for full ahead. He had room to attack now, with the sub ahead. Yorke called the course corrections as they closed and yelled, 'contact lost!' after a few minutes. The Skipper ordered half ahead and rudder to 30° starboard to curve around. They might go over him, but if not, they'd be ready for another try nearer to Ullapool. He was glancing at his folded chart and mentally working out a fresh course when McDonald slapped him across the back.

'Well done Skipper, bloody marvellous!'

The Skipper looked over his shoulder and there, off the starboard quarter, a dark shape was surfacing; white water sluicing from its conning tower and foredeck. He grabbed his megaphone and ordered the twelve-pounder to train on the sub, but the barrel was already traversing to starboard. Leaning over the rail to look aft, he saw the starboard Oerlikon was already pointing in the right direction with Number One standing beside it, his thumb raised and wearing a manic grin. He called for dead slow ahead and told the helm to put the sub on the starboard beam. As they came round, he telegraphed 'all-stop'. The sub was signalling and Egdon was writing on a pad. He turned to the Skipper. 'Signal sir, it reads *Good effort White Nab-stop. Next time we should try that in open water-stop. Well done-stop.*'

The Skipper grinned, 'Mr Egdon, please send "We look forward to it, stop. Safe onward voyage, stop."' Through his glasses, he saw the top of the conning tower emptying, an arm waving as the last two men disappeared. A cloud of vaporised water hissed upward as the sub flooded its ballast tanks and slid back under the surface of the loch. The Skipper pulled his hand bearing compass out of his pocket and took a line along the loch. He whistled down to the helm. 'Well done to everyone in the wheelhouse. Could you please pass that on to Yorke as well? Yes, I know it's you George, but it's easier just to say helm when we're in action.

Yes, fine. Look, would you ring slow ahead and steer 309°? Good man, carry on.' He grinned ruefully at McDonald, who was chuckling mightily.

On their return to Patrol Base 8, they dropped anchor, and the Skipper ordered all hands to muster in the well deck. Once Arthur reported them gathered, the Skipper stood at the front of the bridge deck. A crowd of faces looked up at him, most of them smiling. 'Well done, everyone. That was a great team effort. It was only an exercise, and conducted in confined waters, which makes it easier to catch a submarine. However, this was the first time we've ever handled her as a warship. Every member of the crew contributed to a very satisfactory outcome for our first effort. There'll be harder tests ahead, but I know I can rely on every man to rise to them. I shall now ask Billy to provide his finest brew and best dinner to everyone except the harbour watch and the two men who are about to volunteer to row myself and Captain McDonald ashore.'

McDonald noted that quite a few hands raised to volunteer for the trip ashore and he shook his head in wonder. For once, he had absolutely no doubt about the person he had selected for the work ahead. In his line of work, that was a very great luxury.

Sawdon and Boulby pulled them ashore, where the young sub-lieutenant met them. After saluting, he said, 'Welcome back gentlemen, my heartfelt congratulations for today's effort!' his head bobbed in enthusiasm as he led them off toward the shack.

Captain Stevenson was beside himself, 'A brilliant effort Skipper, well done indeed. Our shore-based observers, by which I mean Sub-Lieutenant Cooper here, armed with a pair of binoculars and his motorcycle, report a very positive outcome.'

The Skipper smiled, 'Thank you sir, but I think the small search area and the restricted ability for the sub to manoeuvre were perhaps not a reflection of the reality we will encounter on actual operations. However, I am pleased with how the crew operated together on a task that was purely academic until today; and of course, a positive outcome on our first effort gives them a great deal of enthusiasm and confidence.'

'Of course. Yet, while there were fewer variables than if you'd been in open water, the skills needed to be successful in the task are not as common as you would think. This was your first exposure to this kind of work as a commander. You must have been quite junior in World War I. To be successful or even nearly successful at this early stage is both a surprise and a very firm endorsement of Captain McDonald's views. He thinks that both yourself, and your vessel, are perfect for the clandestine work we are planning. From what I've seen so far, I am inclined to agree with him. You have been told that transportation of assets in and out of foreign territory will be part of your job, and indeed that is true, but there is more. Someone who can think their way out of trouble, without use of force if possible, is a rare personality, but a personality we believe you possess.'

The Skipper glanced at McDonald, but could read nothing in his face. He couldn't decide whether he was being patronised, or being recruited into a very naïve organisation. He carefully smiled at Stevenson, 'Well thank you sir, it's nice to be appreciated. I'll pass on your praise to the crew.'

Stevenson beamed, 'Excellent. Tomorrow, I'd like you and your officers ashore to get an overview of some security and tactical issues. Say, 09:15? Good show Gentlemen, carry on.'

They both saluted and turned. As they left, the Skipper was patting his pocket for his pipe, so McDonald carefully stayed upwind of him. 'Don't worry about Stevenson Skipper. He came out of retirement for this job and he's bursting with enthusiasm now he's escaped his rose garden. Fact is, he did something like your role in the first war. Ferrying agents, landing materials and, on one occasion, he snatched one of ours from a pretty sticky situation. There could be more hiding in the files, but I can tell you they thought well of him in his day. You never know: some word or idea from his experience might help you this time around. He'll give you his slant on the work as an overview, but then you'll get further tutoring from some regular Navy types on anti-submarine work, codes and wireless discipline, that sort of thing. I'll deliver some training for you and your officers and some colleagues will do some physical training for the crew, basic self-defence and so on. Captain Stevenson will cover security from the Navy's point of view, but

I will probably develop that in more detail. The aim, from my perspective, is that we want you to understand and empathise with the operatives you might encounter and comprehend enough of their world to give help. Questions?'

'Yes, how many others will do this work? Are we part of a larger fleet?'

McDonald frowned. 'I can't give you a number, I'm afraid. If they captured you, that information could give the enemy a feel for the scale of our operations, so it's best you don't know. I can tell you this; you won't be the only ship doing this. As you'll have gathered, however, you are definitely the first to use this training facility!'

The Skipper laughed around his pipe stem. 'Yes, I can see it's an unfinished work! Which reminds me, I was going to suggest my lads lend a hand with the buildings if needed. Assuming they can be spared from the training schedule, that is.'

'Good point Skipper. Perhaps they can build it into the physical training syllabus. I'll speak to the instructors and let you know, thank you for that. Now, I must get back to Inverness, so thanks for giving me a look at the realities of what you do. I know I've only experienced a simple task in sheltered waters, and during early autumn; how you cope with the cold in the arctic winter is beyond me.'

The Skipper grimaced, 'Aye, well, I'd go mad if I was stuck in an office so each to his own, Captain. I'll be seeing you!' With a wave, the Skipper strode off to fetch Sawdon and Boulby.

The next day, the Skipper, Arthur, and Number One sat in Captain Stevenson's office. Before they left the ship, they had detailed a work party to go ashore and assist Sub-Lieutenant Cooper. The Second Engineer, Archie Lythe, and three stokers were helping Svein rig an addition to the telephone system connecting the twelve- pounder, Oerlikons and depth charge launchers to the yard's system. The Skipper had remarked how strange it felt being unable to give direct orders to the helm, engine room, and ASDIC during the exercise. Svein had realised that by using his spare parts, he could fit another handset on the flying bridge and wire in speakers on the flying bridge, engine room and wheelhouse. This enabled broadcasts both to and from the flying bridge and wheelhouse during an action. Svein also had plans for intercoms at the gun positions but needed more parts.

They all stood when the Captain entered but he cheerfully called, 'As you were gentlemen, no need for excessive formality.' The Skipper noted Number One's deep frown at this remark.

Captain Stevenson gave an unexpectedly engaging lecture on security. He explained how enemy intelligence gathered a lot of small and innocuous pieces of information which, when put together, gave a picture from which they could draw reasonable conclusions. He gave examples of airborne reconnaissance in World War One. A photograph revealed a large extension to enemy trenches and, on the far side of a nearby hill, a field canteen with long queues. The sappers then tapped a field telephone line, and discovered that a major local offensive was imminent. He asked them to consider some photographs he handed round. They showed a light cruiser in a harbour, with lighters alongside and a tug nearby, clearly signalling that the ship was preparing to sail.

'This, on its own, is nothing. A routine patrol by a cruiser with a couple of destroyers in company, perhaps. But let us consider how we might think of it if local partisans, or an agent of ours, reported a large capital ship 50 miles away loading ammunition and bunkering the day before. Suddenly there may be a much greater threat developing. This, gentlemen, is the cat-and-mouse game of intelligence gathering. Unremarkable, mundane, pedestrian facts being analysed for patterns and links. I tell this to you for two reasons: first, when your crew members interact with others, regardless of how well they know them, they cannot reveal even the smallest details of their work; the second reason is that when on operations, it is vital to be observant; recording and reporting what you see as soon as possible after the action.'

The lecture continued in this way for a while. They discussed security onboard White Nab, particularly focusing on encoding of signals. He then spoke about their role.

'We will split your time between anti-submarine operations on the coasts of Scotland and England, some convoy escort duties when needed, and your special duties. You've made an excellent start in the anti-submarine field, and we will develop those skills using some tuition and as much practice as we can organise. You will also learn the theory and practice of convoy protection. The Admiralty have already issued orders requiring merchant ships to join convoys rather than sail alone and get picked off by u-boats, so this part of your role will assist us in keeping supply lines open, not only for the military but also for the civilian population.'

They then discussed the theory of convoys and their effectiveness, management from the point of view of convoy escorts, and command structures. They learned the 'submerged approach zone' concept; if a u-boat was approaching, submerged, then its slow submerged speed resulted in it approaching from ahead in a cone defined by the ratio of the speeds of the u-boat and the convoy. This meant that regular zigzags could put the u-boat outside of the submerged approach zone, forcing it to surface in order to intercept the convoy and thus possibly revealing itself if in daylight. Zigzagging could also spoil the submarine's firing solution, but this would require very frequent course changes, which would be likely to result in disarray within the convoy. For inshore convoys, zigzagging was not practicable because of the proximity of minefields, or at least unswept areas. It became apparent to the Skipper why the Escort Commander, in charge of the military escorts, and the Convoy Commodore, in charge of the merchantmen, must be very capable people. He also recognised the challenges to communication, and the hazards involved with the zigzag manoeuvres. Of course, the most encouraging part of their capability was ASDIC, and the Skipper had already learned how vital Yorke had been to their exercise success. He made a mental note to speak to Number One and

Arthur about getting Yorke to give Pickering more training on ASDIC to ensure that Yorke did not get over-fatigued and they could replace him at sea if injured. On a more sombre note, Captain Stevenson pointed out that many of the evasive or protective measures were not available for inshore convoys sailing in restricted channels or close to shore.

Over the next week, the team arrived to erect the Nissen Huts and, as suggested by the Skipper, many of the crew assisted as part of their physical training regime. During the weeks after that, there were many exercises in open sea with submarines from Holy Loch. They proved beyond doubt that a submarine in open and deeper waters was very much harder to locate and catch. They discovered that there was some hope because at the point of attacking, the submarine's position would be confined to a much smaller circle than it had been during its initial approach pattern. There were lectures on everything from seamanship to first aid and repairing battle damage. Eventually, the lectures became less frequent and the practical exercises turned into drills, constant repetition making the correct actions for a certain circumstance almost automatic. They also received an extra crew member. 'Nev' Danby was a trawler man like themselves, but he joined the RNR pre-war. He had trained as a wireless operator. The Skipper was relieved because he had worried no professional 'sparks' was on board.

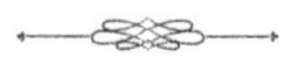

On the 20th of November 1939, the training changed completely. Captain McDonald's men started what the crew called the 'underhand training.' They were taken to a house in the Cairngorms where they learned self-defence, both unarmed and with a knife. Sergeant Smith showed them how to fight with knives and kill an enemy sentry as quietly as possible.

On the second day of Sergeant Smith's training, the Skipper had taken McDonald to one side. 'Look here, Captain, this cloak and dagger business is making me wonder exactly how risky this job will be. Why do my lads need all this?'

McDonald met his eyes, tight-lipped and glaring. 'You are being given this training on my orders, Skipper. As I've already said, I want you to empathise with our people, to understand their world. This won't make you into trained agents. That would take months or years. No, taking empathy aside, this is my way of fulfilling my promise to you. By giving your men this information, I am equipping them with the ability to protect themselves and their mates when they go ashore to deliver people or supplies. I think I've already mentioned that they may need to set up a defensive perimeter and they'll do that as silently as possible if they are to avoid alerting the enemy to their presence. That would endanger them, but also stack the odds of a safe withdrawal very much against them and your ship. This is not an extension of your duties, but an important part of them. In most cases, we can insert people using submarines, but sometimes that's simply not practical. In those instances, you will run inshore, launch your boats and drop the cargo, then be gone before anyone has time to get suspicious. If you encounter a coastal patrol, then you can protect yourselves, the vessel, and my assets. So please realise that I am doing the best I can within the very large constraint that we are fighting a war!'

The Skipper looked away, eyes downcast. 'I understand. I suppose the novelty of this training takes me away from what I know. It goes beyond the reach of my experience, and therefore, my confidence. You have my apologies.' He held out his hand, which McDonald shook with a wry smile. The Skipper turned away to rejoin the crew.

McDonald looked around at mist shrouded trees with skirts of frosty grass underneath, thinking that the war would get very much worse before it got better. His colleague Paterson strolled over, cigarette hanging from his lips. 'How are your chaps doing, McDonald?'

'In a few days, they'll be as ready as they can be. I've got a milk run job coming up, which I'll use to break them in, but after that the Admiralty wants them on a convoy down the east coast of England. I just hope that we don't lose them to a mine after the time I've invested in them.'

Paterson grimaced, 'Absolutely old chap. The boss asked me to tell you that C wants an update on our capabilities and status so could you call the boss to bring him up to speed please?'

McDonald nodded and Paterson strolled off toward the house. Watching the Skipper and crew zeroing the sights on their rifles, McDonald privately acknowledged that he was more attached to these men than he should be, yet he still promised himself that he would do everything he could to avoid sacrificing them unnecessarily. He shook his head as he questioned his world. How short a time it seemed since the last murderous war, and what scars would these men bear when this one was over?

One week later, the Skipper was in the wheelhouse with his officers, preparing for an exercise at sea when the wireless office buzzer sounded insistently. He picked up the handset. 'Skipper here.'

'Sir, I picked up a distress signal from SS Trincomalee and then exchanged signals with their wireless operator for a few minutes. They fell out of their convoy because of a mechanical problem and were heading into the Clyde for repairs. A submarine attacked them after they left the escort, and they are now taking in water. One of our aircraft was circling to keep the sub at bay but left to refuel. They repeatedly altered course while the aircraft kept the sub down; and have suffered no further attack. They're heading for The Minch and are 45 miles northwest of the Butt of Lewis light but only making around five knots.'

The Skipper frowned, 'Thanks Sparks. Is the wireless station manned in the Patrol Base?'

'It is Sir, I helped them do some training yesterday.'

'Righto, call them up please and ask for permission to provide some help.'

'Right away, sir.'

The Skipper turned to his chart table and picked up his dividers. If the damaged ship was making five knots, then she would be around 30 miles north-west of the Butt of Lewis by the time they reached her.

'Number One, call the crew to stations for leaving harbour. We'll call them to action stations some time after we've cleared the Butt of Lewis. Arthur, I won't weigh until we get permission to go, but please make sure everyone is ready to hop to it once we're given the OK.'

Arthur dashed off down the wheelhouse ladder while Number One hit the toggle on the Tannoy to call the crew.

The wireless office buzzer sounded, and the Skipper snatched the handset. 'Skipper here.'

'Permission granted, sir. They were just about to contact us with orders to assist. Base 8 asked me to inform Trincomalee.'

'Thanks Sparks,' the Skipper walked out onto the bridge deck as Arthur looked up, 'Weigh anchor Arthur!' the Mate waved acknowledgement. The Skipper nodded to him and returned to the wheelhouse. He tapped the intercom. 'Svein, we're weighing anchor now. I'll ring for dead slow ahead shortly. Warn your lads that we're going to be pushing her hard in the next few hours. We have to escort a damaged freighter to safety.'

'OK Skipper, ready when you are.'

Arthur shouted up 'Anchor's aweigh Skipper!'

The Skipper waved acknowledgement and swung the engine-room telegraph to dead slow ahead, swinging the wheel to starboard as he did so. Once clear of the headland he rang for half ahead and reached for the Tannoy, 'Gentlemen, we are going to find and escort a damaged ship which is approximately three hours steaming northwest of the Butt of Lewis, the northern point of the island. She suffered a breakdown, after which a submarine damaged her. She is now making water.' he glanced up as Danby entered the wheelhouse and placed a torn off signal slip in front of him. He sighed. 'Sparks just informed me she's a troopship, so we need to get this right. There could be hundreds of lives at stake.'

Once in mid-loch, with the crew at stations, he rang for full ahead and let George Sneaton take the wheel. He pulled on his newly issued duffel coat and headed up to the flying bridge. After briefing the lookouts, he left Number One on the flying bridge, asking him to order 'for exercise, action stations' which brought the ship's company to fighting readiness for sea. The Skipper returned to the wheelhouse and laid off a route for the search area on the chart, making sure they passed through the gap in the mine barrage going north from the Butt of Lewis.

As they reached the entrance to the loch, he gave George a course to clear the Butt of Lewis and called the wireless room. He asked Danby to contact SS Trincomalee and say help would be with them in two to three hours. He then returned to the flying bridge and briefed Number One and Arthur. They secured from exercise action stations and set the hands to cruising stations.

The Skipper tapped his teeth with a pencil. 'Gents, we may have to screen around Trincomalee using ASDIC when we find her. Once we're sure the enemy aren't in immediate firing range, I'd say we give what help we can and then perform random sweeps to deter the submarine if it catches up with us. If Trincomalee remains limited to five knots, it'll be a long day, but every mile nearer to the Minch, I'd say, will be to our advantage. The Nazis know about Holy Loch and of course there are coastal command aircraft patrolling so hopefully they'll be less willing to risk themselves as we near land.'

They rounded the Butt of Lewis at 12:15 and an hour and a half later; they went to action stations. It was choppy, but the seas were not large enough to cause them problems. The light was still reasonable, but the clouds were dark and low. They knew that by 16:00, they would lose the light. The Skipper had told Trincomalee two to three hours deliberately. They would have a higher lookout position than White Nab and if they were watching carefully from 14:15, they were likely to spot smoke before his own lookouts. Sure enough, at 14:45 the wireless cabin light glowed as the Intercom buzzed. 'Sir, Trincomalee reports smoke bearing 040°.'

'Thanks Sparks, well done,' he turned to George, 'Five degrees port George and keep her steady. We should see smoke in the next half hour.'

He alerted the crew they were likely to meet Trincomalee at around 15:15 and he asked Billy to get a brew to the gun positions and flying bridge before that time as they might soon be extremely busy.

Trincomalee acknowledged their signal, but there was no further contact until Len Egdon sighted smoke ahead. Everyone on the flying bridge trained binoculars, but Trincomalee was still hull down. The Skipper ordered an ASDIC sweep to start immediately. He turned to Arthur and Number One. 'If the sub got ahead of Trincomalee to a firing position, then being pinged may persuade the sub skipper to bugger off.'

As the distance closed, he reminded lookouts to keep watching their sectors and not to concentrate on Trincomalee, 'Same drill as always, lads: periscopes, surfacing submarines and, always, torpedo tracks coming toward us!'

Arthur called out, 'Skipper, I can see Trincomalee's upper works now. Looks like she's listing to port, but not a huge amount.'

Pickering grabbed his signal pad as a lamp began flashing from Trincomalee in the fading light. The Skipper swept around and astern with binoculars until Pickering had the signal down, 'Just read it please, Pickering.'

'Yes sir. Signal reads *Trincomalee to White Nab-stop Taking in water through damaged plates but pumps coping-stop No further enemy contact-stop.'*

The Skipper considered for a few moments before replying, 'Please send: *Will escort you and carry out precautionary sweeps as we proceed-stop. Please advise if any help needed-stop,'* he nodded to Pickering. Picking up the intercom, he buzzed Yorke at the ASDIC position. 'Yorke, if I steam at around eight knots, will you be able to listen without pinging? I'm tempted to believe that the sub either lost contact while the aircraft circled or went off in pursuit of the main convoy.'

'Yes sir, in fact I can probably listen well enough at our full speed.'

As they neared Trincomalee, the Skipper wondered if the damage might be more severe than her master knew. She appeared to have a slight hump in her sheer-line forward of the bridge and he wondered if the attack had almost broken her back; if that were the case, then her hull integrity would be degraded. He knew there was little they could do at sea if that were the case. She had been a liner in happier days and had attractive lines, now marred by extra boats, Carley Floats, and scramble nets hanging over the side. His opinion of her condition seemed further borne out when he noticed that hundreds of troops were on deck wearing what appeared to be cork-vest life preservers.

He ordered a search pattern, which involved an expanding oval around Trincomalee, increasing by half a mile or so once complete. Yorke heard nothing underwater apart from White Nab and Trincomalee. He reported Trincomalee seemed to have a propellor out of balance or damaged, and the Skipper surmised this might be what limited her speed.

When they finished the pattern just over two hours later, they formed up ahead of Trincomalee and the Skipper went down to the wheelhouse to work up an estimated position. He ordered Svein to set revolutions for 5 knots, asking Eddie Raw to take a bearing on the Butt of Lewis light. Suddenly Yorke yelled, 'Torpedoes Skipper, two went astern of us, I think. They've already passed us and came from the port side. They must have missed Trincomalee!'

The Skipper hit the Tannoy button 'Hands to action stations, engine room give me all she's got!'

As he spoke, a searchlight came on, lighting up Trincomalee. 'Cheeky bugger has surfaced!' yelled Raw.

The Skipper slammed the tannoy again. 'All guns open fire on that light! Range is about a thousand yards!' The Oerlikon crew on the port side were fastest to the draw; their string of tracers passing right of the light. As they adjusted their aim the light went out and at the same moment, the twelve pounder fired.

Yorke turned. 'He's diving, sir! I can hear the compressed air sounds clearly.'

The Skipper hit the tannoy transmit again, 'Set your charges shallow Arthur,' turning to Yorke he hissed 'Let's start an ASDIC sweep and see if we can give him a headache Yorke!'

Yorke grinned widely. 'Aye aye, sir! He's bearing red zero four five. He'll be dead ahead shortly.'

The Skipper held his breath for a second, 'Stand by depth charges, Arthur,' he looked expectantly at Yorke.

'Contact lost, sir!' Yorke yelled. They had hit the dead zone.

The Skipper ordered a turn to starboard, counting sixty seconds. 'Fire depth charges!' they heard the launchers but not the splashes and after a few seconds, they both heard and felt the charges going off astern.

Yorke turned again. 'No contact, sir. I'll continue sweeping.' Pickering stood at his side wearing a second set of headphones, excited and tense, a hunter.

The Skipper nodded, 'Hard to starboard Eddie, come around to 155°.' He watched Yorke as they turned. The lad was leaning forward, holding his earphones hard against his ears. The Skipper was thinking hard. What would he do if he was the submarine commander? Perhaps get to the other side of Trincomalee for another shot. They steamed at full speed under the stern of Trincomalee before coming to port and paralleling her course around 1500 yards from her.

Yorke glanced up. 'No contact, sir.'

The Skipper glanced at the lighthouse around 45° off the bow. As he looked, the light flashed again. The Skipper whipped out his hand bearing compass and noted the bearing and time. As he straightened, he realised the loom of the lighthouse might silhouette Trincomalee, and ordered Raw to steer a couple of degrees to port. He then waited until they had drawn far enough ahead of Trincomalee to cross her bow safely. Yorke closed his eyes and listened intently as they turned, explaining various noises to Pickering, who either nodded or made a note. They steadied on their course, but still no contact. The Skipper would have given much to light his pipe, but preferred to survive rather than smoke. After a few minutes, he ordered a turn to port, running back parallel with Trincomalee. Yorke was pinging as they turned and continued on the new course. Yorke and Pickering both pressed their headphones to their ears.

They repeated this for just over an hour, roughly circling Trincomalee and pinging as they went. The lighthouse came abeam, still with no contact. The Skipper noted bearing and time and used his sextant to estimate the height of the light above sea level so he could calculate its approximate distance. He had gone up on the flying bridge for a breath of air and had just returned to the chart table when Danby buzzed on intercom, 'Coded signal sir, they are sending a corvette and two tugs from the Clyde and they will rendezvous with us one mile east of Neist Point. They have asked for our ETA.'

The Skipper stepped out the distance to their rendezvous with his brass dividers, 'Thanks Sparks, Tell them 10:30hrs tomorrow at present speed.'

'Will do, sir.'

The Skipper relaxed readiness after another hour of sweeping, allowing the crew to rotate below for hot food and a brew and, once well inside the Minch at around 20:00, they did a wide sweep and then he secured from action stations. He sent Yorke off watch. The lad seemed exhausted from the concentration, and might be needed again before the night was over. He knew also that their action would have given Pickering valuable operational experience and letting him have the watch might add to confidence. In his guts, the Skipper didn't believe the u-boat would risk more populated waters in The Minch, but reminded himself that u-boat operations were all about subterfuge. Checking that Pickering was happy to do the listening watch, he said they would only call Yorke if there were a contact. The Skipper busied himself with an after action report and log updates before the next sweep. There was no contact as they circled and Pickering continued concentrating with his eyes shut as he listened to the underwater noise but reported nothing suspicious. All was quiet until Arthur spelled the Skipper at 23:00. His friend had turned up an hour early for his watch, knowing that the Skipper must be tired by now.

The rest of the night passed peacefully, regular sweeps revealing nothing. At 08:00, the Skipper joined Arthur on the flying bridge. 'Well, there we are, Arthur, we survived our first action. A strange feeling, eh?'

'Aye Skipper, but everyone did well. I can feel their confidence in themselves. We need to watch for overconfidence but I'm sure the crew will be alright!'

Number One joined them fresh from his 08:00 divisions and ships administration. There were no faults or machinery issues, so he could make the report brief. The Skipper had his pipe lit, so the young officer decided he would inspect the gun mountings while he had light. Arthur smiled because the Skipper never noticed the effect his pipe had. Or perhaps he pretended not to notice.

Trincomalee had slowed slightly, so they did not make rendezvous until 10:50. The corvette signalled they were relieved as escort and as they turned back toward the patrol base; they heard ragged cheering from Trincomalee. Hundreds of soldiers lined the railings, and the officers were waving from the bridge wings. The Skipper gave a toot on the steam horn to acknowledge them and smiled as White Nab turned away.

That afternoon, they anchored off in Little Loch Broom and were tidying up when Number One reported the base was signalling for the Skipper to go ashore.

After a brief delay, Boulby and Dunsley were pulling the oars to deliver the Skipper and Number One.

Ashore, they trudged up to the shack, now the seaside residence of Captain Stevenson, as he called it. Most functions of the base had moved to the forest of Nissen huts behind the old shack, rendering it unnecessary but Stephenson liked a quiet place to work.

He was his usual beaming self, shaking their hands as they entered. 'Well done once again, chaps! We were worrying, but you got your charge home safely, I hear?'

The Skipper smiled wearily. 'We did, sir. The officers and crew did well.' He related the events of the previous day and night. Captain Stevenson became more excited as he learned about the encounter with the u-boat.

'Your first actual operation and you not only encountered the enemy but beat him off! I expect you'll claim the u-boat as probable Skipper?'

'No sir, we don't believe that he had spotted us and, while we probably cleared his bridge with the Oerlikon, we saw no evidence of a strike with the twelve pounder. Also, after our depth charge pattern, there were no sounds of a sub breaking up from ASDIC, so I don't believe we sank him. Our chief priority was to shield Trincomalee. I felt, and still feel, that another sweep risked leaving her and the troops onboard her without protection at a critical time.'

Stevenson nodded slowly, 'Of course. If you'd picked the wrong area to search, he might have got another salvo of torpedoes on their way. Faultless reasoning Skipper, and well done again. Now I suspect you two might need some rest, but I wanted to let you know that Captain McDonald will arrive tomorrow morning and has asked for a mission planning session with all of us. Would you be ashore at 09:00 tomorrow please?'

'Definitely sir. I'd like to bring the Mate as well, if I may? I think the more my officers are familiar with the plan, the better they are placed to execute it. Especially if I were out of action for any reason.'

'No objection from me Skipper, now you fellows do what you need to, and I'll see you tomorrow.'

They saluted and left for the boat, which bumped against the pontoon while Boulby and Dunsley smoked on the jetty.

'So if McDonald is leading the planning, Number One, this will be an outing on behalf of the sneaky beaky club, I imagine.' The Skipper looked at the misty hills over the loch, wondering what tomorrow might bring.

Chapter 8

57° 51' 42" N, 05° 18' 35" W

('Patrol Base 8' near Badcaul)

Tuesday 5th December 1939

The Skipper, Arthur and Number One sat in a Nissen hut, waiting for McDonald. The building was utilitarian, but at least it was dry. Curved, corrugated steel panels were bolted to a frame and blocked at both ends with wooden boarding, into which was set a door. It felt like a steel lined rabbit hole with the ends blocked in. In the middle of the room a pot-bellied stove, burning peat, did its best to raise the air above freezing with little success, so nobody had removed their coats. At the end of the hut opposite the door they had built a wooden Dias, raising the floor level by a foot. On it was a table, and they had painted the wooden wall behind white. Three rows of seating faced the Dias in the smoke-hazed room.

They had made sure that the ship was ready for sea again on the previous afternoon. A steam lighter had come alongside from Ullapool and fully bunkered them. The Skipper had commented, 'It's grand to be coaled on our mooring, and even better not having to pay for it!'

Captain McDonald entered the room, waving at them to sit. 'Good morning to you all, gentlemen. Apologies for the slight delay. There was a good deal of fog about this morning further inland. I'm told that you've been giving the Kriegsmarine a drubbing and saving hundreds of troops?'

The Skipper grimaced at the floor. 'We just did what we're paid for, Captain.'

McDonald smiled internally. Yet another confirmation of the Skipper's personality; he was no glory hunter. He smiled broadly, 'Of course, but well done anyway, especially as I learned that there were sixteen hundred Canadian troops on board.'

Stepping on to the Dias, McDonald opened his bag, placing it on the floor next to the table. 'To business, then. Gentlemen, I have a mission for you. Nothing glamorous and hopefully it will be a very simple job. I'd like you to drop two of my people off in Norway. I believe you know Slyngøya Island,' the Skipper and Arthur nodded, 'well, I need our people to be dropped at a beach which is south of Talga harbour at 03:00 on Saturday the 9th. To be clear, there are two beaches and this is the furthest away from the town, southeast. We'll provide a chart before you go back onboard.'

The Skipper did some mental maths, 'That'll be roughly 60 hours steaming, so we need to be away early afternoon tomorrow. I'll check the weather and sea state and calculate an accurate figure later, leaving a contingency for unforeseen circumstances. One question, Captain, is it essential to use that beach? I know a private way to get into the town from the inlet, if it's of use.'

McDonald shook his head. 'They're heading away from the town, so I'd rather they landed south. Their contact will meet them there and won't want to be seen by any insomniacs in the town.'

'I'm assuming we are going in dark and silent?' The Skipper asked.

'Absolutely Skipper, I was going to ask if you have spare berths in the aft cabin. I'd prefer the two passengers to be kept out of sight if possible.'

'We can quarter them in the aft cabin certainly, and they can access the boat deck if they need to stretch their legs. It's unmanned mostly. I'll speak to them once they're on board. Returning to the approach, I'd like to come around the south side of the island, which is almost deserted, and then round Talga Poeng toward the beach. We can send the boat in from there with minimal line-of-sight from the town.' the Skipper looked up at McDonald, who nodded.

'Yes Skipper, that sort of detail I'll leave to you. You're far more aware of the geography and sea conditions than ourselves. I'd just like to be very clear on one point. Norway is a neutral country, so use of weapons is out of the question. All your guns should have muzzle caps fitted and tarpaulin covers over the top. You are off-course and seeking shelter if challenged, so sabotage some equipment if you need to make it convincing. I will provide a code pad for the operation and, if you are to be boarded, you are to send the relevant code word on the frequency specified, then throw the codes overboard in a weighted bag. It is likely that they would intern you under those circumstances, but we believe we could quickly negotiate your release. Questions?'

They clarified a few points of detail and studied the chart McDonald had rolled out, then began moving toward the door. McDonald handed the Skipper the code book, asking him to remain for a few minutes.

'Thanks for your input, Skipper. I just wanted to check that you're happy with arrangements?'

The Skipper looked deadpan, saying, 'Well, I'd rather be in the Mariner's Rest, but in the circumstances I'm tolerably content.' McDonald laughed, 'As would I Skipper, but needs must, I suppose.'

The Skipper's mouth straightened, a slight frown appearing. 'I'm happy enough with the ship and crew. We're a tad short handed but I expect that's the same for everyone. Sparks will train up some lads to read morse as the opportunity arises.'

'Good, I'm glad to hear that all's well. I want to clarify this mission a little. Obviously, it's better if you know nothing about details, but I know your engineer originated on that island. I can assure you, my men are not operating against the interests of Norway, but we need to speak to their government without German intelligence being aware. Therefore, we're not openly flying our people in.'

The Skipper met his eyes. 'Thank you for that. I hadn't considered that aspect at all. I'll have a quiet word with Svein before we sail.'

They shook hands, and the Skipper went off to Captain Stevenson with their bunkering records. They made their way back to the ship, dodging workboats who were laying moorings about a cable offshore.

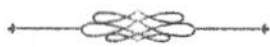

They slipped their new mooring at 19:00 on 6th December. It was cold, with a sharp northerly breeze and sleety rain. The Skipper had donned his old oilskins and was up on the flying bridge until they reached open water. One or two crofts were lax in their blackout measures and the lights shone liquid, as though half dissolved. The chuckle of the bow wave and the sleet made it seem like the entire world was water.

McDonald's men, introduced as Able and Baker, went straight to the aft cabin. The Skipper had spoken to Svein about the purpose of the trip before they arrived. As expected, there had been no real need. 'I trust you Skipper and I know that if there were a problem, then you would be open with me or resolve the issue differently. Also, don't forget that I'm legally a British citizen, though I suppose, like you, I'm really a citizen of this ship, wherever in the world she is!'

All was quiet as they steamed steadily north, then north northeast to round Cape Wrath. They altered course to run roughly parallel with the Orkneys and Shetland. Daylight came, grey but clearing fairly quickly as the breeze freshened from the northwest. By 0930 they were west of the Orkneys when George Sneaton called, 'Aircraft sir, high and coming from southeast. I think it's a Heinkel!' The Skipper ordered a turn to starboard to hide their course until the aircraft had gone over. After a few minutes Sneaton called again, 'It is a Heinkel, sir, and he's descending!'

The Skipper hit the tannoy, 'Hands to action stations, engine room, give me full ahead.' Feet clattered on decks and ladders all over the ship as the crew ran for their stations. The Skipper trained his glasses on the aircraft and saw it was in a gentle dive and headed straight for them. Fortunately, their course-change had put the aircraft abeam. He ran to the back of the flying bridge and shouted, 'Number One, tell the guns to hold their fire. He may not spot that we have the Oerlikons if we're lucky. When he's close, tell the starboard gun to fire and have the port gun fire upwards, as they taught us. Make him fly through the shot!'

'Aye aye, sir!' Number One sprinted toward the gun mount.

As he turned to track the aircraft, he saw Egdon fixing the Lewis gun to the starboard bridge-wing mounting, 'Keep him busy as soon as he's in range, Len!'

'Will do Skipper!' his face looked savage.

The Skipper trained his glasses again. No sign of the bomb doors opening: so a strafing run, and not long to go. He hit the tannoy again. 'We are about to be strafed. Non-essential personnel take cover.' His heart pounded, but his voice stayed calm, just as T'owd Skipper had taught him.

When the aircraft fired, he saw flashes from the nose gun and could hear rounds clanging as they hit the ship. Len emptied his drum of ammunition to no apparent effect and the Oerlikons opened up; starboard first and port a second afterward. Shortly after the aircraft passed over, it suddenly jinked hard right. A strip of something fluttered from its port wing to splash into the waves. For a second the Skipper thought the Heinkel, with those obscene black crosses under its wings, would slide into the sea, but it levelled off and arced round, climbing as it went. Again, he reached for the tannoy toggle. 'Hold hard lads, he may come round for another try!'

To his relief, he was wrong. The aircraft seemed to wobble slightly, although he couldn't be certain, and it climbed away and was gone. Once again, the Skipper reached for the tannoy, 'Secure from action stations, and well done everyone! Inspect for damage.' he was worried by all the clanging noises he'd heard.

The Skipper ordered a course change to resume their original course and spoke to Svein on the intercom, asking for revolutions for eight knots. He lit his pipe and was just about to send someone to ask Billy for a brew when Arthur appeared on the bridge ladder. 'Any damage, Arthur?' He looked up and saw Arthur's expression.

'Would you come with me please, Skipper?' Arthur didn't wait, but turned to clamber down the port side bridge ladder. The Skipper followed, face knotting with concern. At deck level, he saw a circle of men blocking the way, so gently pushed through. He stopped as if someone had punched him when he saw the sight beyond. Number One was sitting on the deck muttering, his back against the deckhouse, cradling young Eddie Raw. Blood spattered the deckhouse behind them and Eddie's eyes stared out at the horizon. The Skipper instantly knew they were sightless. He knelt next to the dead man and his young officer.

'Number One, we should move Eddie, I think?' looking up, he found the Cook. 'Billy, take these and bring two bottles of rum from the bonded cupboard in my cabin. Every man is to receive a good tot.' He handed some keys to Billy. Number one was clearly deep in shock, so the Skipper told two lads to fetch a stretcher so they could lay Eddie out and clean him up.

He lowered his head to get into Number One's eye line and spoke quietly, 'Number One, listen to me. Eddie is dead and we'll deal with our feelings in private. Right now, you are a Royal Navy Officer and you have a responsibility to those under your command. I'll lay this man down and, when I do, you must stand and walk with me to the aft cabin. Do you understand?' Number One's eyes flickered up to him so he gently prized his officer's hands apart to release Eddie, before lowering him gently to the deck. The lads had returned with a stretcher, so the Skipper asked Arthur to supervise laying Eddie out on the afterdeck while he got Number One below.

Billy had returned and was tipping a tot into Number One, who spluttered but seemed to recover awareness. The stretcher was disappearing around the corner. The Skipper adopted a businesslike air. 'Right Number One, time to get below and change, I think? I'll come with you,' he turned to the remaining crew and said gently, 'time to break it up, lads. We'll have a service for him later. I want him buried in British waters and before we go into action again. Arthur or myself will come and speak with you all before then. I'd be grateful if someone would swill the deck clean.'

His last words caused his voice to catch and Dave Roxby put his hand on the Skipper's shoulder before standing back respectfully and straightening, 'Don't worry Skipper, we'll sort it.'

Billy and the Skipper got Number One to his feet and half dragged him to the companionway in the galley passage. They were careful to block the view of Arthur and the lads tending to Eddie as they frog marched Number One across the afterdeck. Once into the corridor, he seemed to shake himself a little, so the Skipper stood behind him and eased off Number One's blood smeared jacket. 'Right, get yourself below Number One and take some time to gather yourself. I'd suggest you go into your own cabin as our guests are in the aft cabin and they're not family.' As Number One shuffled numbly down the ladder, the Skipper turned to Billy. 'Check he gets in there, would you, Billy? Then sponge off Number One's jacket if you can. Hopefully, he didn't see the blood on it. I'd appreciate a brew after that. I'll be in the wheelhouse.'

The Skipper walked slowly back toward the wheelhouse ladder. He had almost forgotten how swiftly and efficiently icy death struck down the innocent.

The Skipper checked course and speed and updated the bridge crew on what had happened. He then climbed to the flying bridge and broke the news to the lookouts before lighting his pipe. He noticed the lookouts covered their sectors diligently, but they also scanned the sky, as well as the horizon now. That reminded him, and he turned to George Sneaton. 'Well done for spotting that aircraft early enough, George. The attack had an awful consequence for us, but if the lads hadn't knocked a lump off the aircraft, he'd have circled back and may have killed others. You did well.'

The Skipper got to the wheelhouse as Billy appeared with his tea. Billy nodded toward the tin mug, saying, 'I've strengthened it Skipper.' The Skipper had already smelled sweet rum. Billy gave a forced smile and went to give the lookouts on the flying bridge their tots.

Arthur appeared on the bridge deck. 'I've updated Svein and Archie in the engine room, Skipper. Number One seems better, but a long way from recovering.'

The Skipper thought for a moment, 'I'll speak to him after I've done my report, Arthur. Well done back there. Did you see what happened?'

Arthur's eyes slid toward the companionway to the Skipper's cabin and the Skipper got the message, 'Maintain course and speed please, I'll be in my cabin with the Mate.'

As they settled, Arthur apologised, 'Sorry Reggie, I didn't want to talk in front of the lads. I was checking the depth charges were secure and disarmed, in case they bombed us. I was going forward and Eddie came around in front of me. He'd apparently been helping Svein and was slow getting out of the engine room so he was running for his action station. It was pure chance Skipper, Eddie went ahead of me and we both ducked as the plane went over. All hell was breaking out from our own guns, but I saw flashes and smoke from a backward pointing machine gun on the plane. There was a glass window thing on the plane's underside. Anyway, Number One was coming down the deckhouse ladder. I think he was going to the twelve pounder when Eddie flipped back against him and they slid down. Number One was busy shouting about assaulting an officer or some such rubbish when he realised Eddie was dead and clammed up. Poor Eddie, he never knew what happened. A bullet had gone straight through his heart by the look of things and another hit him in the belly. I didn't even hear him shout.' There was a long silence. 'Billy has volunteered to sew him into the weighted bag and a couple of off-watch lads are helping.'

The Skipper sighed. 'Well, at least we can tell his family that he didn't suffer. Right, I need to write the after action report, Arthur. I'm thinking that we'll bury him this afternoon. I'm not comfortable taking the poor lad's body into an operation. Are you happy with that?'

'Definitely. We can heave-to and call all hands. Maybe the RN lads will stand watch while our lads attend.' Arthur's head dipped. 'Who'd have thought an hour ago that we'd be arranging a funeral?'

The Skipper put a hand on his shoulder. 'We both know that war is vicious, Arthur. Even when it's unavoidable. We just have to get the job done, one day at a time.' There was a long silence. 'Can you spell me for half an hour in the wheelhouse while I write the after action report? If I don't do it now, I probably never will.'

Arthur nodded and took his leave. The Skipper had so much to say but realised that his log and the after action report weren't the places to say it so he painstakingly recorded a cold series of facts and times save for one entry, 'At 09:35 on 7th December 1939, Able Seaman Edward Raw, aged 20, gave his life for his country and his ship. God rest his soul.' After that he wrote a letter to Eddie's parents, praising the lad and reassuring them that his death had been instant. He also apologised for the need to bury Eddie at sea but explained that they were on active service when he died, so it seemed more respectful to bury him with full honours than to store his body. He felt better when he finished, but not much.

Arthur and the Skipper went to see Number One at 13:00, finding him more alert but very sombre. He held a cigarette in fingers which trembled slightly. They checked him for physical injury, wondering if he'd taken a blow to the head, but there was nothing to be found. The Skipper stood him down until 20:00, thinking that they would stand watch together and he could make sure Number One was fit for duty.

At 15:00, the horizon and sky were clear, so they stopped the propellor and gathered in the well. Arthur fetched Number One from his cabin. They all stared at the body laid under a red ensign. They had agreed that Eddie was more fisherman than naval rating, so the merchant flag was the right one. The sky was grey but some watery beams of light broke through as the Skipper briefly spoke about Eddie's life and his value in the crew, then read the service from his book of common prayer. Before they consigned the sailcloth bag to the water the Skipper walked forward and laid his hand on Eddie's chest, 'When you get up there Eddie, you find the lad with the long white beard and tell him he'll have me to answer to for this.'

The Skipper nodded, so Arthur and George lifted the end of the fish room shelf on which they had laid him, letting Eddie slip into the water. The Skipper grabbed the red ensign and turned to his crew. 'From now on, when we fight, we will fly this as a battle ensign and every shot we land will be for Eddie.'

The crew filtered back to their work in ones and twos, but Number One stared out at the horizon for nearly an hour before returning to his cabin.

As afternoon became evening, the Skipper sat in his cabin looking sombre. He decided a pipe of baccy and a mug of tea were needed. He recognised Arthur's tread as he came down from the wheelhouse.

'Now then Skipper,' as he spoke, Arthur's face looked worried.

'Everything alright?' The Skipper asked.

'I'm not entirely sure, to be honest,' Arthur sucked his teeth, 'I've been down to see Number One and I can't make head nor tail of him. It's like he's only half there. All the stuffing has gone out of him and I don't know what to do.'

The Skipper shook his head. 'I've seen this in the last lot, Arthur. We had a young coal trimmer come up on deck just as they torpedoed a ship. He was in a trance for days and we had a job getting him to go out on deck when we were at sea. A strange reaction. He stayed like that as long as I knew him.'

Arthur raised his eyebrow. 'So what's doing with Number One, do you think?'

The Skipper tapped his front teeth with his pipe stem. 'Leave him to me, Arthur. He's big on naval tradition and his father's expectations, so I think I've got a lever to prise him open again. One thing's for certain though, we can't carry a watch keeping officer who can't get out of his bunk...' Arthur nodded and looked at the Skipper. 'Are you OK Reggie? you look tired.'

The Skipper looked at the grey linoleum. 'Oh, you know Arthur, young Eddie is in my mind too. I realised that, in my head, I've always wanted to preserve ship and crew; in that order. It's very logical, without the ship the crew have no living and so the ship must come first. Now I'm not so sure. Arthur carefully studied his friend's face, 'Reggie, so far as I've seen you look after the ship as needed, and the crew when they have a problem. I'm not so sure it's as black and white as you think. Don't forget, we're at war now. The enemy's job is to kill us and ours is to kill him.' The Skipper looked up, 'Aye, well that's the pure evil of war Arthur. To defeat an animal, we must become beasts ourselves!'

19:45 came around and Arthur turfed Number One out of his cabin. Whatever the Skipper had to say would go down better if he didn't have to dress him down for turning up late for his watch beforehand.

The Skipper looked at his first officer in the light from the binnacle. The young man looked tired and slightly bedraggled. His reactions were slow, his voice lethargic. Once they'd taken over, the Skipper tried fresh air and conversation first. 'Right Number One, you and I shall take in the sights from the flying bridge. Tropical sunshine and grass skirts galore, I expect!'

George Sneaton snorted as he gently eased the wheel, 'Len's up top Skipper. If he's wearing a grass skirt, I'd like permission to jump overboard!' Number One glared at him.

The Skipper grinned, 'If I have to bear the sight, then so do you, Mr Sneaton. Permission denied!' With a wink, he led Number one up the steps to the flying bridge.

Outside, the cold was biting, and the wind had gone southeast. The Skipper was hoping for a fast moving anticyclone so that rain or sleet would give them some cover as they neared the island. For now, there was a tear in the cloud cover through which the stars glittered gloriously. He checked the lookouts were alert, and the compass agreed with the binnacle, an old habit from the last war. Clouds were closing the little window on the stars, but all was clear on the horizon.

'Strict blackout gentlemen, no lights or cigarettes and minimum noise from here on in.'

'Right you are Skipper,' a voice whispered out of the darkness.

'So, Number One. Time for some chart work.'

The Skipper got no response as they descended the steps. When they entered the relative warmth of the wheelhouse, the Skipper turned to his first officer. 'Would you stand watch here for a short while, please? I want to check our arrival time at Slyngøya'. He disappeared down the companionway toward his cabin. Number One had barely responded to him since coming on watch and the Skipper was losing patience fast. He pursed his lips, then slapped his table and called the wheelhouse. 'George, could you ask Number One to bring down my North Sea Pilot from the table up there?'

After a couple of minutes, Number One appeared in the doorway. He stopped and stared at the floor. The Skipper glared at him, 'Out with it Number One, what on earth is the trouble?'

Number One blew out his cheeks. 'I'm surprised you have to ask. I assume you saw what happened today.'

The Skipper's voice was tight and low, 'Too right I did. I saw a lad I respected become...'

'A side of meat, that's what became of him!' Number One screamed, spittle flying.

'I wasn't speaking about Eddie Number One. I was speaking about you. A promising young officer, a man I previously respected, who fell apart in front of his men. Now, I can forgive a lapse if it's an initial reaction: the first time under fire can make or break a man, and death is never easy to watch. What I'm finding difficult to accept is the pit you're allowing yourself to dive into. Good God man, you're an officer in the Royal Navy and First Officer on my ship, yet you're sulking like a child! I know your story, a square peg in a round hole and the old man moulding you into an image of himself. All this I accepted when I made you part of this crew. I let you find your voice and your position. After a "get to know you" period, the lads respected you, but respect is hard won and easily lost. I saw your face earlier when George cracked a joke: it was utter contempt, and believe me when I say that George will have seen it too.

What you clearly misunderstand is that fishermen and naval ratings alike have a gallows sense of humour. They know if they whine and let themselves get bogged down by their situation, then they'll break. These lads, this amazing crew, are stronger than that. They accept their situation, dealing with it as best they can, but work to better it. If death strikes, they pay their respects and then move on to get the job done, but understand this, Eddie was family and they're all hurting inside. None of us feel like joking, but those small moments of relief open a door. That door leads to accepting what happened, so as a leader, I welcome them. I do this because I am their skipper. The man they look to when things are bad. I simply don't have the option to stop and grieve or have some kind of breakdown. They need leaders. Arthur does it quietly, they know he's like steel if someone is buggering him around but their respect for his constancy, his ability to teach them skills and his commitment to them as a crew, well, that means he seldom has to raise his voice. You were doing well. They saw you working for the ship, for this little family, but now, Number One, you need to make a big decision. You can either develop a way of putting hard things in a box and dealing with them later, or you can sink into oblivion. If you can't pick up the reins of leadership, you have no place in my crew!'

Number One looked ashen; he took out a cigarette, tapping it on his case before shakily lighting it. The Skipper knew he was taking a risk, but he had to stop the descent into nervous exhaustion, as the navy described it. After a time, Number One softly spoke, 'Sir, I am deeply sorry. I've let you down. When Raw fell on me, I was yelling at him to get off me and asking him what he thought he was doing. When I saw the blood and his eyes staring, a switch clicked and I was stuck inside a sort of echoing room. Everything became distorted, unreal, with no way out! At the funeral, the darkness came down again, even though I thought I was getting better. I watched the mate and yourself dealing with things, doing things right instinctively, and it occurred to me I will never be like that. I'll never live up to what those around me do as a matter of course,' his voice tailed off.

The Skipper looked at his hands for a moment, then spoke gently. 'Listen; what you are describing is nothing more than youth and inexperience. When I was in this ship with T'owd Skipper, I was fine. It was just my dad teaching me about life and work. When I got apprenticed into a boat sailing out of Hull, I felt many of the inadequacies you described just then. During that time though, I came to realise that my father had given me everything I needed to make good: a strong work ethic, listening to others but speaking my truth, being honest, accepting others for what they are but standing up to them if they were wrong uns. These things are in you too, Number One. I've seen them since that first passage we made. Learn to look at yourself honestly: see your strengths and recognise weaknesses. Where you can improve, and we all can, just set about learning whatever you need to make that improvement. Never dwell on the failing, just focus on the route to overcoming it. If you can't work out what that is, then ask myself or Arthur, but not in front of the lads. To them, we are rocks and never doubt ourselves. Does that make sense?'

'It does, sir, and thank you. I can't say it'll be easy, but I can promise I'll try my best to put my role on this ship above all else.'

'Do that, and everything else will fall into place, lad. Oh and, if it helps, I won't object if you take the trigger yourself the next time some Nazi bugger points an aeroplane at our ship!'

The edges of Number One's mouth flickered up, just for an instant, and the Skipper dared to hope.

For the rest of the watch, Number One remained quiet, but he became responsive and made eye contact when spoken to. The Skipper noticed, when Number One fetched a brew, he quietly handed a mug to George, then took two up to the flying bridge for the lookouts.

Chapter 9

62° 55' 06" N, 06° 52' 37" E

(Slyngøya Island, Norway)

Saturday 9th December 1939

As Arthur took over at the end of the watch, the Skipper calculated they were just over an hour from their course change, which would begin the run in toward the Norwegian coast. He gave instructions to reduce revolutions to avoid arriving early at the beach.

Number One looked all in, so the Skipper sent him to his bunk as soon as Arthur arrived. Arthur smiled at the Skipper. 'Someone looks happier, Skipper?'

'At the moment, Arthur, yes. I ended up giving him a roasting to bring him out of his black mood. I'm uncertain it was the right thing, but we need him sharp for the operation, so let's both monitor him. Right, if there's nothing else, I'm going to turn in. By the way, Arthur, let's watch the lads too. You never know, there might be more people struggling.'

'Aye Skipper, sleep well.'

The Skipper ached as he got into his bunk. It was now his turn to recriminate; he couldn't help but wonder whether, if he had turned away rather than let the aircraft hit them abeam, Eddie might still be alive. Intellectually, he knew the bullets would have raked them from stem to stern, so more people could have been hit. As his eyelids drooped, he could hear his father saying, 'Make the best decision you can, then live with it. But always remember this; if you have to decide quickly, it'll rarely be perfect, so be kind to yourself afterwards.'

The Skipper dragged his head up to find Arthur waking him once again. Arthur had insisted they resume their normal watches, so the Skipper could rest before they closed the shore. He had initially resisted but eventually realised that Number One's confidence would take another knock if he didn't let him stand his watch. As he had gone off watch at 08:00, he had broadcast on the Tannoy, 'We will shortly enter Norwegian waters. Norway is a neutral country, so we must cover all guns, fit muzzle caps, and they must remain unmanned until we leave Norwegian jurisdiction. Let's dismount the Lewis gun as well. As we near shore, the Chief will be on the bridge with me to handle communications, but we don't expect to encounter any patrols. Sadly, there'll be no opportunity to go ashore for akvavit on this trip!'

Before turning in, he had checked whether 'Able and Baker' had everything they needed. They said they were fine, and the Skipper suggested they stretch their legs on the boat deck after dark so they could 'get the creases out' before disembarking.

He went to the wheelhouse with a mug of tea, feeling refreshed. Nodding to Yorke and Pickering, who were listening to the hydrophones, he checked the log. All seemed well, so he tapped the barometer, which remained obstinately steady. Despite the relatively high pressure, the clouds were dense, if high, and squalls of fine snow occasionally crossed their path so they might have some cover.

Around 14:00, they saw smoke off to starboard but pressed on at their current speed. The Skipper felt they seemed more innocent by doing so. Around 15:30, it was already dark, and they spotted steaming lights as they emerged from a snow squall. They were not showing lights, so once again, they maintained course and speed. The other vessel's starboard green light eventually disappeared, and they saw only a stern light so they were clear.

At 01:30, they had a firm fix using the light on Moøya and the Start Klippe (Start Rock) light on Slyngøya. They slowed to 6 knots and warned their passengers to prepare. Number One had seen to the inflatable and had it ready in the ship's waist so that they could go quickly when needed. They crept along the rocky southern coast of Slyngøya; the Skipper holding their course, until he could see the lights of Talga past Djevelens Peong (Devil's Point). Once there, he knew he was safe to come to port and head due north until he could see the harbour lights beyond Talga Poeng. He slowed to three knots and came around to 285°, which would put them just off the beach when the last lights of Talga were abeam on the port side. He dropped speed until he just had steerage way and Arthur heaved the lead line until he had three fathoms, at which point he whistled and the Skipper called for all stop and noted the arrival time as 02:45. The engine-room telegraph bell sounded very loud as they stood on the flying bridge, as did the rattle of the anchor chain.

Able and Baker waited until they saw two flashes from a red lamp and clapped Number One on the back. Over went the boat, without a splash. Boulby, Dunsley and Number One were quickly in it, holding her in with a line through the ship's scuppers. Able and Baker went over with a wave to the flying bridge and they pulled away toward the line of surf. The Skipper took precautionary bearings on the last light in the village and the one on the entrance to the distant harbour as a snow squall hit them. The snow passed quickly and at 03:10 they heard the paddlers labouring back. Once they were safely aboard and the rubber boat recovered, the Skipper called for dead slow ahead and wheel hard to starboard. They gradually gained way until she answered the helm and then came round to 105°, the reciprocal course to their approach, and crept away. At no point did they hear any sound or see anything to alarm them. Once they were in deeper water, the Skipper called for revolutions for six knots.

As Number One climbed the steps to the flying bridge to report back, the Skipper looked around at the dark shapes around him, saying, 'OK lads, we can start breathing again.' He shook his head at the strangeness of sneaking into a place they had visited openly so often.

The trip out of Norwegian waters was completely uneventful and once in international waters, they hoisted their white ensign at the stern and reversed their outbound course. As they passed west of Orkney, they all tensed a little, but the only aircraft they saw was a high level reconnaissance over Scapa Flow. Whether it was friend or foe was unclear, because it was too high to be recognisable.

They captured their mooring buoy and rang 'finished with engine' at 21:46 on 11th December 1939.

The following morning at 09:30, the Skipper, Number One and Arthur sat in Captain Stevenson's hut with Stevenson and McDonald present for a debrief. The haze of Stephenson's cigar and Number One's cigarettes hung heavy. The Skipper gave them the bare facts, saying an aircraft had strafed them, but they suffered no damage. He then described their approach to the beach and the two red flashes which prompted McDonald's men to ask to be delivered ashore. McDonald was visibly relieved when they mentioned the signal. Waiting until the end the Skipper said, 'A smooth mission, but I have to report that I lost one of my crew who was machine gunned from the aircraft as it withdrew. I have a full report of the entire mission here.' He handed the envelope to McDonald, seeing pain in the other man's eyes.

'I'm so sorry to hear that, Skipper. Who was it?'

'Young Edward Raw sir; he was a promising lad. I'm only sorry I had to bury him at sea, but I didn't want his body onboard in case they intercepted and interned us. At least he rests in home waters.'

McDonald and Stevenson both commiserated, then moved on swiftly. Arthur noted Number One's lip tremble as the Skipper spoke, but the lad controlled himself well.

Stevenson straightened, 'I have good and bad news Skipper, the bad news is that you're needed in Southend on Sea as part of a convoy escort up the east coast from the Thames to Methil in the Firth of Forth and sailing on Christmas Eve. The good news is we have nothing for you before that, except re-provisioning tomorrow morning. There's no reason you can't call in at your home port on the way. Just be at Southend Pier by 11:00 on the 23rd and report to the Naval Control Service HQ on Royal Terrace for detailed orders. The only information I have is the convoy will marshall that afternoon and you'll sail in the early hours of the 24th. Your engineer requested some spare parts which are arriving by truck early tomorrow, so just drop ashore and collect them if you would. Skipper, I'm genuinely sorry about what happened to your crew member but, once again, you put up a good show on the mission.'

The Skipper took his letter from his pocket. 'Thank you, sir. One last thing. I wonder if I could post this to the lad's family. There are no details of our mission in it. I thought it might be better if the news came from me, rather than a just telegram. I'll visit them when we get to Scarborough, too: not sure of the protocol, to be honest.'

'Send your letter Skipper, by all means. In fact, leave it with Sub-Lieutenant Cooper here and he'll get it off for you. It says much for you, both as a man and a commander, that you do this yourself. Godspeed, and we'll see you here after your convoy, unless our paths cross in the morning.'

'Thank you, sir.' They stood and saluted, then McDonald walked outside with them, pulling the Skipper to one side as they closed the door, 'Skipper, I can't give you details because it's classified but I wanted to let you know that this mission was important to the interest of our country. You can tell the lad's family that he died doing something that could shorten the war and ensure victory against the Nazi's.'

'Thank you for that, Captain. I'm sure it will be no comfort at first, but as time passes, it may mean something to the family.'

'I hope so Skipper, but it's a small return for the life of their boy,' he sighed and shook his head, 'righto then, I'll let you get on and we'll see you back here in the New Year; safe voyages!'

Once back on board, the Skipper slumped into his cabin chair, writing letters to Mother and Mavis before turning in.

Chapter 10

54° 16' 59" N, 00° 23' 25" W

(Scarborough, North Riding)

Saturday 16th December 1939

The night was dark, and the cold almost paralysing as they approached Scarborough. The fog was so dense it felt like their ship was the entire world. Sound was muffled and distorted. The dim, red light from the binnacle made the wheelhouse seem homely, somehow safe. The Skipper had put men on the whaleback as a listening watch and they rotated every half-hour throughout their watch. It was exhausting, but better than a collision.

They reduced speed to three knots to keep machinery noise down and give them more time for collision avoidance. In happier times the Skipper would have gone much further offshore, but there was now a minefield outside the coastal shipping routes which limited options. The passage had become horribly slow as soon as they had changed course off Duncansbury Head to follow the coast down past Peterhead. The frost and fog had worsened and their speed had steadily reduced the further south they went. Arthur kept his own counsel because he sensed the Skipper was hating this. They were well used to freezing conditions, ice and fog, but there were fewer ships that could run them under in the Barents Sea than on the convoy route between London and the Firth of Forth! Luckily, there were buoys marking the safe channels every half mile or so. Dim though they were, they could use them to 'buoy hop' from port to port, though they knew that care had to be taken as the buoys often dragged in bad weather or the lights got damaged in collisions.

But they had steadily made progress, and the Skipper had telephoned the harbour master from Patrol Base 8 to inform him of their intended arrival. He also had the foresight to mention that operational demands might vary their arrival by 24 to 48 hours.

Svein spent the voyage utilising the 'spare parts' from his delivery. Like all talented engineers, he had taken steps to secure his supply line. Over the years, he found that a favour here, or a bottle of akvavit there, was enough to promote goodwill, easing the flow of spares and equipment. Because of this, he had secured everything he needed to fit intercom handsets and control boxes at the twelve-pounder gun, the after deck for the depth charge launchers and on top of the deckhouse for the oerlikon gun positions. He was happy that the Skipper could now control the ship without having the tannoys on deck blaring out as often. His finest achievement, the one that had earned him a large tot of the Skipper's best malt, came from a note he'd received from Mr Dennison at Fellows' yard. Dennison had received a badly damaged trawler which, when surveyed, had been beyond repair. On discovering three Lewis Guns on board he had realised that the crew must have liberated one of them from somewhere so in recognition of all the help Svein had furnished at the yard, he had put a gun aside for them, which they could collect next time they passed. He'd even amended their inventory to add the gun's serial to their ship so that it was officially theirs. The Skipper was relieved they could mount a gun on each bridge wing and planned to put into Great Yarmouth on their way south under the pretext of checking some of their repairs with the yard. The Skipper knew it would cost them a day at home, but the additional firepower seemed worth it after Eddie's death.

Entering the harbour, they moored to a 'dolphin,' a conical structure piled into the harbour bed and protruding above the high-water-springs water level so that vessels could moor at all states of the tide.

Before anyone went ashore, the Skipper and Arthur assembled the company in the ship's well. They spoke about Eddie, and the Skipper said he would go to the family when they finished their talk. He explained they had to call at Great Yarmouth and would leave mid-morning on the 20th to arrive at Southend in good time. Arthur told them the RN volunteers had stepped in to give the rest of the crew a clear first night and had already said they'd do the last night, too. They appealed for volunteers to spell them on the other two nights and got them immediately. With the organisation complete, the Skipper asked them to remember that the location of their patrol base was secret and they were only to say that their job was convoy escort and anti-submarine patrols, the 'Sneaky Beaky Club' was an off limits topic.

The Skipper and the first group of shore-goers embarked in one of their boats and headed for shore. The Skipper called to Arthur, 'I'll come straight back and we'll sort out the admin.' Svein said he'd let Mother and Elsie know their men would be home later.

It was a long walk up the hill to Eddie's house. The Skipper felt like a condemned man as he climbed the slope, puffing out clouds of steam in the cold air. Even a view of the castle, sitting timeless on the rock and looking mysterious in the fog, didn't cheer him as it usually did. He knew many folk in the town, but he'd not been on first-name terms with the Raw family, which he now regretted. He straightened his cap as he knocked on the door, mouth dry.

The door opened, and Eddie's brother, Dan, asked him in. Eddie's parents sat on a sofa and beckoned him to sit in an armchair by the window while Dan sat on the arm of their sofa.

Mr Raw smiled warmly, 'Now then Skipper, we don't shoot messengers in this house. No need to look so nervous. First off, thank you for your letter and for coming today. Dan said you've not long tied up and you must be busy. Your letter was brief, so we'd just like to know a bit more about what happened to our Eddie?'

The Skipper nodded. 'An enemy aircraft attacked us, unfortunately. As he passed over us, his rear gunner sprayed us with machine gun fire. Poor Eddie was hit in his heart and died instantly.' Mrs Raw was weeping and her husband's eyes were damp but he nodded to the Skipper to continue, 'well, Eddie couldn't have felt anything. My First Officer grabbed him and lowered him to the deck, but he had gone by the time he was down. I'm sorry I had to bury him at sea, west of the Orkneys. It felt right to lay him to rest because we were on an operation and I didn't want to risk taking the poor soul's body along with us. It seemed disrespectful. I've noted the exact position; and after the war, I'd like to take you there, so we can lay a wreath or some such.'

Mrs Raw met his eyes. 'You're a decent man, Mister Hurton. We've always thought it. Please don't fret about the burial at sea. Our Eddie was a fisherman by trade, but he loved the sea, so we have no problem with what you did, not least because you did it for the right reason. Once this is over, we'd love to lay a memorial for Eddie. That's incredibly kind of you.' Her eyes swam, and she tailed off.

'Your lad was a credit to you, and to his ship,' his eyes flicked between the three of them, 'I never knew a lad before who would whistle while he hauled nets. The rest of us were panting like spent horses, but Eddie just whistled away as he worked. Same with his training. He never complained and lapped up everything they taught him. One of the best he was, and you should be very proud.'

Mr Raw smiled. 'That was Eddie. Tell me, if you're allowed to, what happened to the aircraft? Did you escape him?'

'Well, the lads knocked some lumps off him and we sent him home wobbling a bit, but we didn't bring him down, I'm afraid.'

The Skipper chatted with them for a few minutes more, trying to leave them with his fond memories of Eddie before judging that he ought to leave them to their themselves. They stood as he rose and he shook their hands before being led to the door by Dan. The lad looked about thirteen and was barely controlling his emotions. The Skipper shook his hand, 'We are flying the flag we used for Eddie's funeral as a battle ensign so we never forget him Dan, but after the war is done and we've beaten Hitler, I'll bring it here for you so that you know your brother was with us to the end; in here, if not in body.' His hand was still on his heart as he stepped outside, walking downhill with a heavy tread. Behind him, Dan smiled tearfully, his face a mixture of sadness and pride, before gently closing the door.

The Skipper and Arthur were heading ashore with Danby at the oars after securing the ammunition lockers and putting sensitive papers and charts into the safe. The Skipper had agreed that Number One could stay on board, but had insisted that he must join them for dinner later that evening. He felt that letting him brood alone would be bad for him at the moment.

It felt strange as they pulled toward the harbour wall in the blackness of early evening. Ordinarily the seafront and harbour side would have been well lit, as would many of the vessels in the harbour, but today all was dark. They were used to it in Scotland because a military base was supposed to be unobtrusive but in their home port it jarred. Everything felt alien despite the familiar smell of bladder wrack and mud from the steps. Once ashore, the sense of strangeness didn't dissipate. Every window had tape from corner to corner, intended to prevent or reduce flying glass in the event of bombing or shelling. The front of one shop reminded the Skipper of a child's game of noughts and crosses, and sandbags surrounded PC Osgodby's box. Along with the cold and fog, the effect was distinctly eerie.

As the Skipper stood before the front door, he realised that mother had made the same modifications to their own home. He bade Arthur good night; the crew had agreed to postpone their post trip pint until the next day. Once inside the front door, things seemed more normal. The hall stand, tiled lobby and a wall lamp his father had installed, all these things called out 'home' and safety. He shook his head; this would be a long war and he shouldn't allow himself such sentimentality.

On entering the parlour, he was delighted to see Mavis sitting with Mother. They were listening to a concert on the wireless and hadn't heard him arrive. Mother got up and hugged him and, to his delight, Mavis also gave him a demure squeeze. His cheeks coloured, but neither lady commented.

Mother sat him down and brought him tea and malt loaf. He mentioned that Number One would join them for dinner, but he really wanted to talk about Eddie's family. The ladies had other ideas. There were a lot of questions and comments, from smart uniforms to the Scottish weather, but eventually they slowed down.

'I visited the Raw family before finishing onboard. Such a waste of a good lad.'

Both women were understanding and Mother said what they were all thinking, 'Sadly Reggie, I don't suppose he'll be the last young man to die in all this mess. God willing, there won't be more tragedies for our people, though.'

They chatted on for over an hour: the news in town, who had joined up, what the papers said, talk of food rationing. They laughed or frowned as the mood took them and relaxed as they had never done before. All tension between Mavis and the Skipper was gone.

The Skipper looked down at his empty plate thoughtfully. Ever watchful, Mother said, 'I'll get more malt loaf and freshen the teapot.' As she delivered them a further slice each, she noticed her Reggie gazing at Mavis so for the sake of giving the young folk space, and with the thought of grandchildren springing unbidden to her mind, she clattered around in the kitchen and scullery making things ready for dinner and reboiling the kettle.

In the parlour, they chatted pleasantly for ten minutes. The Skipper was gazing admiringly at Mavis; her auburn hair catching the firelight was stunning as she sipped the last of her tea. She looked over at him as he leaned toward her. 'Reggie dear, may I say something?'

'Yes Mavis, of course,' his heart soared at the use of the term 'dear' and he smiled in hopeful anticipation of what she might say next.

'Well, Reggie, it's just that you've tipped a slice of malt loaf into your lap while you were leering at me.'

It was a dagger to the heart. He glanced down in the vain hope she was joking, but no. The truth was writ in butter-smeared testament to his adoration of Mavis. His uniform trousers must now go to the cleaners, and he felt he had plumbed new depths in terms of suave seduction.

Wiping up the worst with his handkerchief, he looked up at her, cheeks glowing brighter than the fire. '*Why does she do this to me?*' he thought bitterly. He knew why, and he knew he had to speak. Clumsiness be damned, 'Mavis, well, it's like this. Since I've been away, well, I've realised how fond I am of you.' He checked for progress and saw her listening with shining eyes.

'Reggie, last time you said anything like this you asked me, and I quote, "to correspond" with you. Is this going to be another showstopper?'

He felt that his romantic ambitions were being shredded like a torn net. If his love life were a ship, she'd be tipping her rudder up to the sky and slipping beneath the waves. They had reached the point where he would normally slink off to the pub to massage his aching heart with a fine ale. Today though, he felt fate was looming over him, this time he would get it right, 'It is not Mavis, no stopping shows today, this time I want to say,' he hazed lovingly into her round face, 'I want to say that I think I'm in love with you!'

Time seemed to stand still. Only the crackling of the fire and the thumping of his heart reassured him things were still ticking along. Mavis looked at him with genuine affection and he dared to hope.

'Oh Reggie, what a lovely thing to say,' her eyes glistened, reflecting the flames from the fire, 'I need to be very frank with you Reggie.' He nodded expectantly and her lovely lips parted as she spoke, 'When you've made your mind up whether you love me, I'd like you to let me know!'

His emotional barometer plunged yet again, but this was his moment. Mavis had beaten him back repeatedly; but this time he would show her his metal. He had warned off a u-boat and a Nazi aeroplane for goodness' sake. He would not let her crush him again. 'All right then, I know beyond all doubt,' he took a breath, 'THAT I LOVE YOU!' He winced as he realised he had yelled.

Mavis looked shocked and there was utter silence, disturbed only by the sound of Mother's second best teapot shattering on the kitchen floor.

Mavis sat back in her chair, looking shaken, 'Well, that's very clear, Reggie, loud perhaps, but very clear. Well, you need to know I am very fond of you. I would even say that I love you, despite your dithering; which has driven me to distraction! But here's the other side. I have waited, Lord knows how I've waited, for you to speak, but when you did, you went straight from correspondence to fiery passion! What I expected was an invitation to see a film at the Odeon perhaps, or for tea at Bonnet's. What with the war, and Eddie's death, I think I understand why you want to rush. But I also know we must find out how we work as a couple: away from church, school, families, and so on. To know how we function together, just us two. So here's what I think. We love each other, I'm sure of that, but perhaps we should take time to do the things courting couples do: dancing, the pictures, dinner or tea, that sort of thing. Then we'll know we really are as good together as we hope. What do you say Reggie?'

The Skipper realised instantly that he had over-committed, and that Mavis was right. Life was so fragile in wartime that he had subconsciously needed to take uncertainty out of his personal life. Part of him felt disappointed, but the rational side said the relationship she proposed was orders of magnitude better than their current situation. He smiled happily, 'Of course Mavis, that would be just grand; very sensible.' He reached out and held her hand as Mother walked in.

'Reggie Hurton, could you please make sure I'm not holding valuable crockery when you shout out things like that?' Her smile was as wide as her son's.

The rest of their evening was memorable. Number One arrived for dinner and brought a bottle of red wine for the table and a box of chocolates. It shocked the ladies that he had found either on a late winter's evening, but Number One said a gentleman must preserve his mysteries and would not divulge his source. The Skipper recognised one of Gerald's better bottles of wine and the chocolates, he suspected, were those peddled by Tunny's friend, Sid, who bought in cocoa powder and made his own sweets. He kept his own counsel on that one. Number One took him aside after they exchanged the pleasantries and told him they had asked him to get the early train to London for a meeting with his father. He said he was unsure of the purpose of the summons, but suspected his father would want a report on his progress. The Skipper said not to worry; it was a quick hop to the Thames so he and Arthur could manage. He suggested Number One rejoined at Southend rather than waste more of his leave travelling back to the North Riding.

Mavis noticed that Number One was tightly coiled as he sat tappping his cigarette on his case. She thought of his youth and decided to make efforts to make him feel at home. 'We can't call you "Number One" all night. What's your first name?'

'It's Piers, Miss Everley. I was never terribly struck on it, but it's a family name, you see.'

'Well, in that case, Piers, you must call me Mavis. We'll have no more ranks or surnames.'

The evening went along well. Mother had done some delightful belly pork, and they tucked in enthusiastically. The wine went round, and conversation flowed. They even diverted the Skipper away from lecturing on cricket. Mavis could see that Number One was relaxing quickly as tall tales and laughter flew across the table. She could see this was therapy for him.

After the steamed pudding, the Skipper excused himself and disappeared into his study, saying he wouldn't be long. He returned ten minutes later with an unsealed envelope addressed to Admiral Sir Nigel Fortesque-Smythe KG and, leaning in toward Number One, he said quietly, 'Read this when you're alone lad, then seal it and give it to your father would you?'

Number One (the Skipper simply could not bring himself to say 'Piers') looked nervous, but seeing the Skipper's nod of encouragement, he tucked the letter in his jacket pocket and returned to the table.

Mother turned to Mavis, 'Shall we share our chocolates now?' she asked.

'Ooh, good idea, then the gentlemen get a taste too!' said Mavis.

They all took a chocolate, but the Skipper held off before popping his into his mouth.

'Oh Lord, what have I inflicted on you all?' Number One exclaimed, 'this is the most ghastly chocolate I've ever tasted!' They were indeed extremely bitter, as the Skipper had expected.

The Skipper roared with mirth and wagged a finger. 'I know your source, Number One!' They all laughed, aside from Mother, who commented with a bulging cheek, 'Well, I like them. They're a local delicacy if you ask me.'

After a glass of port, the evening tailed to an end. Number One rose to make his goodbyes, and they all shook his hand. Mavis commented she was feeling a little tired, so the Skipper offered to walk her home before Number One could get all chivalrous. They bade goodbye with lots of handshaking and smiles.

As they strolled away, Mavis commented on Number One's obvious tension and asked what the Skipper had written, 'It's to his father,' the Skipper explained, 'he's a bit of a tyrant it seems, and is forcing his lad to do things which he considers are necessary for a naval officer. Number One is doing a fair job, however, what he's naturally good at is, I suspect, the work they selected him for during training, which was the paymaster branch. He's good with figures and organisation, that sort of thing. I've pointed out that he is an excellent member of the crew and a promising young officer. Also, I mentioned he had been exemplary during his first time under fire.'

Mavis looked up quizzically, her breath steaming in the cold, 'Was he? Exemplary, I mean.'

'Well, the lad wobbled initially. He was a fish out of water really, but we encouraged him and brought him along as best we could and he's responded well. He was deeply shocked by Eddie's death. When Eddie got hit, he fell back against Number One and they went down onto the deck, so he effectively held Eddie as he died. It shocked Number One, and I had to be firm to shake him out of it. I didn't feel it was the best way to deal with it but we were about to go into action and I needed him to manage the gun crews you see.' He didn't mention the boat and the beach because he knew how curious Mavis was and he didn't want the awkwardness of telling her he couldn't speak of it.

At her door, she looked at him. 'It's not just the ship, navigation, the war and all that. You carry the weight of their problems as well, don't you?' she smiled. 'You're a good man, Mr Hurton.' She put her gloved hands on his cheeks and kissed him softly, lingering a second or two longer than a parting of friends. She went inside, waving as she gently closed the door.

The Skipper felt afterwards that he might have actually flown home.

As with all leave, it was over too quickly. As he waved goodbye to Mavis, the Skipper thought of their evening at the Odeon, watching Laurel and Hardy in 'The Flying Deuces'. Mavis had loved it, but it left the Skipper cold, aside from a few involuntary chuckles. Despite the limitations of the film, being with Mavis felt liberating. Even being beside her in church on Sunday had been wonderful. Not even the short eulogy and prayers for Eddie Raw could spoil it, sombre though they were. On Monday evening they had Svein, Arthur and Elsie round for tea and Mavis had also accepted his invitation. That led to an uncomfortable moment when Mavis mentioned Svein had dropped in on Saturday, saying the Skipper wanted to invite her over. The Skipper had rounded on Svein with, 'What?' but Svein had simply grinned.

'Well Skipper, you were so engrossed in Eddie's parents that I was concerned. I was certain you *would* invite Mavis, so I took it upon myself to give her as much notice as possible.'

Mavis opened her mouth in mock horror, 'Svein Bergland, you are a crafty one! You said, "The Skipper sent me to ask you to dinner," without even blushing! I shall be very careful to check everything you tell me in the future.' She gave him a glare, at which he visibly reddened, and the entire room degenerated into laughter.

The Skipper knew these were golden moments. Times he would remember for all his days; but now he must get back to the cold, hard business of running his ship.

Chapter 11

51° 31' 22" N, 00° 43' 03" E

(Southend-on-Sea, R. Thames)

Friday 22nd December 1939

They were slowly steaming south with very frequent fog banks, especially at night, and almost arctic temperatures with an ENE wind and heavy snow squalls. The Skipper could only recall such severe ice formation on masts and rigging in British waters once, years before. Wire stays looked like trees with branches of ice crystals radiating outwards. He studied the charts showing the war channels around East Anglia: these were the buoyed routes, regularly swept for mines, through which the convoys travelled.

They were searching for the East Holm Channel, which served Yarmouth and Lowestoft and the Skipper had hands on the whaleback, looking for the number four buoy which marked the fairway toward Holm Sand. Someone yelled on the whaleback, and the intercom handset from the twelve-pounder sounded. 'Skipper, there's a man clinging to the buoy! Just off to starboard.'

The Skipper ordered full astern to get the way off her, then manoeuvred nearer to the buoy. He didn't want to launch a boat because there was a fair tide running and he couldn't risk losing the boat in the fog. He could hold the ship up-tide and pay out a line tied to the boat, but he was hopeful he could get the man without that. As they neared the buoy, going astern, they realised there were two men clinging to it. Only one was waving. They put a ladder and scramble net over the side. Two lads stood ready to go over and help. Arthur yelled up to the Skipper on the bridge-deck, 'Skipper, one lad is badly hurt. Sid is going over to hold him. The other lad is being helped up. Can we come round and stem the tide? I think it might take a bit of time to get the injured man up.'

The Skipper nodded. 'Let me know when you're set, Arthur. We'll go about and hold alongside the buoy.' In these shallow waters, the tide ran fast, and it was harder to hold position while going astern. Five minutes later, they had gone about and were edging the last few feet toward the buoy. Arthur gave hand signals to the Skipper, who shouted instructions into the wheelhouse. Sid did a spectacular buoy jump and got a canvas sling around the injured man.

They then got him aboard as gently as possible. Sid looked sombre as he came back on board. 'He's burned Arthur, badly.'

Arthur yelled up to the wheelhouse, 'All clear, Skipper!' They reduced revolutions and let her drift astern until the buoy was well north of them, then went ahead with full starboard rudder to swing around and head south again. They quickly found the number four buoy and negotiated the East Holm Channel, then entered the River Yare without incident despite a channel that was only two cables, or four hundred yards wide.

The uninjured man gave the name of their ship. They had fallen behind in a southbound convoy which had passed about three hours earlier. He stood shivering, and said his mate Ned was a trimmer who got scalded when a torpedo, launched from an E Boat, he thought, had broken some steam pipes from the boiler. There was confusion, and he got Ned into a boat being launched. Then another explosion broke the ship's back and the wash from the blast had capsized their boat. Their ship must have gone down in around two minutes, but they were unsure because by that time they were being swept away and the man, Davey, had been keeping Ned's face out of the water. It was pure chance that they'd fetched up on the buoy, he'd said. Six other men who had been in the boat with them had disappeared. The old World War One destroyer which escorted the convoy had steamed past some time later, so they hoped it had rescued their mates. The destroyer was further away from the buoy than White Nab and had not seen them. Davey said that getting Ned out of the water had been the hardest thing he'd ever done, and he'd been close to exhaustion afterward.

Arthur took a still shivering Davey off to get him another blanket. The ambulance arrived from the Naval Hospital. They moved Ned carefully, but the medic came back for Davey a few minutes later and told them Ned had just died in the ambulance. The medic gentled Davey away, his head down and shoulders slumped as he trudged through the thick snow.

As they watched the scene with heavy hearts, a man with a barrow approached. 'Delivery for White Nab courtesy of Mr Dennison.' Svein had leaped over the rail and thankfully taken the gun, wrapped in oilcloth, carrying it onboard carefully. Arthur passed over the curved mount.

The Skipper waited until they stowed the gun, then ordered the deckhands to cast off, heading downriver and out to sea.

As they neared the end of the East Holm channel, the Skipper saw a northbound convoy approaching from starboard. There were two columns of ships. Many were clearly in ballast, their propellors breaking the surface. As they passed, the length of the columns seemed incredible to the Skipper. He spotted the escorts, which, so far as he could make out in the fog, comprised an ancient-looking destroyer and two trawlers.

The rest of their passage was uneventful and despite the biting cold, the fog lifted somewhat in the afternoon watch, which helped them navigate into the Thames and work their way up to Southend, where they moored to the pier head outside another trawler at 15:30.

As they had approached, the pier seemed to go on forever. The pier head structures were like an island, with a thin umbilical disappearing into grey mist and occasional snow flurries. The length of the pier was a simple board walk supported by vertical legs going into the sea, with a spider's web of bracing holding it all together. They later learned it had a small railway running along it.As they squared away, there was a call from the pier, and Number One waved down. He clambered across the well of the other trawler and came aboard. Behind him came three ratings who formed up on White Nab's well deck, two of them looking uneasy and shivering in their greatcoats.

Arthur went to greet them and immediately recognised one man. ' Fred; Fred Braithwaite! My God, how many years has it been?'

The man grinned. 'Arthur Stainton, as I live and breathe. It's been a few; that's for sure! I knew I'd like this ship. Is it true that your skipper lays about him with a cricket bat if he's in a bad mood?' The other two hands looked at each other in horror.

Arthur shook his head. 'Not so much when he's in a bad mood; more often if someone curses, mistreats folk or proves to be a slacker!' They clapped each other on the back in welcome.

'Well, I've heard he's a good bloke and a fine skipper, Arthur,' Fred's eyebrows lifted in a question.

'Aye, you heard right. He's a man who works with a crew instead of stamping on them, if you know what I mean. All my years fishing and I've not met another like him. He's a stickler for doing the job right, mind, but his aim is to do what needs doing, then get us all home safe.'

'Can't ask for more than that, Arthur.'

Arthur turned to the other two; who introduced themselves as Sid Benson and Danny Williamson. Both were from the Royal Naval Volunteer Reserve. Unlike White Nab's crew and Fred, who were all Royal Naval Reserve and therefore experienced seamen, the volunteer reserve came from civilian life and this was Arthur's first exposure to them. Both were gunners. Neither had been to sea before. Arthur took all three to the fish room (as he still called it), telling them to settle in and get a brew from the galley. He promised he'd be back in 20 minutes to give out their assignments.

The Skipper and Number One were in the wheelhouse, so Arthur joined them. Number One looked much better and seemed content, if not wildly happy. Arthur shook his hand as he entered. 'Good to see you back, sir.'

'Same here, Arthur. I saw you took the new hands off. What do you make of them?'

Arthur sucked his tooth. 'Well, the eldest, Fred Braithwaite, will be fine. I've not seen him for years, but he was the Mate on Bill Carson's boat. Do you recall Bill, Skipper?' He turned.

The Skipper nodded, 'I do. He was a decent bloke, if I recall, and so was Fred. What do you think, Arthur?'

'I agree. Hard as nails but always ready with a smile is Fred. I'll check, but I think he has his watch keeper's ticket Skipper, if it helps.'

'Another watch-leader might be a good idea, especially as Number One here has grabbed the Gunnery Officer's job on top of his own.' He winked at Number One. 'Leave it with me, Arthur, I'll have a think. What about the other two?'

'I'm not sure, Skipper. Volunteer Reservists and they both seem green. Very green, to tell the truth.'

Number One grimaced, 'My father promised to get us an extra hand or two, but as usual...' he tailed off.

Arthur glanced at the others. 'Well, all we can do is to try them out and work out how they fit in. I'm told that they're both gunners, so I'm afraid you'll inherit your Father's gift sir!' he grinned a at Number One's rolling eyes, 'If you're done with me Gents I'll nip down and get them familiarised. Would you like to speak to the gunners, sir?'

Number One nodded. 'Yes please Arthur, send them to me when you've done with them. We'll do an hour of gunnery drill this afternoon to get them up to speed.'

The Skipper pursed his lips. 'Well, you're both busy, so I'll cut along to the Naval Control Service and report in. I'll see you both later and brief you.'

Arthur nodded and disappeared down the steps of the wheelhouse ladder, but Number One held back. 'Sir, before I go, I'd just like to thank you for your help with the letter.

The old man was pretty happy once he'd finished reading. I'll be honest, when he began reading he started with, "Who the blazes does he think he is," but ended up sort of glowing. It's not what I'm used to from him, I can tell you!'

'I'm pleased, Number One. I can empathise with you. My father was an exceptional teacher and leader. Any skills that I may possess have come straight from him, so when I hear of people with domineering fathers, well, it just seems wrong and self-defeating. Anyway, I thought it might take some load from you if the Admiral wasn't riding you.'

'Well, it worked sir, I can't thank you enough,' he held out his hand and firmly shook the Skipper's work hardened mitt, 'oh, I've left you a bicycle on the pier, sir. I've borrowed it because I find it saves a lot of time on the pier.'

The Skipper smiled, 'All in a day's skippering, Number One; and thanks for the bike. Right, I'll go get the bad news!'

As the Skipper went ashore, he looked along the incredible length of the pier and, smiling, reached for the bicycle lock key Number One had given to him.

The Skipper returned at 17:30, his eyes watering from the lancing cold of his bicycle ride back along the pier. Arthur and Number One were in the wheelhouse with the doors buttoned up, drinking steaming tea in the binnacle's warm light.

Arthur reached for the intercom and pressed a button. 'Sparks, would you poke your head out and ask Billy for a hot drink for the Skipper while we chip the ice off him, please?'

The Skipper was leaning over the heater at the back of the wheelhouse, chafing his hands. 'Right lads, I've had a good session with the Controller. He's glad we're early because the convoy will begin marshalling in the morning and we'll act as a sort of runner for the Commodore of the convoy as he gets them in the right place.'

Number One grimaced, 'I fear we might lose some paint tomorrow, sir!'

'I'm afraid you could be right, Number One.' The Skipper shook his head, then continued, 'Apparently, these convoys can be pretty bloody. The Nazis are infiltrating, using their submarines when they can. There are mines laid by submarines or aircraft, and occasional attacks by aircraft.' He had watched Number One, but there was only nodding, no signs of the strain that had gripped him after Eddie's death.

Number One piped up himself, 'That's what I heard, sir. At least we're heavily armed for a trawler and we might keep their heads down.'

Arthur smiled, 'We now have two Lewis guns, sir. Thanks to Svein and his ability to make friends everywhere!'

Number One looked delighted. 'Marvellous! Also, my father lent me a pair of Purdey shotguns and some buckshot cartridges. He's certain they can cause a lot of damage to aircraft if we aim for the propellor disc as they approach or go over. Hardly a battleship, but hopefully we can sting them.'

The Skipper laughed nervously, 'Go to it Number One, but for Heaven's sake, wear your tin hat! Anyway, the Controller said there is less risk from aircraft at the moment, they are only attacking sporadically. Apparently, the weather and icing conditions are hindering aircraft operations, so that's also good news. He also reckons the river is iced over, just upstream of the city!'

Arthur grinned. 'Well, if the Londoners are saying it's like the arctic, then most Yorkshire folk will put their winter coats on, I expect!' Number One just shook his head.

'You Northerners and your in-built sense of superiority, honestly!'

The Skipper wagged a finger. 'We are two separate races, Number One. The French did not conquer the North, you see. They burned our crops, yes, but we managed by eating granite until spring, then they buggered off north and failed to subdue the Scots as well.'

'To each their own, sir. I'm off for some kip anyway.' he grinned at them both as he left.

When he had gone, Arthur nodded, saying, 'That one seems much improved, Skipper.'

'I think he is Arthur. I hope it lasts: the signs are good at the moment. Let's hope the signs remain good after this convoy of ours!'

Chapter 12

56° 10' 21" N, 02° 58' 58" E

(Methil Roads, Firth of Forth)

Friday 26th December 1939

The next day didn't really dawn. Things just gradually came into soft focus, revealing a world of swirling grey fog and thick hoar frost, like some faerie kingdom with strange ice spikes everywhere. It would look truly incredible if the sun could penetrate the fog.

Mercifully, by lunchtime the fog lifted, reducing to a hazy mist. Aside from a few snow flurries, which were light, the weather was much improved. That was the only good news White Nab had for the day. As the Skipper put it, getting the ships in line was like herding treacle. Skippers of colliers were intent on doing precisely what they wanted to do; rather than what they were ordered to do. The Skipper thought he'd encountered undisciplined trawlermen in his life; but this was a whole new game.

They plied away for hours, signalling and shepherding until the newly arrived Escort Commander signalled them to stop in the mid-afternoon. They were told to anchor off and wait for instructions on the following morning while his elderly destroyer went off to exchange presumably angry signals with the Commodore.

The Skipper had chatted with Number One and Arthur about Fred. Given his history as a mate and his possession of a watch keeping ticket, he would use Fred as the third watch leader. This freed up Number One for divisions, ship tidiness and cleanliness, assisting the Skipper and drilling the gunners. His action station remained as the gunnery officer, which he could perform either from the Oerlikon positions on the deckhouse roof or at the twelve-pounder using Svein's new intercom. The Skipper felt that separating Number One from duties as a bridge officer would help efficiency and prevent overloading him. Number One seemed happy with this decision.

So the morning of departure came around. Unusually, as daylight did its best to penetrate the icy grey dawn, there was little fog. Occasionally, flurries of snow swept across the Thames, trailing from darker, pregnant clouds.

As the light levels rose, they made out, with horror, a mass of ships labouring under clouds of smoke. The

Escort Commander signalled to prepare for departure and instructed White Nab to take a position outside the right-hand column, ending somewhat cryptically, 'Prevent merchant ships leaving the swept channel.'

Number One reported the ship ready for sea and Arthur had the deckhands casting off smartly. As they gathered way, cutting across the two columns astern of the Commodore's ship, they were almost run down by a tramp steamer going hell for leather up-river. As they swerved around her stern, the Skipper could see Arthur looking up and blowing out his cheeks. Each knew what the other was thinking: this would be a miserable day!

Eventually, the convoy was arranged in two ragged columns, and the Commodore signalled to get under way. The Escort Commander was in between columns, to port and astern of the Commodore, who led the right-hand column. White Nab was on the starboard flank toward the front, with another trawler on the port flank around five ships from the rear. A battered corvette brought up the rear. There were twenty-one ships in this small convoy, with three more due to join from Harwich and one from Lowestoft. Some ships would go into the Humber, but more would join. Many of the colliers and some merchantmen would go into the Tyne, with the remaining ships all heading for the Firth of Forth where the convoy would disperse in Largo Bay off Methil, a coal port in Fife which is on the north shore of the Firth.

The Skipper felt like Methil was very distant, perhaps not in miles, but certainly in hardship and suffering.

As they sailed into the Black Deep, the convoy was probably as orderly as it was going to be. After passing Long Sand buoy, however, the contingent from Harwich joined from the port side and the Commodore seemed to increase speed by half a knot. The Escort Commander went after him and tried to drop the freighter's speed by going ahead of the starboard column and slowing slightly, weaving either side of his mean course as he did so.

The Skipper had his own problems: one of his charges, five ships astern, had veered to starboard in a snow squall and needed shepherding back. The Skipper asked Fred to do the navigating while he looked after tactics from the flying bridge. Navigating was difficult when visibility closed in: there were no obvious landmarks visible, and a dead reckoning plot had to be kept up. This allowed them to work out an estimated position until the next buoy or landmark became visible so they could take a reliable fix. The Skipper asked Fred to plot their current position so that he knew approximately how much leeway they had before they left the channel.

As they turned to go back to the wayward merchantman, the ship seemed to realise it had gone off-track and turned to rejoin the column. As she straightened her course, there was a massive explosion. The sea all around her turned white and erupted upward like some obscene geyser. She visibly lifted and her back broke as she reached the highest point. The two parts came down together, but the bow section went under immediately. The aft section rolled slowly sideways. A gaping hole in what must have been the engine room bulkhead was belching steam as she settled. There was another explosion, probably as cold water reached the boiler. Then she rolled on her side and disappeared.

The entire event took less than five minutes from the explosion to an empty sea. Everyone on the flying bridge stared at the few pieces of flotsam left swirling in the water. The Skipper shook himself, 'Helm, five degrees to port and hold our present speed. We'll check for survivors.'

The Skipper felt mines were not so densely laid that the ship was in danger, even if they were outside the swept channel, so he was content that he wasn't putting the crew in imminent danger.

As they arrived at the oily-looking patch of water, full of broken wood and unidentifiable floating detritus, a deck-hand called out, pointing to port. The Skipper swung his binoculars and spotted two men clinging to a baulk of timber. He ordered the lookouts to sweep all around and told the helm to come round to port, calling midships as the ship's head came round to a point to starboard of the men. In a few minutes, they were clawing their way up the net and over the bulwark. They sat on the deck, shivering in shocked silence as Arthur sprinted off for some dry coveralls.

Once satisfied these men were the only survivors, the Skipper ordered full ahead and set off to regain their previous station. They signalled the Escort Commander to let him know they had two survivors on board.

It took some time to regain their station because the convoy was doing seven knots, so they weren't overtaking fast as they cruised along at nine. Arthur climbed to the flying bridge to let the Skipper know both survivors were well. Speaking quietly, he said, 'One lad was a lookout, thrown off the bridge wing by the explosion and the other a deckhand who had been greasing boat davits near the stern when he also got thrown into the water. They reckon that the ship's complement was twenty-two. I should also say, Skipper, that Number One came to help, and he seemed fine.'

'Thanks Arthur. It's a pitifully small number of survivors; but nothing we could do to change that, sadly. I'm glad Number One is coping,' he slammed his hand on the rail, 'This is worse than the last war Arthur! Why the Admiralty haven't devised better strategies in the years since the armistice is beyond me.'Arthur nodded, 'I know, but think on this. We were lucky in the last war. T'owd Skipper often told us that anti-submarine patrolling was a doddle compared to convoy escort, but you lived through the convoys and learned. We are in the thick of things this time, but you've made the right choices so far based on your experiences. It's bad, but I can't see how you could have made it better. We can't change the Admiralty's decisions Reggie. Just trust your judgement. We do.'

The Skipper felt great sadness: the desolate certainty of wasted lives, 'Well, the scale of loss this time is huge compared to what we saw taking coal to France and food to the Netherlands in the first war. But you're right. We won't change the Admiralty's strategies, so all we can do is act more like the Navy and just press on.' They looked ahead, both hoping there would be no further drama.

For a time, it seemed they were getting their wish, but as dusk came, there was an explosion from the rear of the convoy. This time, the vessel, a collier, took around twenty minutes to sink. After firing at something hidden in the gloom from their position, the rearguard corvette went alongside the sinking ship, which was on fire as they took off survivors. The Skipper thought that, if it were a torpedo from a u-boat, then stopping for survivors was a brave thing to do. The corvette rejoined, just as deep twilight faded to complete darkness.

Around fifteen minutes later, Pickering called up to report a strong SONAR contact, around a mile away and fine on the starboard bow. The Skipper suspected the contact proved the last sinking must have been a submarine, and the commander was preparing for another go. He was just about to signal the Escort Commander when the destroyer itself took off like a hare. The Skipper edged slightly forward up toward the head of the convoy so that he could cover for the destroyer if needed, while still guarding his flank of the convoy.

They heard two loud 'crumps' and felt a slight shock in the hull as depth charges went off. Shortly afterward Pickering reported no contact on SONAR but no noise indicating a sinking or damaged submarine either. He commented that noise from the convoy made listening difficult.

They settled down to the routine. It was impossible to shepherd their charges at night because nobody showed lights. They were hopping along the dimly lit channel marker buoys and praying that the buoys hadn't dragged from their position. Periodically, a snow squall would hit them and they relied on their last course to steer to fetch the next buoy. It wasn't uncommon to miss a buoy, and the Commodore would wait a few minutes before altering course for the next buoy.

At midnight, the Skipper broadcast on the tannoy, 'Merry Christmas to you all. I'm certain we would all prefer to be elsewhere on Christmas Day, but we've a job to do and I know you'll all do your bit, and do it well. Just to show Jerry he can't take everything from us, Billy has a plum duff to go with your lunch and there'll be a tot of rum to go with it.'

The rest of the night passed without incident, but was intensely cold, with heavy snow squalls from time to time. As the visibility increased after dawn, a pulse of finer snow blew across them and, as it moderated, there came the sound of a steam whistle. The Skipper scanned aft and saw that two ships were veering out of the starboard column. He went about smartly and headed back toward them. As they neared the two ships, the leading vessel, another collier, signalled a minor collision had taken place. As the bow of the tramp steamer behind came into view, there was a hefty dent at the top of her stem and a bent guardrail, but nothing worse. Her crew were checking the anchors were secure, it seemed. The Skipper asked Egdon to check if the collier could steer, and the reply came, 'Steering undamaged.' They sent a last signal for both ships to return to their stations. The back end of the convoy had compressed somewhat, and more ships had gone off station to avoid a risk of collision. It took some time to get everyone back in line, causing the Skipper to repeatedly thump his fist on the handrail.

Following a good feed by ship's standards, they toasted each other with their tot of rum. Billy had been hoarding to make Christmas Day lunch filling and, of course, there was a small portion of plum duff for everyone. There were some sombre faces as they returned to their duties, but morale was standing up well enough.

Later in the afternoon, the contingent for the Humber peeled off, accompanied by the other trawler. They had lost six merchantmen and one escort from the convoy, but three merchantmen came from the Humber and joined the rear of the convoy near the corvette. Again, station keeping became ragged, and they spent two hours of the long pull up the Holderness coast trying to get them on station before dark.

The night passed without further incident, aside from the bridge crew unsuccessfully trying to pierce the darkness as they passed Scarborough, but daylight revealed what, to the Skipper, seemed utter chaos. The starboard column astern of White Nab had split off and veered out of the swept channel. Despite the nagging about station keeping, it seemed the port column had kept station on the ship to starboard while losing the ship in front. As a result, the convoy had split into two parts. The corvette was busily darting about, heading them back into the swept channel. Many ships had gone independent, in particular the port column, and were heading back to their stations alone. Ahead, the first three ships in each column were miles away, so they now had three sections! The Commodore had clearly increased speed during the night, while the mid section had held steady at just under seven knots, according to the patent log, so it wasn't the main body who had lagged. The Escort Commander signalled for White Nab to take the lead in the centre, then the destroyer shot off once again.

Eventually the corvette had everyone approximately on station astern. The Skipper held his speed and signalled the lead ships to take station on White Nab. Many colliers peeled off into the Tyne and Blyth, with a single coaster joining. They never regained the front end of the convoy and so the Skipper simply stuck to the plan, rounding St Abbs Head, then Bass Rock, before crossing the Firth toward Methil. Once in the Firth, the Convoy dispersed, so when the Skipper spotted the destroyer ahead, he anchored astern of her. After a short time, a motorboat came into sight, heading toward them. The crew put a boarding ladder over and a young RN Lieutenant Commander came on board. Number One gave a salute and took him to the Skipper's cabin.

The officer entered the Skipper's cabin with a warm smile, and his hand extended. 'Good afternoon Skipper,

James Wilson, Captain of HMS Gordon anchored ahead of you. I wanted to congratulate you on a job well done. That was your first convoy, I understand, and you handled it well.'

The Skipper shook his hand. 'Well, thank you very much; I'll pass on your comments to my crew. I'm glad you came, actually. My orders are unclear at the moment and I don't know the lay of the land ashore in Methil. I've never had occasion to put into the Firth of Forth.'

Wilson smiled. 'I plan to go ashore in the morning to see the Naval Controller. I lodge a complaint about the Commodore racing off after every northbound convoy, but they do nothing about it. It's shocking really.'

The Skipper grimaced, 'He's a man who knows how to bugger up a convoy, that's a certainty!'

Wilson eyes twinkled. 'Quite! Anyway, you can get your orders from the Controller in the morning, I'd say. If not, there's a telephone you can use. Normally we'd dock in Rosyth, but this is a quick turn round, so we're loitering here. One bit of good news: the Commodore for the southbound run is less of an independent thinker, so we can expect more cooperation on this one! I'll swing over and pick you up in the morning if it helps?' the young man's eyebrows lifted in enquiry.

'That would be useful, yes, please. In which case, would you like a nip of the whisky I mentioned as part payment?' The Skipper was leaning toward the locker as he asked.

'Decent of you, just a small one, as it's the festive season.' The peaty aroma of Islay malt filled the small space.

They both leaned back to savour their drink, and the Skipper asked whether they had hit the submarine. Wilson seemed surprised. 'What makes you say that?'

'Well, my ASDIC operator said it was a strong contact, but he couldn't hear much afterward. There was a lot of noise from the convoy itself.'

'Great Scott, you have ASDIC! I didn't realise that. You're very well equipped for a trawler, aren't you?'

The Skipper adopted a conspiratorial attitude. 'Ah, there's an excellent reason for that. Their Lordships want to sleep at night knowing their Dreadnoughts are safe, so I normally have the honour of steaming up and down near Scapa Flow pinging away for nonexistent submarines!'

They both laughed and Wilson grinned. 'I'd swap that for trying to get the irascible Commodore to toe the line! To answer your question, however, no. We weren't sure if it even was a sub, but my ASDIC rating said it had to be because there was pinging. It made no sense to me. Why did it have to be a submarine because somebody else pinged it? I assumed it was the corvette who was pinging, but clearly not. At any rate, I dropped a couple of charges as a precaution, with apologies to the whale community if it was one of theirs!'

The Skipper nodded, 'Quite right too. I blame the Nazis, though. Nobody should prosecute a war from under the water. They should face us on the surface like gentlemen.'

Wilson smiled as the Skipper clenched his pipe between his teeth and lit it. As the aroma replaced the sweet smell of whisky, Wilson drained his glass and headed for the companionway with a cough. 'Right, I'll see you in the morning. Probably 08:30, but I have an injured rating who may need to be taken ashore, so it may be later if our sawbones prefers to move him using the boat.'

The Skipper leaned back contentedly, 'Until tomorrow then!'

Wilson gasped his way to the wheelhouse before going onto the bridge deck for a gulp of clean air.

The Skipper jumped down the ladder into Wilson's motor launch at 08:15. Wilson explained their surgeon had treated the injured man's leg and so they were free to leave straight away. The Skipper asked what to do with the two survivors on board, which he had completely forgotten about the previous evening. Wilson suggested they take them ashore now, so the Skipper whistled to Arthur and asked him to send them over the side. When the huddled men were onboard, the launch crew cast off. The snow drove horizontally across the surface of the water, so conversation was virtually impossible. They all sank into their duffels and folded up collars to shield their ears.

Once ashore, Wilson pointed out where the naval control office was on Commercial Street, saying he needed to get the survivors sorted, then would meet him at the office in about an hour. The Skipper waded through the snow and slush toward a wet, grey stone-built building which was grimed from smoke and coal dust.

The Skipper asked for the Naval Controller. The harassed-looking clerk pointed to an office on his left without looking up. Inside the office, a Wren sat at desk. He asked where he could inquire after his orders. She asked, politely enough, for his identification and the name of his ship, then when satisfied with his credentials, began searching through a filing cabinet.

'Ah, White Nab, here you are, sir. There's also a note for you to telephone Captain McDonald. It says that you have the number?'

The Skipper smiled and nodded as he opened the buff envelope she had passed over. He asked if there was a telephone he could use, preferably where he could hold a private conversation. She pointed him to the end of the room: there was a wooden cubicle with concertina door. He thanked the Wren and wandered through the haze toward the door. Once inside, he first looked at his orders, which were unhelpful in that he was required to continue convoy escort duties until he received further orders. He rolled his eyes. Belonging to two separate chains of command might get a little complicated. Then he dialled McDonald, who answered after a few rings.

'Hello Captain, Hurton here. I'm in Methil and had a message to telephone you.'

'Oh hello Skipper, how did convoying go?'

The Skipper involuntarily rolled his eyes again. 'Fine, but it's a nasty business. We lost two merchant ships: one got mined, they probably torpedoed the other, I can't be certain. We may have depth charged a porpoise!'

McDonald laughed heartily, 'At least you've got your sense of humour, Skipper. Right. To business. We have another job for you, so I asked you to call. I had a tussle with the Admiralty, who wanted you to remain on convoy duties, but I got your release after your return south. I'm not sure when you sail, but I expect you to be there well before I need you. The job is completely routine. I've sent young Cooper down to Methil to meet you in the Naval Controller's office. He'll give you more detail.'

'Thank you, much appreciated, Captain. If that's all, I'll go to find him, I'm in that office now.'

'Yes, that's all Skipper, good luck and I hope we meet again soon!'

The Skipper replaced the receiver, then strolled over to the Wren, 'Excuse me Miss. I'm expecting Sub Lieutenant Cooper to see me. Would you know where I should meet him?'

The Wren smiled. If only they were all as personable as this one! 'You're very organised sir, he's on his way to you as we speak. There's an empty office outside and to your left. Sub Lieutenant Cooper said it would be a short meeting.'

The Skipper smiled. 'Thank you very much. I'll pop my head in when we're done so that you know the office is free.'

As he opened the door, he nearly collided with Cooper. 'This way, young man, we've a room allocated to us.'

Once inside, they shook hands and sat down. Cooper opened his satchel and took out some papers. 'These are for you, sir. Captain McDonald also asked if I can take passage with you to Southend so I can liaise with your passengers?'

The Skipper was skimming the papers and looked up, 'Of course Mr Cooper, we have a sea berth free in the aft cabin.' He returned to the papers: the official order for HMT White Nab to detach for special service, a note about the passengers and their destination, and a handwritten note from McDonald. They were to take two people from the dock at Garrison Point, Sheerness, and ferry them to Boulogne, dropping them on the Quai Gambetta near the fish market without drawing unwanted attention. Cooper would accompany them and would go ashore to make some minor purchase from a chandler on the docks, so they had a reason for putting in. They would then await a confirmation that their passengers had found their contacts ashore and leave as soon as possible. If the contacts failed to arrive, they were to report to the authorities that they had to make a repair before they could put to sea and the passengers would return to the ship. McDonald closed by apologising for the cloak and dagger work, but stressed that it was vital that their passengers got into France unnoticed and that the French intelligence service was aware, and had approved the operation.

The Skipper put the documents back into the envelope and stood, 'Right Mr Cooper, let's find our lift back to the ship and go wreck the Nazi's efforts to sink our merchant fleet before we go on holiday!'

He popped into the office once again tell the Wren their room was now free. She directed them to another room, where Wilson was in conversation with the Naval Controller.

After introducing Cooper as a liaison with the Royal Naval Patrol Service, they learned the convoy would muster on the following day, sailing as soon as they formed up.

Outside on the quayside, the wind was slicing through their duffel coats as they clambered into Wilson's motor boat. Reaching White Nab as low cloud crawled across the water, trailing snow like shirt tails, they said goodbye to Wilson, who called out as they pulled off, 'Good luck chaps, we'll make a good run of it tomorrow I'm certain!'

The run south was cold with short, choppy seas and night time fog, but was uneventful until they reached Hartlepool. They had rounded the Heugh in reasonable visibility and were crossing Tees Bay. As Wilson mentioned, this Commodore was a reasonable type and navigated well. The swell was running heavily as the seabed shoaled into the bay, but the sun had put in a rare appearance. White Nab was in her now customary position on the starboard flank and had closed the tramp steamer which was two vessels astern of the Commodore after the lookouts spotted an enormous tree trunk, half submerged and almost dead ahead. They had cleared the obstacle, and the Skipper turned to order a change of course away from the tramp when there came a load slam. White Nab lifted bodily as a tidal wave rolled her well over to starboard.

As she paused at the end of the roll and came back, freeing herself of green water through the scuppers in the well deck, they all had a second or two of numbness which rapidly faded as realisation dawned. The tramp must have triggered a mine on her port side and even with a 2000 ton steamer to shield them, the shock wave had been vicious. An immense tower of white water hung above the doomed ship. It paused in mid-air for a fraction of a second, crashing back over her superstructure as they watched. She, too, had rolled to starboard, but further than White Nab. Slowly, she rolled back; the movement continuing until she was on her port side, propellor out of the water but still turning. She quickly settled. They could hear the booms and splintering wood as her hatch covers blew off because of compression of air inside the hull, and the loud whistling of steam.

The Skipper had ordered a sharp turn to starboard as a reflex action, and now called out, 'Midships the wheel!' He instinctively looked aft and was relieved to see the next ship in line had altered to starboard to avoid hitting the rapidly settling victim. He quickly realised that any survivors would be in the water on the other side of the ship from his current position. Before acting, he called Svein on the intercom, 'Is everything in one piece down there, Svein?' he yelled.

'Yah OK Skipper, I think so. The machinery seems sound and I'll check things in more detail as soon as my ears stop ringing. Archie has gone to sound the slush wells to make sure we're not making water, and I'll report back when he returns. The stern glands look OK. Danny just shone a light down the propellor shaft and the after peak looks dry.'

'Thanks Svein. I'll keep manoeuvring to a minimum, but I need to look for survivors. She's answering the helm all right, but I'll try to keep course changes gentle until you confirm any damage.'

Replacing the handset, the Skipper looked at lookouts around him. They looked pale and shocked so, thinking quickly, he flashed them a smile 'You should see your faces, they're a picture. All's well below gentlemen. We won't meet Davy Jones today. There may be men in the water on the other side of that ship. So unless you want to pay me a penny for a trip around the bay, we'd better steer off to port and look for survivors.'

Len Egdon smiled as he swung the wheel over. You could always rely on the Skipper. They curved around ahead of the foundering ship and scanned the water. As they straightened to head back to her, she seemed to split across her deck near the main hatch and, with a rush of air and steam, she was gone.

Ordering, 'Dead slow ahead please,' the Skipper went out and up to the flying bridge where he whipped out his hand bearing compass and his glasses. He first took a bearing on the lighthouse on the Heugh and another on the greenish white bubbling water marking the ship's new grave and then swept the area between their position and that point with his glasses. Without taking his eyes from the binocular cups, he said, 'Starboard lookout, please scan on your side. The tide should bring them toward us, but maybe someone is down-tide of us already. Let's keep our eyes open, gents.'

After two or three fruitless minutes, he turned to port. They went close to the position where the ship had gone down. The Skipper called dead slow ahead and all off-watch personnel were manning the rails. Sub Lieutenant Cooper had come up to the flying bridge to help. Sadly, all they could recover were three bodies. They covered them with canvas on the afterdeck, where they would be least disturbed.

Once up-tide of the sinking site, they turned and slowly picked their way through the detritus popping up from the broken ship below. Reluctantly, the Skipper ordered the search to be abandoned. The Hartlepool Lifeboat had arrived and hailed them. The lifeboatmen agreed to take the bodies ashore: if more were found, the families would want them together.

With that, they left the Lifeboat to its miserable task and turned. Svein had reported the ship dry and functional, so they upped their speed, signalling to the freighters who had passed them to return to their stations. HMS Gordon had taken their station on the starboard flank so, as they caught up some time later, the Skipper had a signal sent by lamp to report themselves fully operational but no survivors and recovered bodies put aboard the Lifeboat.

Young Cooper was staring aft with vacant eyes and the Skipper clapped him on the shoulder, 'London and the south-east needs around 40,000 tons of coal per week Mr Cooper. They need it for heat, power: the things a country needs to function. The railways can't yet cope with that volume, so this thankless job is actually vitally important. Let's hope future generations never forget; whatever the outcome of this war, these men did their bit and a great deal more.' Everyone on the flying bridge nodded as the Skipper went to write up his log.

The rest of the trip south was uneventful. They moored to the pier at Southend just after 19:00 on the 30th, tied up on the outside of HMS Gordon. The Skipper, Cooper, and Arthur, together with Lieutenant Commander Wilson, trudged along the end of the pier. They hoped to find bicycles; but discovered the Naval Control Office now had an office on the pierhead where they could report to the duty officer.

The Skipper reported their arrival, handing over his orders for detachment, and Wilson was on the telephone behind the counter. Cooper had trudged off up the pier, promising to return as quickly as he could with news of their passengers. Formalities over, the Skipper and Arthur went for a ten-minute stroll on the pier to stretch their legs before returning to the ship. The other trawler from the southbound convoy was ordered up-river, so they were exposed at the end of the pier. The Skipper and Arthur ate in the Skipper's cabin with his heater quickly warming them.

The Skipper slurped from a tin mug of Billy's tea. 'I think Fred is doing very well Arthur, what do you reckon?'

'I'd say so Skipper. He's got a sound head on him. Number One seems a lot more settled too, so I think that the new arrangement is working.'

'I agree Arthur. We'll monitor it, but I think we're set fair.'

Arthur nodded. 'I meant to ask you, is Svein happy after that mine business?'

'He is Arthur. He said they'd dried out the slush wells and we're not making water.'

'That's good, Archie was telling me it was one hell of a thump when you're working on the waterline.'

The Skipper chuckled, 'I bet. A ship is just a big drum, I suppose, and water transmits sound much better than air.'

The conversation drifted on, as it does with old friends. The Skipper brought Arthur up to date with their orders, expressing the secrecy of the operation.

Arthur said, meditatively, 'I don't suppose we'll ever find out what these folks are up to.'

Shaking his head, the Skipper replied, 'True enough. To be fair, it's better we don't know if ever we're captured. I'm happy enough to concentrate on our part of the job and let McDonald deal with his.'

As he spoke, they heard a thump on the deck and feet treading above them in the wheelhouse. The Skipper shouted up, 'Down here Cooper, and bring a mug. We've still got tea in the pot.'

The young man came down the steps, mottled with cold, 'Thank you, sir. I'd appreciate a drop of char.'

'What news?' the Skipper asked as he poured.

'The passengers have a briefing in the morning and we are to pick them up at 10:30 tomorrow morning, Skipper.

Everything else remains as per your orders from Captain McDonald.'

'Marvellous; once we have them onboard, I plan to stay north until we're between Dover and Folkestone and then cut across. That way, we should look like a coastal passage maker: unremarkable to prying eyes.'

Cooper smiled. 'You've been working with Captain McDonald for too long, sir. You're thinking like him!'

The Skipper was hunting his pockets for his pipe. 'Well Mr Cooper, I'm hoping there'll be a special sneaky beaky club medal at the end of the war.' Cooper returned the smile and made his apologies quickly before the Skipper could light up.

'The trouble is Arthur, I suspect this secret stuff is all very well unless you get caught. It will probably go downhill at a fair rate of knots at that point!'

Chapter 13

50° 43' 43" N, 01° 35' 47" E

(Boulogne Harbour, France)

Sunday 31st December 1939

They were alongside at Garrison Point at 10:30 the next day. The Skipper looked up at the old grey stone fort as Sub Lieutenant Cooper came along the jetty with the passengers. It surprised him to see that one of them was a young woman. He shuddered to think of it. He didn't doubt her ability: Mavis and Mother had taught him how competent and self-reliant women were: it was the fact that not only were young men like Cooper and poor Eddie being put in harm's way, but now young women too. As he thought about it, he realised that the war at sea was misleading. All-male crews went to war with other all-male crews, but ashore, women were in the same danger as men every time a bomb dropped. As he often said, war is a dirty business.

Cooper settled the passengers in the aft cabin as they cast off for Boulogne. They left the Thames on an ebbing tide via the Oaze Deep and Knob Channel. The weather seemed set to change: a little warmer and the fog less dense. As the morning progressed, it had turned into a cloudy day with a light breeze; still cold, but not as bitter.

Rounding the North Foreland, the Skipper had just given the course to steer in the wheelhouse when he heard a call from the flying bridge, 'Aircraft, bearing red zero two five!' He sprinted up to the flying bridge as action stations sounded and he saw Len Egdon sprinting to his Lewis gun. He screamed to the deckhands, 'Get that red ensign up on the starboard cross tree, NOW!'

It was a large twin engine floatplane, he could see it side-slipping as it descended. He realised Number One was on the ball, because the port gun was already aimed and they were elevating the starboard gun to put up a curtain of fire through which the aircraft must fly, so the Skipper yelled for the port Oerlikon to open fire. It looked as though its bomb doors were open already when the port gun opened up with short, rapid bursts of fire. Len gave a few bursts from the Lewis at an optimistic range, but the firing of the Oerlikon made the aircraft sway. Their Oerlikon fired a long burst as Len was changing the drum on his Lewis. The nose gunner fired back, but the rounds went over the funnel, making the sea sprout geysers of ice-white spray. As the aircraft went low over the ship, the Skipper heard a flat double crack, which he feared was the sound of rounds hitting the ship. The starboard Oerlikon's fire seemed ineffective because the aircraft turned hard as it flew over, but as the engine noise began to fade, he heard a wild cry of, 'Got the bugger: a left and a right, just like shooting grouse!' Number One was waving his father's shotgun in delight.

The Skipper grinned despite the seriousness of the situation. The lad had certainly overcome his fear! Looking up, he saw the aircraft trailed a thin line of white smoke and the engine note seemed to have changed a little. He was hugely relieved when it swept around in a wide circle and disappeared off, heading east. He pressed the Tannoy button, 'Secure from action stations and lower the battle ensign.'

As he reentered the wheelhouse, Arthur came in from the opposite bridge wing, grinning. He belly laughed as he fished in his pocket, then held something out for the Skipper. It was a sliver of black metal about three inches long, grey and abraded on one edge, bright and granular on the other, with a dimple at the bottom. 'What's so amusing about this, Arthur?'

Well, it's like this Skipper. When the aeroplane went over, I saw something out of the corner of my eye and this thing tinkled along the deck. I thought it must have come off the plane, so I pocketed it. On the way up here, Sid told me Number One had a go with his shotgun, so judging by the size of the dent in this, that he might have actually shot part of its propellor off!

The Skipper's eyes boggled, 'Pass it here, Arthur. Not a word about it from any of you. We'll make a formal presentation of it when the opportunity arises, but let's keep it under our hats until then.'

The rest of the passage went smoothly, and they tied up to the Quai Gambetta at 16:00. Before they entered harbour, more accurately the River Liane, Cooper had taken the passengers into the forepeak, asking them to get into two bunks and close the curtains. A French customs official strolled over as they rigged a gangplank and went ashore, so the Skipper tried out his best French (with Cooper correcting when necessary). He explained they were carrying out a minor engineering repair and his officer would go ashore for supplies. Whether French intelligence had spoken with him, they never knew, but the man gave a cursory glance at their naval identification cards before telling them to remove the Q flag from their rigging.

Once accepted by customs, Cooper went off about his task. Returning 30 minutes later, clutching a pump impellor, cheese, wine and a red ribbon, he reported to the Skipper. 'No problems sir, I found the shore contacts. Everything is fine, but they suggested waiting half an hour for the late shoppers to disappear before we disembark the passengers. We'll just need to cover them as they leave the ship.'

'I have just the thing to allow them to get off unobtrusively, Mr Cooper. Leave that to me. I'll muster the crew on the dockside. You get the passengers up the gangplank behind the men and then sidle off to the left. Only cross the open square when the cheering starts. Oh, and could I have my ribbon please?'

Ten minutes later, the Skipper had spoken with Arthur and they had the ship's company fallen in on the quayside, the rear rank around three feet forward of the gangplank. He asked Number One to bring the company to attention and then said in a loud voice, 'Gentlemen, we are here this afternoon to mark a very special occasion,' he could see Cooper and his charges strolling slowly behind the crew and continued, 'Mr Bergland, do you have the item?'

Svein marched forward smartly and presented a cardboard box to the Skipper, saluted, then marched back to his place in the front rank. The Skipper continued, 'There is one among us who is unique, having performed a feat which no ship's company has seen in the service's history, and today I am proud to honour that man. Gentlemen, we are in the presence of a member of the honourable order of Heinkel Killers.' he turned smartly to his right and asked Number One, who was now laughing uncontrollably, to remove his hat. Opening the box, he lifted the red ribbon, which now had the propellor fragment attached using a split-ring, over Number One's head calling, 'Three cheers for the First Lieutenant.' Some local people stopped to look as they gave three rousing cheers and, as the crew dispersed, the shore party melted away with their fellow spectators.

Number One was still chuckling and when they got into the wheelhouse he looked at his award in the light, 'Good God sir, is this real?' the Skipper smiled, 'It is Number One and we know this because the shrapnel nearly took the Mate's ear off. Luckily, he thought to pick it up!' Arthur shook Number One's hand. 'You'll be able to tell the Admiral that his buckshot idea seems to work, sir!'

Mr Cooper walked in smiling, 'Well done Skipper, a masterful diversion. The passengers are safely on their way.' He neglected to say that the young lady had turned to him as they left the open area outside the fish market, saying in a very thick French accent the crew were fools, but very brave and efficient fools, and she liked them. Given the sour face she had maintained since their acquaintance, he felt that to be high praise indeed!

The Skipper called the party to a halt. 'Right lads, let's get ready for sea before we get interned for wine smuggling.' He had thought to wish them all a happy new year, but given their circumstances, decided not to tempt fate.

They returned to Southend in the darkness without incident. HMS Gordon had left, and they berthed outside another trawler which was fitted for minesweeping. The Skipper reported in to the duty officer and received orders to join a northbound convoy leaving on the 4th. The Skipper was glad they could have a couple of full night's sleep. One or two of the lads, the bridge crew in particular, were looking weary. He asked Arthur to let the lads know the next two days were 'make and mend'.

The first few days of January 1940 were very mild, but on the 6th the weather clamped in as never-before. The conditions were almost arctic, with deep snow and winds causing drifting across Britain. It seemed like it would never end, but actually lasted just over a month. Despite the weather, convoys went on and after the turn of the year, they seemed to see more aircraft during their FN and FS (Forth North and Forth South) convoys.

The grinding drudgery of winter convoys was profound, and broken only by short spells of shore leave, a quick job for McDonald where they collected three people from a Norwegian drifter north-east of Shetland, and one three-day stopover for repairs after a collier did her best to ram White Nab. It happened in thick fog just south of the Humber. While it was a glancing blow, it resulted in a section of the bulwark on the port side of the well deck being replaced. They left the ship in Cook, Welton and Gemmell's yard near Beverley and took a train to Scarborough, where they spent a wonderful two nights at home. The Skipper had taken Mavis out for afternoon tea; Scarborough seemed very grey, what with rationing, the weather and all the air raid precautions. The Skipper thought that war ashore smelled of wet sandbags, gun oil, and fear.

Other than that, the breaks from routine were, mostly, tragic. A tanker covered the sea in burning oil after being mined and the survivor's injuries were terrible to see. They said afterward they should carry ampules of morphine on board, but the admiralty seemed loath to give them more than the handful in the first aid box. The Skipper requested a professional medic, but to no avail. In the end McDonald said he'd try to pull strings, but the army was getting the lion's share of trained medics as things stood. The Skipper added it to his 'outstanding items' list.

On another occasion, they pulled a British airman from a tiny dinghy which was adrift near Bass Rock. He said he was an observer in a battle, and his pilot and gunner had died on impact with the sea. They later discovered that the aircraft he came from was called a Fairey Battle: a type which, because of its weight and three-man crew, was often mauled by the Luftwaffe. Yet still the crews flew their missions with great courage. Sadly, the airman died from exposure before they reached Methil.

They had a couple of tussles with enemy aircraft and hit the tail of one plane, who was lining up to bomb the Commodore's ship. There were some lighter moments when Number One blazed away with his shotgun at any enemy plane even remotely in range, but he hadn't so far added a bar to his 'Heinkel Killer' award. Number One remained confident, and the crew now accepted him as one of their own. No mean feat for the officer who made them parade every morning. The Skipper took to joining him on the well deck if he felt the crew needed a push to improve, or a pat on the back.

The little wireless that Svein had rigged up was a godsend. When their watches allowed, Arthur and the Skipper would eat in the Skipper's cabin and listen to the wireless for an hour. It was their link with their old life, a reminder that life had not always been, and would not remain, the way it was at the moment. Yet the wireless was not the only way to unwind. When they laid over awaiting their next convoy, the Skipper had persuaded the authorities to let him berth in Methil harbour. He cited extra protection for the harbour from his Oerlikons, but in reality, it just felt more like their old life. The lads were happy and had a 'local' pub. The Skipper had purchased the Oxford Book of English Verse as a way of unwinding during their shore leave periods. Arthur accused him of trying to be romantic for Mavis, claiming he had only previously read cricket almanacs, all of which earned him a glare. The Skipper and Arthur often left the ship in the morning for a long walk, each clutching a canvas haversack containing an apple, some cheese and a flask of tea. They would frequently be gone for hours, following the course of the River Leven or tramping up the hill near Glenrothes if visibility was good and weather allowed. They spent late afternoons and evenings following such walks in companionable silence, listening to the wireless and reading. These rare rest days kept them sane.

After a gruelling convoy in the last week of March, during which aircraft sank two larger merchant ships by dropping mines on them, they laid up for 48 hours in Methil. The Skipper and Arthur were resting in the cabin with Svein when the wireless news, sounding hollow and crackly, reported the sinking of two warships by u-boats in the North Sea. The Skipper seemed to explode. 'Why can't these silly buggers send the airforce to bomb their docks? God's teeth, the Luftwaffe, seem to bomb us often enough! The thing that really gets my goat is the merchantmen we lost didn't even get a mention!'

Arthur stiffened. It was unlike the Skipper to yell like that, 'Are you alright Skipper? You don't normally let it get under your skin?'

The Skipper sighed, 'You're right Arthur. I'm sorry lads, it's just being penned into the swept channels. The Nazis know just where to find us, and it seems like stacking the odds against us. There are ancient destroyers and converted trawlers protecting the convoys, yet they tell us that these supplies are important. It makes little sense!'

Arthur nodded. 'I was thinking the other day, I believe that we've seen more ships die from mines inside the channels than outside them, even that time when nearly half the damned convoy was outside the swept channel.'

Svein shook his head. 'I remember a storm many years ago that sank maybe a hundred fishing boats in Norway. The headline in the newspaper next day said the King had opened a new opera house. It's just the way it is, I suppose.'

As the Skipper opened his mouth to reply, there was a shout from the wheelhouse, 'Boat approaching Skipper!'

They tidied up and went up into the wheelhouse. The Skipper and Arthur glanced at each other as they recognised Captain McDonald being led toward the wheelhouse ladder by Number One.

As McDonald reached the bridge deck, he shook the rain from his hat and followed Number One through the wheelhouse door. 'Good afternoon Gentlemen, does anyone fancy a change of pace?'

They grinned and frantically nodded. McDonald laughed as he clapped the Skipper on the shoulder, saying, 'You chaps are so reliable. How quickly can you put to sea Skipper?'

Chapter 14

57° 51’ 42” N, 05° 18’ 35” W

(‘Patrol Base 8’ near Badcaul)

Saturday 30th March 1940

McDonald had asked for passage to Patrol Base 8 with White Nab after their initial reunion. He’d said a very important mission had arisen which would need their expertise, and they needed to return to the Base as quickly as possible.

Arthur and Svein went ashore to round up the lads, finding them in a snooker hall not far away. Number One was readying the ship for sea and the Skipper had worked up a quick passage plan.

McDonald was sitting in the Skipper's cabin reading and drinking a mug of tea when the Skipper went down. He looked up as the Skipper came down the steps, 'How goes it Skipper?'

'Not too bad. Arthur just got back with the lads. Fortunately, they were just playing snooker and not in the pub, so we'll square away soon and we can set the watches.'

'Great news Skipper, thanks. I've just had an intelligence update which I need to share with you. We'll have a more detailed briefing at Base 8, but in short, we believe the Germans will invade Norway shortly. At the moment, the Norwegian, French and our own government are wrangling about the appropriateness of mining Norwegian waters and we fear that issue distracts them from the primary threat.'

The Skipper's eyes widened, 'My Lord!, they'd invade a neutral country?'

McDonald nodded. 'They'd invade Heaven's gates if they thought there was a strategic advantage for doing so. Fortunately for the angels above, they don't own a long coastline bordering the North Sea; Norway, however, does!'

McDonald stopped; silent for a while. 'Look Skipper, there is a lot that I can't say, but I can tell you this. The Germans are interested in an area of science which could generate new and powerful weapons. We, as yet, would have no reply if they were successful. We are therefore allowing several Danish and Norwegian industrialists and scientists to travel to Britain and France to help us develop our own programme as soon as possible. One chap, in particular, has expressed a desire to travel to Britain should Norway fall to the Nazis during the war. That chap, a scientist, is the subject of this mission. The plan is this: you will land a party of ground troops to provide an escort for the subject and his son to a rendezvous point. When they arrive, you will collect them all and return here. Simple enough perhaps, but the trouble is, we don't know when the Nazis will attack, though we believe it is imminent.' The Skipper shook his head slowly, letting out a quiet whistle, 'Unknown weapons, imminent invasions... How do you sleep at night?' McDonald nodded and shrugged, 'A good malt on my bedside table helps. Sometimes! Anyway, we have made some preliminary contact with anti-Nazi Norwegian patriots who will form resistance and sabotage units, but we can't be sure where the Nazis will concentrate once they invade, nor how many of the resistance fighters will actually take up arms. Despite that, we have one advantage. The subject has a house on the mainland close to Slyngøya Island where your contacts live. We don't want to jeopardise your friends, so we can't involve them in this operation, but the subject has friends, a couple on the mainland, who will definitely help get him to Slyngøya. He frequently goes there to fish and takes a boat from Bud, so he shouldn't arouse suspicion among his neighbours when he leaves. We believe your First Officer would be a good choice to go with the troops and act as naval liaison. He did well in establishing control of landing beaches during training, so we're confident he can handle that part. You can drop him ashore with an army patrol and they will bring the subject across the island to the small jetty you described to us, then signal you to pick them up. We want absolute radio silence on this. The Nazis can detect the origin of a signal, and we can't bring down their wrath on the islanders. This suggests a night-time drop, with pickup the following night. We'll try to pick a new moon or at least a crescent that won't be too bright. That should allow you to approach unobserved. I'd like your view on whether you'll be able to blend in with local boats or hide somewhere nearby, so have a think about that as we travel to Base 8. Of course this is all outline at the moment and you'll be involved in detailed planning of the operation as the situation develops. There are a lot of unknown factors, but I think your local knowledge could swing it for us if there are any developments we can't plan for. As I say, this mission, along with other extractions to Sweden and France, could decide the outcome of this war.'

The Skipper's eyes narrowed. 'I'll cross my fingers. From your tone, I suspect the plan may be a sight more complicated than we expect.'

'Well, it's really just lack of knowledge. If I knew the situation on the ground and still felt our plan was workable, I'd be a sight less worried. At this moment, I simply don't have that information. What I'm working toward is a point whereby, when you sail, we will have those details, which, of course, will be much nearer the invasion. Perhaps even after it.'

The Skipper pursed his lips. 'I think the basic idea is sound. Avoiding the harbour is good. The folk at Friyatoft inlet are anti-fascist from run-ins with the Norwegian Fascist Party, or just Norwegians who want to live their lives as they always have. So we shouldn't have any issues with them reporting us to the enemy. Most will simply close their curtains and ignore any strange noises. By crossing the island, the soldiers can hide in the hills above Talga in daylight. I can't imagine there would be many people up there, but we can check with Svein. So yes, we have at least the basis of a plan, I'd say.'

McDonald grinned, 'I suspect you're right Skipper, I certainly hope you are. Once we get to Base 8, we can work up the plan properly. We'll work with all involved as the situation unfolds over there. By all means, have a chat with Mr Bergland about my invasion suspicions, but clarify we aren't certain and definitely can't pre-warn anyone over there.'

'Svein is sound, Captain. Don't worry about him. Right, I'll round up the lazy buggers on deck and get us moving!'

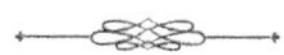

Their passage over the north of Scotland was without incident. In fact, there were some significant periods of sunshine which lifted everyone's spirits. As they rounded Cape Wrath and entered the Minch, it almost felt like a second home.

That feeling became stronger as they entered little Loch Broom. The yellow of gorse and broom flowers patched the lower south-facing slopes of the hills with shimmering colour. As they coasted to the mooring, water chuckling at the stem, Arthur breathed deeply of that highland air and wished away warfare.

Yet warfare was their business, for the time being. Within half an hour of mooring, they were sitting in the Nissen hut by the pot-bellied stove. A sign on the door now identified it as, 'Briefing Room'. The rear wall now had a blackboard added. The Skipper, Number One, Arthur and Svein sat in a row with Captain Stevenson and Sub-Lieutenant Cooper behind them, while McDonald had mounted the wooden dais.

Right, 'Thank you all for your attendance, Gentlemen. Skipper, did you bring your chaps up to speed?'

'I paraphrased what you told me, sir, yes.'

'Thanks Skipper. So, we all know the bare bones. One or two clarifications first. We want to launch the operation from here. Lerwick has too many prying eyes and we might appear out of the ordinary. They watch Scapa Flow using reconnaissance aircraft, and no doubt some people who may be sympathetic to the enemy. Also, we may have an unquantified wait before we go, so that would beg questions. I've had conversations with the team here, and we're still in the same position I described to the Skipper. That is, we have governments distracted by other matters and our intelligence is enough to convince us we're right, but not firm enough to convince any of the governments involved. Yes, Cooper?'

'I was just wondering, sir, is there any point at which an infrequent overflight by reconnaissance aircraft might provide concrete proof that our information is correct?'

'Good question. As you imply, we can't make reconnaissance flights too obvious, otherwise they'll know we're on to it and perhaps bolster their forces even further. Also, the RAF is deep in politics over how photographic reconnaissance is to be run, and by whom. We know of troop movements from certain assets within Germany, but aerial reconnaissance hasn't noted them massing in positions we'd expect to see for a major drive through Denmark and Norway, neither are we aware of any major groupings near ports where an amphibious attack might develop. All of which can be summed up as fuzzy!'

The range of resources available to McDonald privately impressed the Skipper. He had thought of spies, secret agents, but not aircraft which could take photographs.

McDonald continued, 'So after a fight which the head of my section thankfully won, the Admiralty released White Nab for an undefined period to assist the Secret Intelligence Service. We can therefore prepare carefully and comprehensively; however, the uncertainty as to timing means we must act on the assumption we have very little time. If we're wrong, then we can decide at the time whether the plan needs revision. One thing which might take time to deal with is the question of how White Nab should hide when the shore party are in action. We considered painting her as a Norwegian civilian trawler, but that increases the risk of the crew being exposed as involved in espionage should the worst happen. We don't yet know if the invaders would seize Norwegian vessels, so we need to decide whether to leave White Nab painted and equipped as a warship, or whether to disguise her as a civilian vessel. Do you gentlemen have any thoughts on how or where to hide? Yes Skipper, go ahead.'

'Yes. I thought about this issue as you asked, and I wonder whether to fit a pair of gallows in the waist and stream weighted otter boards to make it look like we're minesweeping, or fishing. We could then go south around Gossa Island, or even into the Midfjorden to hide in plain sight. In this way we're always moving, we're never over two hours steaming from Slyngøya and we wouldn't pass the same point twice. At least from a distance, we'd seem legitimate. Of course, this all goes west if there are sweeping activities in that area. I suppose, in that case, we might pose as a Norwegian minelayer. As you mentioned, so much would depend on the situation on the day.'

McDonald thought for a time, 'That's useful. At least we have plausible options. In that case, we've answered the first question. We don't need to repaint her. Next thing, we are sourcing some different and heavier Vickers machine guns to replace the Lewis guns you have. The reason is that Lewis guns weren't very reliable when new, so Heaven knows what they're like now!'

Svein grinned, 'Yah, I lost count of the times I've pulled rounds out of the breech with my pliers. Luckily, mostly during practice firing. Thank you for that Captain.'

'Not at all, Mr Bergland. Last year, we took what we could get hold of. Today, we can get better kit if we have sufficient justification. On that subject, I should have mentioned the reason we finally won permission to keep White

Nab, and why we have the new guns. It is the vital importance of the scientists we propose to rescue or recruit. We should always remember that success in this mission could lead to us winning the war.'

They had a break for tea, during which McDonald asked about the convoys. He was both surprised and amused to learn that Number One had damaged an enemy aircraft using a shotgun. He was truly dumbfounded when they told him how much coal was being carried to London each week. After fifteen minutes, they restarted.

'Right chaps. We plan some refresher training to make sure the crew is up to speed and fighting fit. Also, we'd like Mr Bergland to make sure any equipment which is less than 100 percent reliable gets overhauled or replaced as quickly as possible,' Svein nodded happily, 'The wireless operator will refresh his training on coded signals and the First Officer will receive a crash course in army liaison.'

The briefing then covered bunkering and ammunition top ups, all the unglamorous details that ensured the ship could do her job. Everyone was engaged, and they covered everything needed, but the Skipper felt clawing unease that, despite all this detail, uncertainty was at the core.

The next two days passed quickly. Svein was working down his snagging list and getting the ship as near perfect as possible. Number One spent a lot of time ashore with McDonald and a lieutenant from the King's Own Yorkshire Light

Infantry, Brian Jackson. McDonald didn't want the army contingent to be a separate entity from the ship because in his experience that was where confusion, poor communication and inter-service rivalry arose. By ensuring that the shore party understood the naval aspect of the plan, and that the shore party leadership was a joint-service team, he hoped to encourage constant cooperation.

On Thursday, the fourth of April, McDonald and Stevenson called the ship's officers and Jackson into the briefing room. McDonald stood on the dais looking sombre. 'Gentlemen, I can tell you we believe the Nazis are beginning an invasion of Denmark and Norway as I speak. Yesterday, we saw a lot of ships leaving Germany with troops and materiel, so we assume they are planning an amphibious landing or landings. Elements of the home fleet will sail today or tomorrow. However, the Admiralty is adamant this is not a Nazi invasion, but an attempt to break out elements of the German fleet and release them into the Atlantic. My organisation is bending the ear of our own Government but it's hard going. This changes nothing for us, of course. The subject won't leave unless Norway falls to the Nazis and, as discussed already, we need things to be stable enough so that we can execute our plan with the greatest chance of success. As you all know, we could never pull off our mission until the bullets stop flying.'

Captain Stevenson stood, 'So it very much seems like we were right in our assessment, however I want you all, especially you Mr Bergland, to understand that we would much rather we'd been wrong and the Norwegian and Danish people are in our thoughts and prayers. Are there questions?' There was silence, so Stevenson dismissed the group.

McDonald collared the Skipper as he left. 'Are you sure that Svein is alright?'

The Skipper nodded. 'Svein is usually a closed book, but he will talk to Arthur and myself if he has any concerns above the usual. Thank you for thinking of him, though.' McDonald nodded, and the Skipper followed his officers to the jetty.

Everyone at Patrol Base 8 became shocked, angered or depressed by turns as the invasion and debacle of the Norwegian Campaign developed. Reports reached McDonald of failures of approach and communication within the British forces. Norwegian senior officers who either mismanaged their commands or, in rare cases, seemed defeatist from the start. The Admiralty adherence to their theory of an Atlantic breakout infuriated Stevenson in particular and he wrote a couple of unwise letters to contacts which mercifully seemed to have disappeared into the filing system (in fact McDonald had intercepted them before they left the base). It infuriated McDonald when a contact described the botched mobilisation of the Norwegian Army: they sent mobilisation letters to reservists rather than broadcasting an immediate callout. This disaster had the result that un-drilled troops went straight into fierce combat with the Wehrmacht. Yet in his heart, he knew that confusion and miscommunication were a simple fact of war.

In the end, the decision to evacuate all allied forces from Norway came toward the end of May and was complete in the first week of June. The Norwegian King and Crown Prince began a government in exile, based in Britain.

They had summoned McDonald, with a few of his superiors, to speak to the new Prime Minister, Winston Churchill, in mid-May. They had briefed Churchill on their plan, which Churchill said agreed with certain conversations that had taken place between himself and President Roosevelt. He gave them the green light to implement their plans at the earliest opportunity.

As he travelled back from London, McDonald reflected on the test that they were to face, perhaps the greatest of their lives.

The day after McDonald's return, they had a review meeting at the Skipper's request, so they gathered in Captain Stevenson's office.

The Skipper sat straight, biting his lip and frowning, 'We're now getting toward the time of year when there is no such thing as "the cover of darkness", so I think we need to revisit our approach.'

McDonald nodded, 'Fair enough. What are you thinking?'

The Skipper stood and began pacing as he spoke. 'I have mixed feelings, but the more I think about it, the more I believe disguising ourselves as a minesweeper could be too risky as we get into longer days. I can't get away from the idea that, in full daylight, we might be more open to challenge.'

McDonald nodded slowly. 'I understand you may get detected more easily, but why is the disguise less effective?'

'Well sir, for example, we don't know where the enemy put defensive minefields, nor do we know when each area was last swept. Darkness would both conceal us, as you say, but if they spotted us, it also adds an element of doubt in the mind of a lookout. A hazy sighting in the dark could well lead him to believe he'd seen what he expects to see, whether that be a minesweeper or a fishing boat, whereas the clarity afforded by daylight makes us both easily seen and more likely to be identified. If we do anything out of the ordinary, we could be in trouble.'

'I see your point, Skipper. Any suggestions on an alternative approach?'

The Skipper's shoulders slumped slightly. 'I do, but there lies my concern. The only workable disguise is a fishing vessel, but, for it to succeed, we would need to remove the twelve-pounder and maybe the Oerlikons, too. It seems like we'd be entering hostile waters in a pretty helpless state!'

McDonald stared at the floor for a few moments before speaking, 'I see your point, Skipper. I wonder if we could mount a smaller gun without the current large platform, or even one Oerlikon. It would be easier to disguise it at deck-level I suspect?'

The Skipper rubbed his chin. 'Well, we would never sink a destroyer with the twelve-pounder even on a good day, though Number One would probably try, so I suppose the

Oerlikon would suffice if we had to. At the least, it's got a high rate of fire. We can mount the new machine guns when we need them, so there's no problem there. Oh, and we'd have to dismantle the flying bridge. Svein says that most of it disconnects at deck level, so it should be simple enough. I would say we'd need to keep the full crew complement if we're to manage the beach. I'm conjecturing that withdrawal under fire is not impossible.'

McDonald grinned and shook his head. 'You've got a bright future as a naval planner Skipper, I'll say that,' Captain Stevenson's chuckle was audible, 'and, no, that scenario is not impossible.'

The Skipper's jaw set firm. 'Anything else we can do to reduce the chance of it going west?'

'I'll have a word with our sources and ask them to note the location and behaviour of local fishing vessels to make sure that you fit in. Also, I'll widen the net and see if we can find a hide-out for you.'

Arthur sat upright, his eyes gleaming. 'Skipper, can you recall when we lent a pump to that boat who had beached after hitting a growler?'

The Skipper stared for a second. 'By God, Arthur, you're a genius! Why didn't I remember that?' he turned to McDonald. 'We went to help a Hull boat whose Skipper was a pal of T'owd Skipper. Sorry, my father, I mean. Anyway, there's an island southwest of Bud, I'll get the name from my chart, and it has a small harbour on the north side but a pretty empty bay on the south where this chap had careened his boat on a shingle beach. We could anchor in that bay and act like we're making repairs. If anyone comes out to us, Svein can speak to them. I can't imagine the enemy would be interested in that shallow bay.'

McDonald's eyes flicked between the Skipper and Arthur, 'Well if you chaps are happy, then so am I.' He glanced at Stevenson who was smiling and nodding, 'So Captain Stevenson and I will organise a yard to remove and store the twelve-pounder and one Oerlikon. We'll keep the Oerlikon under lock and key. Yours were original trial pieces supplied in thirty-seven and the army get all the guns we ordered pre-war for anti-aircraft service. We convinced them that the trial pieces had a slower firing rate and were no good as anti-aircraft weapons, so it's our secret. Well, one of our secrets at least!'

The Skipper turned to Arthur and Number One. 'So we need to give her a lick of paint. I'll let you two break it to the lads!'

Chapter 15

57° 51' 42" N, 05° 18' 35" W

('Patrol Base 8' near Badcaul)

Monday 10th June 1940

On the tenth of June 1940, the Norwegian Sixth Division laid down its arms after British and allied forces were evacuated. As the Skipper listened to his wireless, he realised that this could herald the start of their mission. He wrote letters to Mavis and Mother, making light of their work but warning they would be busy, so not to expect any letters for a while. As he had got used to it, he started to enjoy writing and receiving letters. The post had become much more regular during their prolonged stay in Scotland.

As a result, Mavis' letters became longer and more personal, which pleased the Skipper.

During the waiting time, they exercised with submarines to assist in training sub commanders and had tested the new machine guns, but once the conversion to 'fake trawler' as Arthur had christened it, was complete, they had no further sea time. The Admiralty had insisted that they remove the ASDIC, but McDonald had borrowed a hydrophone unit so that they could listen but without accurate range and bearing. He explained the Nazis had at least that technology, but he didn't want to give the enemy ASDIC if the worst happened.

The Skipper and Arthur had walked for miles as the evenings lengthened, and McDonald occasionally joined them. The smell of gorse flower and rising sap was intoxicating, but the Skipper liked to catch the tang of salt air to remind him that the sea was near.

McDonald called a briefing on the eleventh of June. He stood on the dais, looking relieved. He smiled as he began, 'Gentlemen, we are entering the period when our opportunity will arrive. The Subject would like to leave with his son as soon as possible. The Nazis have taken over the civilian governance of Norway, having pushed Quisling's puppet leadership aside, so we hope the invaders will now feel more secure. We have scaled up our detailed intelligence analysis of the enemy's disposition between Bergen and Trondheim to identify the best date for the operation. We are utilising reconnaissance overflights, military intelligence and our own sources to determine where threats may be and to estimate the risk to our operation from those threats. So far, we have identified an armed trawler, very much like your own, in Talga harbour on Slyngøya, but it hasn't sailed at all during the period we've been monitoring it. Frankly, we're uncertain whether it's Norwegian or German, but we think probably Norwegian. The enemy bombed both Ålesund and Kristiansund in late April and early May, so the Nazis clearly have some plan for them. We believe that these two ports will ultimately become bases for shipping and lighter military vessels, such as minelayers and minesweepers with the larger warships at Bergen and Trondheim. We don't believe the harbour on Slyngøya is large enough to be important, so we are not expecting a naval threat from there. Clearly, two Nazi held ports close by are a concern. As you know, Ålesund is just over thirty miles southwest of Slyngøya and Kristiansund about the same northeast, so we will be closely monitoring events at those locations. Depending on analysis of intelligence received in the next few days, we will decide on whether to go before the enemy organises further, or to wait until their disposition is better understood. We'll therefore ask you to be ready to raise steam and go with very little notice and any exercise taken ashore is to be within the bounds of Base 8. Your refresher training has been extensive, you have rested from operations, and I have absolute confidence in your ability to pull this off. I think we're ready.'

The grating buzz of his intercom tore the Skipper from sleep. He rolled from his bunk, whacking his heel into one of the drawer handles underneath the bunk base.

'Skipper here, go ahead.'

'It's Arthur Skipper. We're to go ashore with Svein and Number One immediately. I've told our chaps already.'

'Thanks Arthur, I'll be two ticks.' He massaged his heel, then wearily stood and opened the tiny wardrobe for his clothes. Glancing at his clock, he mused that something really was brewing if they woke him at three in the morning.

A few minutes later, he was in the wheelhouse with the others. Arthur had called Archie, the second engineer, and asked him to have the firemen ready to bring the boiler to full heat. The Skipper nodded. 'Right lads, let's away and get the latest news!'

Once again, they sat in the briefing room, shivering despite the valiant efforts of the pot-bellied stove. Arthur mused. It said something about the climate in that part of the world when they needed a stove in June.

McDonald and Cooper entered with a bleary looking Captain Stevenson following. Cooper handed a sheaf of photos to the Skipper as McDonald stepped onto the dais.

McDonald rubbed his hands together, his eyes shining. 'Gentlemen, it looks like the gods are smiling at us. Skipper, if you could have a look at that first photo, then pass it down the line, I'd like to flesh it out a little. You'll recognise the harbour at Talga, and on the quayside you'll see the trawler, still in exactly the same position. Now we've had some information from our asset, to whom you handed over the two people you carried to Slyngøya. The trawler is indeed Norwegian, but the enemy has seized her and is converting her to, he believes, a minesweeper. So far, they have only got as far as fitting some machine guns, apparently. Also the caretaker, Nils Heiberg, is a known anti-fascist and has promised to let our man know if the Nazis plan to send her to sea. So the good news is the local presence is not a threat. As regards the Ålesund and Kristiansund contingents, there is one e-boat and one corvette which alternate between the two ports and sometimes both ships are in the same location. These vessels seem to patrol irregularly, and we now have enough sources to tell if they are both in port. We think this is the best situation we are likely to have in the foreseeable future, and the top brass agrees. So I'd like you to work up your passage plan Skipper if you would. We're all aware that the very narrow window of deep dusk means that darkness and moon phase are almost irrelevant, so we're thinking of timing your arrival when people are at low ebb, say 03:00, approximately. Then you can reach your hide-out in the early morning.'

The Skipper's cheeks blew out like apples. 'Do you have any analysis of wider range naval patrols and the frequency of Luftwaffe patrols? I'm thinking we'll probably have to go fairly far north before running in toward Slyngøya if we want to avoid any close inspections.'

McDonald pursed his lips. 'It crossed our minds, too. I wondered about a diversion, but couldn't think of anything within our resources that would be effective. One thing we have in our favour is the occupying force currently has very few airfields. The Norwegian airforce bases that the Nazis have taken over are often grass strips, unsuitable for fully laden bombers. Our understanding is that heavier aircraft undertake convoy attacks in the north and British coastal shipping attacks in the south, but it's all new to both sides. The Norwegian coast seems to get comparatively few patrols at the moment, so given the nearest airfields are over a hundred miles away from Slyngøya, I think an approach from an unexpected direction is enough. Work up your plan so you head up toward the Faroes and head across to Slyngøya. Once we have an ETA, then we'll alert the Subject.'

The Skipper stood. 'I've already planned such a route. The passage takes six days and four hours. So if we leave at around 23:00 on a particular day, we'll arrive at 03:00 six days later.'

McDonald smiled and shook his head, 'You're a force of nature Skipper, you really are! Right then. I'll contact the Subject and agree a date.'

Chapter 16

65° 00' 55" N, 00° 28' 47" E

(On passage, furthest point north)

Tuesday 18th June 1940

On the 16th, HMT White Nab had passed northeast of the Faroes. On the previous day, they saw sheer cliffs with white surf at their bases clearly, but as the day progressed, a haze had hidden them. The Skipper always felt like each island was a fortress; the ones he had visited had only one bay containing crofter's cottages, the rest was dizzying cliffs or steep hills where the grass felt like a temporary coat which might easily slip off. But the place had a wild beauty, and the Skipper appreciated that.

They had departed Patrol Base 8 at 23:00 on the thirteen[th], after waiting for a reply to their message. It had come via a Swedish asset who drove a train shipping iron ore over the border twice weekly, and could telephone the asset in Talga. The Subject was to travel to Slyngøya by boat as he always did, but once ashore would go to ground on the southwest side of the island, well away from any habitation. The Subject would carry food and drink for forty-eight hours and was told; no fires, no lights and no noise, even if he thought that he and his son were alone. He was told where to hide and given a password which the shore party would call out. He also had the response which he must make to show all was well. There had been some debate about the need to hide out through the day, but they had all agreed that moving British troops and the Subject through Friyatoft would be best done at night.

The soldiers, under Lieutenant Jackson, were billeted in the fish room and could exercise on deck when the horizon was clear.

The Skipper's route passed east of the Faroes, where he began a long curve which started heading northeasterly and ended up approaching Slyngøya from the north-northwest. This minimised the time that White Nab was in patrolled waters and once closing the coast, they would stream the two otter boards weighted with a length of steel-cored rope. In addition, they hung a net over the foremast boom as if it were drying, which neatly covered the deck mounted Oerlikon.

The Skipper felt reasonably comfortable, but underneath was the hollowness of knowing their armament was puny and the Nazis outnumbered them. The Norwegian flag fluttering at the stern didn't help his frame of mind, either.

At 16:30 on the eighteenth, they had just over a hundred miles to run. Things were going smoothly. They had altered course twice when they spotted aircraft. The Skipper felt that, if their course were reported, they might appear to be heading to north Norway. Neither aircraft had shown interest, so they had quickly resumed the planned track. At 15:00 they ran into a heavy rain squall, which they had welcomed, but they were now leaving it.

Number One was on the well deck with Arthur making sure that they were ready to stream the fake trawl when he heard the lookout on the bridge deck shout. He glanced toward where the man was pointing, but a greenish path in the water caught his attention. He yelled, 'Torpedo!' but it was too late to take evasive action.

The massive boom seemed to reverberate inside his chest and he looked up as an immense column of white water rose over the stern. The wave raised by the explosion pitched the ship forward, her bows burying deeper as the stern lifted. He could see the lads on the bridge deck sliding around, some on their backs. He himself toppled into the bulwark and as he pushed himself upright, he was aware of salty spray falling like the heaviest rain he'd ever known.

He ran aft, scanning the water in the direction from which the torpedo had come, but could see nothing. Rounding the aft end of the deckhouse, it amazed him to see that the whole after deck was intact! He leaned over the stern and thought that he was hallucinating. Everything was in one piece. Looking aft to the boiling greenish patch of water, he guessed the torpedo had exploded astern, but could think of no reason it should.

On the bridge, the Skipper shouted for silence when too many voices babbled at once. With order restored, he pushed his way to the bridge deck and slid down the steps to the deckhouse. As he turned, Number One's head popped up over the top of the deck ladder and gasped, 'We're all in one piece, Skipper. It's a bloody miracle if you ask me!'

The Skipper turned and raced up to the wheelhouse, with Number One following. He pressed the intercom to the engine room. 'Svein, would you do a damage survey and let me know how things stand? In the meantime, give her everything. I'm heading back into the squall.'

As they swung round, the Skipper went to the wheelhouse door and shouted up to the flying bridge. 'Right, who called out first?'

'Me Skipper,' it was George Sneaton, 'I saw a periscope bearing green four-zero, but it disappeared as that thing went off.'

'Thanks George. Right lads, eyes out for the periscope or torpedo tracks. Usual drill, this isn't new to us.'

Going back inside the wheelhouse, he turned to Yorke, who was listening to his hydrophone. 'Can you hear anything?'

Yorke glanced up, 'Nothing, sir. I didn't hear him fire either, so assuming I haven't got an equipment fault, then he possibly fired at long range. Judging by what I hear now, the equipment is working.'

The Skipper turned. 'Fred, I'm going back into the rain, then turning hard to port and stopping the engine. We'll then listen to see what happens next. The wind is north-easterly, so we may need to alter course and speed to stay with the heavier rain, just follow the darker parts, don't wait for me to notice. We just have to hope the squall lasts!'

Number One leaned against the door and the Skipper gave him a reassuring smile, 'A close call Number One, I suspect the torpedo malfunctioned, apparently there have been several attacks where the buggers have run deep but I'm not sure what made it explode if that's the case. Anyway, would you nip down into the fish room with Arthur please? Reassure the soldiers and check the slush wells, please. Let me know immediately if you find we're making water. Oh, and tell the lads to keep the netting over the gun unless the bugger surfaces, would you?' Number One nodded and disappeared.

Fred nodded to the Skipper. 'She's answering the helm alright, Skipper.'

'Thanks Fred, keep her heading for the squall, please. Any sightings, chaps?' Everyone shook their heads, and the Skipper nodded. 'So far, so good.'

The engine room intercom buzzed. 'Good news Svein?'

'Yah, well, I'm not sure yet, Skipper. That thing exploded under the aft end of the hull somewhere. The stern gland housing is leaking so I'll need to grease it up now and tighten the gland when we stop the shaft. There is water in the after peak behind the watertight bulkhead, and we're making water forward of the bulkhead too. It looks like two buckled plates letting in water, which is also coming up through the concrete ballast right back to the after peak. As things stand, my guess is that the pumps will cope, but we can't afford any more leaks. There is limited space, but if we can stop the shaft for fifteen minutes, then I can make a pad for the plates using mattresses and coir mats, then prop it with timber and wedge it tight to slow the flow. I'm more worried about the leak under the ballast. If it separated the keelson from the keel, or buckled the plates down there, which seems likely, the hull may be seriously weakened.'

The Slipper swallowed hard. 'Thanks Svein. Number One and Arthur are checking the slush wells forward, but from what you've said, the damage is all aft. I'll let you know if they find we're making water up forward.'

The Skipper repeatedly rubbed the back of his neck and paced the wheelhouse and bridge deck as they neared the squall. He couldn't understand why the sub hadn't fired again. *Maybe they had no more torpedoes. Perhaps they think we are civilian, what if they're aiming at us right at this*

moment? These thoughts bounced around his mind until he had a stern word with himself. They were still afloat and nearly into the squall; these were the relevant facts. He slowed his breathing and thought of the next steps.

As the first misty rain blurred the horizon, he told Fred to hold her steady and rang for half ahead. The rain was slightly heavier, which gave some comfort. As soon as the horizon disappeared aft, he ordered full ahead and a turn to the northwest. Then, after about a minute, he rang for a reduction to slow ahead and told Fred to make the turn on to 195°. After five minutes he called for 'all stop', and let her coast to a halt. The Skipper turned to Yorke, who shook his head, 'Nothing sir, I can hear marine life but nothing else at all.'

The Skipper pursed his lips. 'Good news, Yorke. Keep a listening watch and we'll hold our position for a while.'

As he descended into the normally rowdy engine room, the Skipper was acutely aware of the sound of people sloshing in water. He could hear Svein and Archie calling to each other and as he worked his way aft, Svein turned, 'The shaft is impeding Archie's props, Skipper. I'm not sure how much we can slow the inflow. It seemed to get worse slightly after that hard turn and I'm wondering if the loading on the rudder post was putting pressure on the damaged plating. Maybe the pumps are the only way to keep her afloat, so we should probably head back to Aberdeen as quickly as we can.'

The Skipper tapped on the oiler he was leaning against. 'Svein, we have to press on. The job they have given us is vital for the war effort, so unless we're going to founder immediately, then I can't head home.'

Svein tapped his teeth and sighed. 'Yah, alright. Well, the stern gland is OK while we're stopped. Archie has pumped the greaser, so hopefully it will behave. I think the pumps can cope, just, but if we suffer more damage...'

The Skipper banged his fist against the water tank on the starboard side. 'Bugger that submarine! Right then, good work, you two. I'll go slowly and manoeuvre carefully: let's just hope that the sub has gone on its way!'

Chapter 17

62° 55' 06" N, 06° 52' 37" E

(Slyngøya, Friyatoft Inlet)

Wednesday 19th June 1940

As they eased out of the grey safety blanket of rain, the Skipper could barely take his eyes off Yorke. The lad's ability to disappear into his world of squeaks, bubbles, propellor noises and all the rest was amazing. The Skipper was very grateful for Yorke's skill at that moment. Every so often his eyes would open and he'd nod his head at the Skipper. All's well.

After an hour of this, the Skipper hoped the sub had gone on its way and indeed; they encountered nothing more of it.

Svein reported the pumps were holding their own and the Skipper couldn't help patting the teak rail which went around the bridge deck, thinking, *Well done old lass.*

They were in the last two hours of their run. Ten nautical miles to go and the wind had increased markedly, which had knocked up quite impressive seas as they entered relatively shallow waters. They'd seen another aircraft, this time at medium height, and had gently altered course as though heading north, but it had quickly turned south and so they resumed their course after a few minutes. The light had faded, colours being replaced by less intense versions of themselves, and they were now heading into the dusk. The lad on the whaleback, who was on lookout, yelled, 'Mine, it's a floating mine Skipper!'

There was nothing for it. The lad was pointing to the port-side of the stem so the Skipper called, 'Helm! Hard a starboard, quickly!' The ship heeled a little as she went round and the lad continued pointing at what he'd seen, his arm sweeping slowly backward. The Skipper ran to the port side of the bridge deck as they slipped past the mine, black and menacing, its hedgehog prickles revealing it was a contact mine. He would rather have sunk it by gunfire, but he knew it could take many rounds to make it go under, and he couldn't afford to draw any attention this close to shore.

As the Skipper began breathing again and ordered a return to their course, the intercom buzzed. His heart drummed as he saw the engine-room light glowing. 'Svein here Skipper. I think we strained the plates a little more. There is definitely more water coming in now. I'm sorry Skipper, she may not make it home. If it were further forward, I'd pull some canvas under the hull, but with the damage where it is, well...'

The Skipper's head hung forward. 'I assume that we'll make the island Svein?'

'Yah, for sure. No problem there. Archie is just closing off the after peak. It's a watertight bulkhead, and that means we can't get to the stern gland, but once that compartment floods fully, no more water will come from there and we might locate the damaged plates. Bad news is, as you saw, most of the damage to larger plates is forward of that bulkhead. I'll get the pumps to maximum now, but frankly, that will not give us much more pumping than we have now. We will not go down suddenly. We'll just keep getting heavier at the stern until the pumps stop or the water hits the boiler. I think, if I have to guess, that we'd get halfway home if we went straight for Aberdeen.'

'Understood Svein, thanks.' He looked up at the shocked faces around the bridge. 'Don't panic, lads. We might need to take to the boats for the last mile, but we'll be fine. Of course, if anyone can pull a replacement ship out of their pocket, I'd be grateful!' the quiet laughter was the best he could hope for.

Peering ahead, the Skipper froze. *No, not in a thousand years; and yet... could it work?*

The Skipper ran back out onto the bridge deck. 'Arthur, Number One, bring Lieutenant Jackson and come to my cabin!'

A couple of minutes later, they had all gathered. The Skipper grimaced as he looked around the old familiar cabin, but steeled himself. 'I'll keep this short. The torpedo did some damage, as you know, but the hard turn to avoid the mine has made the leak worse, which shows the hull integrity is suspect. Svein says we're not likely to get home before she founders,' he registered shock on their faces but couldn't spare time to soften the blow, 'We all know the importance of this mission and I have a plan of sorts but I need to know that you are all willing to take the risk involved.'

Lieutenant Jackson straightened. 'Sir, from what I've seen and heard, you are a man who finely balances the safety of his men against the mission. If you feel it's worth the risk, then I don't object.' The other two were nodding, too.

The Skipper breathed slowly, his thoughts whirling. As his mind came back under control, one thought dominated: 'This is crunch point and I have to put crew before ship. That was my decision when Eddie died, now I have to live up to it, however hard it may be.' The Skipper smiled as warmly as he could, 'Right, I'm going to steal the armed trawler from Talga,' the silence was as thick as Mother's custard.

The Skipper grimaced, worried their faces betrayed the madness of his idea. He explained, 'We heard the caretaker chap is friendly, so we'll have Svein posing as skipper and go alongside her. That gets over the language problem. We'll think up a story to explain our presence if the harbour master turns up. Perhaps we received orders to convert another trawler and were told to deliver her there. During the day, we'll strip White Nab of everything we can and get it on board the other ship. We'll need a tall tale to explain that activity. Then, in the middle of the night, we'll take the old lass in tow and slip out of the harbour. It's possible we might borrow an extra pump even. If she stays afloat, we'll get her to Aberdeen, but if Svein is right, and I trust his judgement, we may have to cast her off and say our goodbyes.'

Arthur and Number One went through the same process as the Skipper himself had, disbelief followed by a sneaking suspicion it might work, then conviction it was their best option. The Skipper could see they were with him.

The Skipper clenched his fist. 'Now look, lads. As Captain McDonald would say, there are a lot of variables in this plan. I'm going to have to ditch the codes and some charts if I'm deliberately going to expose us to capture, but I'll get Sparks to write the success message pre-coded on a postcard or something and hide it on the other ship. For the shore party, I think we can massage the plan a little. Take a signal flag or something else brightly coloured, which is visible at a distance. We'll try to get there after twenty-four hours as planned but when we arrive, we'll stand off and if you fellows stay on the hill above Friyatoft and wave, we'll reply with four flashes on the Aldis Lamp so you can descend as we come inshore and launch the boats. If we don't show up, then hide out, perhaps up in those central hills, and we'll try again twenty-four hours later. Number One, take a hand bearing compass and, if we haven't arrived on the third night, steal a boat and head for the mainland, then do your best to get to Sweden. Does anything need adding to that?'

They all thought, shaking their heads after a few seconds, so the Skipper sent everyone to prepare and returned to the bridge. He could hear Mother in his head, '*Reggie Hurton. I've never heard of such a hare-brained scheme in all my days!*'

The time was 03:20 on the nineteenth of June. The weather was dry, but some clouds had rolled in, making it darker than they had expected. They savoured their luck and carefully launched both boats to row ashore. Tension hung in the air like a damp mist.

The Skipper shook Number One's hand as they stood in the ship's well, 'Good luck and try not to start a battle,

Number One. I know how much you enjoy taking pot shots at Nazis.'

Number One shuffled his foot as he put on his tin helmet and checked his cigarette case was in his pocket. 'I'll fight the urge, sir, and good luck to you. The enemy will class you as a pirate after tomorrow, I expect. Captain Stevenson will love that one!'

The Skipper chuckled, 'We'll see Number One, oh and I'll make certain we take your shotguns with us!'

Number One waved as he slung his rifle across his back and clambered down into the boat. Forty minutes later, they heard a muffled noise, and the boats emerged from the gloom. Len Egdon looked up as he came alongside. 'Clockwork Skipper, not a soul awake and our lot just melted away up the path past the houses.'

As Arthur supervised getting the boats back onboard as quietly as possible, the Skipper stood watch on the bridge. He couldn't help tapping the intercom, 'Svein, sorry to interrupt. How are you doing down there?'

Svein knew the Skipper was really asking whether a miracle had happened. He looked at the plating on which he stood. 'I'm sorry Skipper, if anything it's slightly worse judging by Archie's soundings.'

Chapter 18

62° 52' 00" N, 06° 55' 12" E

(Slyngøya, Talga Harbour)

Wednesday 19th June 1940

At 05:30 they were approaching Talga harbour, having ditched the fake fishing gear and the codes in their weighted bag. Anyone not needed on deck was in naval uniform in the fish room with loaded rifles. Svein, Arthur and the Skipper were in the wheelhouse dressed in fishing clothes. The Skipper and Arthur both wore knitted woollen caps, while Svein sported the Skipper's old Breton fisherman's cap, with its black braids on the peak. Fred and Len were on the port side of the well deck, putting out fenders. Svein had taught them all to say 'takk skal du ha', stressing the first and last parts so that they could say 'thank you' in Norwegian and could all mimic his 'Ja'.

The entrance channel had a forty-five degree dog leg in it because of underwater rocks. As they coasted forward at two knots, they could see the stone blocks of the two small harbour arms. Further away was a hut and sentry box halfway down its length, which hadn't been there before the war. Svein picked up the glasses, but the sentry box seemed unmanned.

As they turned the corner to line up between the harbour arms, they all gasped. Dead ahead, at the opposite end of the harbour, was a corvette flying the nazi naval ensign. The Skipper turned slowly to Svein, 'We can't run lads, it'll look too suspicious. Our best hope is to ignore them unless we're challenged and tie up to the trawler as planned. If the trawler has gone, we tie up and let Svein go ashore to see if he can rent an extra pump. Arthur, will you pop down and tell the lads on deck to ignore it, please? It will look odd if they stand and gape at it.' Arthur darted off down the steps and strolled across the well deck as if organising his deckhands.

They trickled forward and Svein spotted a man in civilian clothes heading for the guard hut. The man was looking across, so he waved, then ignored him.

The harbour opened to their view. The Skipper felt a real pang as the familiar ochre red and mustard yellow houses came into view. They had painted one hotel white on the street that crossed the end of the harbour where the German boat moored. A couple of her sailors glanced over but took no interest in them, which boosted their confidence.

They could see the trawler was still in harbour and the Skipper, on the helm, took her around in a gentle curve to starboard, ringing for slow astern as he neared the side of the trawler. With the way off her, Fred and Len looped the breast lines around cleats on their new neighbour's deck, leaping back on to White Nab. Svein and Arthur went ashore to fix the bow and stern lines to the harbour wall while Len rigged springs to reduce fore-and-aft movement. After checking fenders, they went into the wheelhouse while Svein went aboard the other vessel to see if anyone was awake.

The Skipper suggested they should go into his cabin, so it looked like the crew was resting. Arthur looked worried. 'Maybe you should lie low, Skipper. There are a good few people here who would recognise your face. We can't afford a slip up.' The Skipper nodded agreement.

Svein rehearsed his story as he quietly walked across the well-deck and stepped over the bulwarks on to the other trawler. He didn't want to stumble if someone hailed him from the harbour and asked questions. The authorities sent them from Harstad in the north to deliver another ship for conversion and they were to assist the caretaker in Talga to remove unnecessary items, as well as delivering some hardware for the ship already under conversion. They would shortly take both ships to Ålesund for more work, they believed. If challenged, he would say they had no papers because things were so disorganised up in the north. The transition to the new administrative council was causing problems. They had been told the caretaker of the existing ship under conversion, a certain Nils Heiberg, would help them move the hardware over.

As Svein peered up the steps to the wheelhouse, he realised that nobody was stirring and turned to go back to White Nab, which for their subterfuge he had named 'Hvit Klippe' or 'White Cliff'.

As he was about to recross, he heard a soft call and saw the man they had seen heading for the guard's hut. Svein beamed. Speaking in his native tongue, he asked, 'Are you the harbour master, sir?'

The man was in his early fifties with close cropped grey hair. 'I am indeed, my name is Leif Johansen. May I ask your business here?' He sounded oily and sly. Svein felt a shiver and decided he was not a man to trust.

Svein trotted out the cover story without mentioning their lack of sailing orders. In the event the name of the caretaker seemed enough evidence for the harbour master, and he wished them a pleasant stay, recommending a bakery and cafe, which was run by his wife, as the best source for fine food in the town and opening for breakfast shortly. Svein gushed and promised to try the place as soon as he could.

Once the man had gone, Svein hopped back to White Nab for a council of war.

Svein entered the Skipper's cabin to find Arthur and the Skipper reading an Admiralty manual. He described his conversation with the harbour master, concluding that they couldn't trust him but that he seemed to be mainly in business for himself, so that made him easier to influence, if needed.

The Skipper pointed at the book on his table. 'We were looking up the Nazi ship over there. She's an M-Class Minesweeper. Fairly heavily armed, and has a complement of just over a hundred men, so we are probably outgunned and definitely outnumbered, I fear.'

Svein heard a scuff on deck. He climbed into the wheelhouse, making a show of tidying up. Hearing a whistle below, he galloped down the steps to find a man of about fifty waiting. Svein adopted the same smiling and confident air he had used with the harbour master. The man stuck out his hand, and spoke in Norwegian, 'Hello, I am Nils Heiberg, engineer and caretaker for the fishing boat next door.' His eyebrows lifted.

'Hello Mr Heiberg, I am Svein Bergland, temporary captain of this ship.'

Heiberg's eyes crinkled. 'Temporary, you say?'

'Yes, I delivered her here from Harstad up north.'

Heiberg laughed: a deep, warm sound, 'Svein you are a very poor liar. I knew you as a boy, forever helping the fishermen or tinkering with machines ashore. I also know you visit your cousin from time to time and that you are the engineer on a British fishing boat.' Svein's mouth sagged as the man continued, 'But you have nothing to fear my friend, I am no fascist and I know for sure that you aren't either, so how about we have a talk somewhere quiet?'

Svein racked his memory but had no picture of this man; though what he described was true. He took Heiberg to the cabin, where he introduced him to the Skipper and Arthur. Heiberg could speak English with a thick accent. Shaking Heiberg's hand the Skipper pointed to the settee seat, and the Norwegian sat down. Arthur went off to the fish room to update the rest of the crew, so Svein sat between the other two. Heiberg spoke to Svein for a few minutes about people he would remember and recounted some tales of Svein's youthful exploits and Svein knew he was genuine. Heiberg then looked curiously at the Skipper. 'This man has an excellent reputation here, Svein. At least among the people that matter. It's good that you found your way to him, I think? Now, first, I heard you talking to Leif Johansen, the harbour master. Be careful there. As long as he thinks there is something for him, he'll ignore you, but make no mistake, he would sell his wife to the Nazis to curry favour. He's a big supporter of Quisling and the Nasjonal Samling, his pro Nazi party. The only thing that trumps his politics is his greed.'

Svein looked at the Skipper, who turned and spoke, 'Mr Heiberg, thank you for your advice and I know you are correct about the harbour master. Now, I have to tell you we are in some trouble. A submarine fired a torpedo at us, which malfunctioned and exploded at considerable depth under our stern. Unfortunately, the shock wave has sprung a few plates and possibly damaged the keel itself, so we are uncertain we can make it back home.' He deliberately omitted all mention of the mission, but Heiberg was no fool.

'Skipper, I will not ask what you were doing in Norwegian waters. Best I don't know, but I will say this; if it damages the Nazis, then it's alright by me!'

The Skipper couldn't help smiling, 'Well, the world seems like a pretty awful place at the moment, but with people of good heart, like yourself, I believe there is hope. So now I must be blunt and ask an impertinent question: what is your interest in the ship next door?'

Heiberg looked surprised, 'Well, other than being instructed by our beloved harbour master to maintain the ship until they complete the full conversion, nothing. According to Johansen, she is to be made into a minesweeper for the Kriegsmarine. I am a widower and have a house on the harbourside, so I obey the fascists and await my chance to fight back.'

The Skipper took a deep breath. 'OK, time is of the essence, so I must tell you we intend to take the ship in the early hours of tomorrow morning. We want to make sure they can't blame you for the removal of the ship. We can leave you tied up or something like that to cover you.'

Heiberg shook his head, 'Svein, Skipper, the King is now in Britain. He left in HMS Glasgow. This I know. I would much prefer it if you could take me there so that I can fight beside him?'

Svein turned to the Skipper and they both imperceptibly nodded. The Skipper thought for a moment before answering, 'The answer is yes, of course we will take you. I need to ask another thing; would we harm local people if we blocked the harbour for a few days?'

Svein frowned, then realised what the Skipper must mean. 'Scuttle White Nab? Is that what you're thinking?'

The Skipper's face looked lined with strain, but determined. 'That's right Svein. We can't have that bugger over there chasing us around, can we?' he nodded toward the minesweeper through the porthole. 'If they sail today, then it may change, but I have to plan for the worst.'

Svein looked away, and Heiberg grimly smiled. 'Not at all. They can sell their catch fresh in Bud; or if it's for salting or smoking, it can go to Friyatoft. They could even go back to the old ways and beach launch the smaller boats. We have two drifters and they won't be back until tomorrow anyway, so I don't think there's a problem. The two herring boats over on the other side of the harbour don't go out nowadays.'

The Skipper thanked Heiberg for his help and his honesty. Heiberg grinned, 'For Heaven's sake both of you, call me Nils!'

Chapter 19

62° 49' 30" N, 06° 43' 04" E

(Sandbukt, southwest Slyngøya)

Wednesday 19th June 1940

Just before they reached the ridgeline in the centre of the island, Lieutenant Jackson called a halt. He sent his sergeant, Payne, and another man to reconnoitre the path ahead while the rest sat down for a breather. The two went forward at a crouching run, flattening themselves to a crawl before they reached the top of the incline. Jackson explained they were avoiding being silhouetted as they reached the skyline. Number One sat on a rock and took off his tin helmet. It was 05:30, bright, and the air was warming nicely. Where clumps of grass and heather grew, beads of dew glittering in the morning sunlight. He tilted back his head and realised the largest hill, which had been on their right as they marched, was a very impressive lump of rock indeed. The three hills in the centre of the Island had family names: Farstopp, Mortoppen and Sønntopp (father, mother and son peaks). They were passing between the father and mother. The son's more rounded top would appear as they crested the ridge ahead. Dattertoppen, the daughter, was on the point between Talga harbour and Friyatoft. The soldiers quickly came back and reported to their officer that all was quiet. Everyone ate a breakfast of corned beef and biscuit and the soldiers boiled water for tea on small folding stoves which burned circular solid-fuel blocks without smoke. Sergeant Payne sent one man ahead to watch over the ridge as he drank his tea and he himself faced back along their path.

As they finished their brief rest, with no word of command, the men picked up all their tins and the wrappers from the stoves. One man unfolded a short entrenching tool, unfolding its small spade end, and dug a hole behind some heather clumps a little way from the pathway they were following. They buried all their rubbish and, as they walked away, a very young soldier wearing a leather jerkin over his khaki battledress scuffed away the small patches where their stoves had blackened the sheep-cropped grass of the trail. As the soldier hurried to catch the rest Jackson smiled, 'Good lad Thompson,' turning to Number One he spoke quietly, 'I think he should still be at school, but ask him his age and he looks you in the eye and says that he's eighteen. Only the set of his jaw when he says it gives him away.' Number One shook his head, smiling as he clapped on his tin hat and adjusted the chin strap.

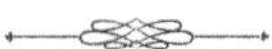

As they crested the ridge, their track became less distinct, but the shortest grass trended slightly to their left, following the lower slopes of the mother, Mortoppen. Svein had advised them to continue until they saw a large copse of birch and alder appear to the left of Sønntopp. This copse was the Subject's hideout. They should then turn right, into grassland which contained thinly spread trees and some folds in the land, heading straight for their destination.

As they descended, Jackson noticed that the 'road' which went two-thirds around the island, from Talga to the Svart Klippe lighthouse, was, in fact, a track. As they looked, Sergeant Payne made a low whistling sound and the soldiers all lowered themselves down slowly. Number One copied their action, and they laid in the longer grass. Jackson rolled on his side to face Sergeant Payne, who whispered, 'Movement on the track, sir.' Sergeant Payne took off his helmet and eased his head up. 'Two armed German soldiers, moving left to right. They're relaxed and showing no interest in the copse where our friend is hiding,' he rolled so that he could see Number One, 'Did you say there is a lighthouse at the end of the track sir?' Number One nodded and Sergeant Payne continued, 'In that case I imagine they'll patrol the length of the track before they turn round so we should have time to get our friend out.'

Jackson nodded, then waited until the soldiers had disappeared before rising slowly. They had briefed Number One during the walk over that 'take cover' meant dive quickly to ground, but any other signal or noise was a sign to move more carefully: apparently rapid movement caught the eye more easily.

Moving carefully at first, then picked up the pace again, they headed straight for the copse.

On reaching the edge of the densely packed trees of the copse, they stopped, Jackson making the internationally recognised 'Psst!' noise. There was no reply. He tried again, a little louder. They all breathed deeply with relief when they heard the word 'Grasshopper' in a stage whisper from within the trees, slightly to their left. Jackson replied 'Mackerel' and started toward the voice, signalling Sergeant Payne to stay there, under cover. He wanted his soldiers to stay hidden so as not to scare the Subject.

Around 20 paces into the trees, a man rose from the ferns, slowly waving. Jackson and Number One pushed through the undergrowth toward him. McDonald had shown them a photograph of the Subject so they looked carefully at his face. They simultaneously nodded and shouldered their rifles. The Subject was tall, sandy-haired, and looked pathetically relieved. Speaking in excellent English, he said, 'Hello, gentlemen. My name is..'

Jackson had held up his hand. 'I'm sorry sir, just give us a first name that we can call you by. It's best we know as little about you as possible, just as a precaution.'

The man nodded, 'Please call me Bjarne, and this is Tor.' He pointed toward a large fern, which produced a boy of about fourteen wearing a tweed jacket and waving nervously.

Jackson smiled to reassure the boy and his father, 'Good to meet you both. I am Lieutenant Jackson of the King's Own Yorkshire Light Infantry and this is Lieutenant Fortesque-Smythe of the Royal Navy. We saw what looked like a pair of guards walking up the road, so we'd like to get up into the hills and under cover as quickly as we can. Do you have any luggage, Bjarne?'

'Just a knapsack each, and my satchel.'

Jackson looked at his watch and held out his hand. 'Come on Tor, let's climb a hill!' Tor turned to his father, who nodded. They both picked up their knapsacks and followed Jackson, who warned that his men had hidden, so not to be afraid when they appeared. As they neared the edge of the woodland, Bjarne turned to Number One and whispered, 'If anything happens to me, the documents in my satchel must reach Captain McDonald, or destroyed if that is not possible. I was told that the naval party worked directly for him, so I assume you at least know how to reach him.'

Number One nodded. 'I'm certain you will be fine, sir, but I will ensure the material reaches Captain McDonald or is destroyed in the event of unforeseen circumstances.'

'Thank you Lieutenant, this is a weight lifted from me, I can assure you!'

Jackson and Bjarne reached the edge of the trees and Jackson turned to tell his sergeant they were moving off. Glancing around, he realised his men had moved and turned to look for them. He froze as a voice yelled, 'Hände hoch!'

Number One stepped in front of Tor and raised his hands. Standing out in the grass were two figures in field grey and coal scuttle helmets. More worrying was the fact that their Mauser rifles were levelled at the British Officers!

Chapter 20

62° 52' 00" N, 06° 55' 12" E

(Slyngøya, Talga Harbour)

Wednesday 19th June 1940

Svein gulped water as he leaned against the bridge-deck railing. He had stopped for something to eat after the most gruelling morning of his life. They were systematically stripping every moveable item of equipment not needed to keep the ship afloat, move her or steer her. They had removed as many Tannoy and intercom components as they could. All the wireless gear was gone, even Billy's pots and pans were in an old sail bag.

Once Nils had agreed to help he had been to the cafe for early morning coffee as was his habit, and sown the seed that the transit crew had orders to inventory the trawler and transfer some useful items to his ship, then to tow her to Ålesund using his ship, where they would convert her to naval specification, assuming she was repairable. He even planted the idea that the new ship went aground and they left her pumps running because one of her bottom plates leaked. He knew the local grapevine would spread this information through the town.

Svein smiled as he remembered the best part of the morning. He had taken the Skipper over to the other ship, leading him down toward his new cabin. In the passage at the bottom of the companionway, he stopped, turned, then slowly moved aside. The Skipper looked at the brass maker's plate on the teak-faced wall: it read Cook, Welton and Gemmell. Shipbuilders. Beverley. 1935. Despite being busy, Svein had polished it a little before he showed it off. The Skipper had looked at Svein, 'Well, I'll be! A Beverley built ship. I might get used to her after all!' Turning, the Skipper had shaken Svein's hand. They said nothing, but each knew that in some small way the fact that she was from a Yorkshire yard favoured by T'Owd Skipper meant something.

Shaking his head, Svein turned his mind back to business. The lads had opened the watertight tunnel between the boiler space and the spare bunkerage aft of the fish room. This allowed them to move from the engine room to the fish hold without going on deck. As far as spectators might see, there were only three or four seamen on deck who were winching cargo from one ship to the other. Nils found six empty coal bags and the trimmers and two deckhands had been filling them in White Nab and emptying them into the coal chutes on 'Ganton Lass II' as the crew had christened the other trawler, whose real name was 'Arktisk Blomst' or 'Arctic Flower' in English.

They had moved the deck cargo as early in the morning as they could because they didn't want anyone to pay attention to the Oerlikon gun. Archie had transferred the whole mount but could not fit it to the deck of Arctic Flower, probably until they reached England. They had therefore bundled the parts in tarpaulins as deck cargo. For the rest of the morning they transferred coal and then, whenever they felt unwatched, they had shuttled items from White Nab's port side deck to Arctic Flower's starboard.

Svein, Archie and Nils had checked over the engine room on Arctic Flower and found everything in order. There was no heat in the boiler, but they didn't want to raise steam until the late evening when Nils would go for his evening beer and lament the loss of his job now that the ship was to be moved to Ålesund. They hoped it would be enough to prevent undue curiosity. As far as Svein and Archie were concerned, the best thing was Nils' report that all pressurised parts were tested and certified when she came to Talga. Arthur had checked the deck gear and found that everything was in order.

Arthur had spent his morning onboard Arctic Flower stowing everything as it came over. They planned for Svein to spend the afternoon checking for common spares, then tell Archie what to transfer. It emerged that most of their spares were useful, so they took almost everything.

By 11:15, Svein had returned below and was doing a last sweep of the engine room. Fred peered down through the open skylight and hissed, 'Svein, the harbour master is coming down the quay!'

Svein sprinted up the ladder and out of the deckhouse, springing over the bulwarks on to Arctic Flower. He was walking around the steam winch as Johansen arrived. 'Ah Mr Johansen, good to see you. Our work is going well. Soon we shall be ready to receive orders to sail for Ålesund!'

Johansen sneered, 'Then you may be here a while. I have spoken to the Hafenkapitän in Ålesund and he is not aware you are coming.'

Svein inwardly flinched at the use of the German title but smiled widely. 'Hah! Typical of the confusion up north. Naval forces do one thing, ports do another, fishermen want to carry on fishing and we all try to do our jobs but nobody seems to communicate! I expect that the Administrative Council will impose order soon enough!'

This was speaking to Johansen's fascist tendencies, 'Absolutely right, Captain! The Third Reich will impose order and bring prosperity to all the countries that are liberated!'

Johansen turned as he heard a footstep behind him. Nils' punch started from waist level and followed up through Johansen's eye socket. The harbour master's head snapped up, and he flipped backward, rolling on to the deck of Arctic Flower like a rag doll.

Svein didn't have the heart to be angry with Nils. He might well have done the same himself. They checked they were unseen and dragged the unconscious Johansen over Arctic Flower's deck, taking him down into White Nab's fish room where they tied and gagged him. The Skipper glared at them but realised they were unlikely to get through the whole day without at least one setback. He told the lads to keep checking Johansen, making sure he was secure and could not shout for help.

The Skipper and Svein went to the Skipper's cabin, now looking bare without his wireless and photos of Mother and Mavis. Billy had made tea for them, which they welcomed, 'Well Svein, you've done a fantastic job as Skipper, I might retire after all,' he winked and smiled, 'Let's just hope that our troubles are at an end for the time being at least!'

Chapter 21

62° 49' 30" N, 06° 43' 04" E

(Sandbukt, southwest Slyngøya)

Wednesday 19th June 1940

After a few seconds, one of the German soldiers yelled, 'Herkommen!'

Jackson walked forward, then veered slightly toward the right-hand soldier with Bjarne behind him. Number One and Tor followed him until Jackson suddenly yelled, 'DOWN!' and dragged Bjarne to the ground. Seeing kneeling figures in khaki to the left of the Germans, Number One turned and threw himself on top of Tor in the bracken. There was a two-second slam of gunfire, and the two German soldiers fell.

Number One gasped. He thought he had landed on a rock, but as he knelt up to let Tor rise, he realised blood was dripping from his fingers. He saw there was a ragged hole in his sleeve and screwed up his eyes as the pain hit.

Jackson ran over as he noticed the blood . 'Hang on, I'll get the first aid kit.' One of his men appeared from the grass and handed him a small khaki satchel. Jackson cut away the sleeve of Number One's jacket, pressing a dressing pad over the wound, then took out a tube from which he extracted a bulb with a needle fitted to it. He stuck the needle into the right arm above the wound and squeezed the bulb, then wiped around the wound. He sprinkled some powder and then tied on the field-dressing properly. Afterward, he placed a length of dry tree bark between Number One's upper arm and torso before wrapping it in a khaki bandage to form an improvised splint. That part was incredibly painful. Finally he folded a sling to support the lower arm, tied it around the neck, and used a safety pin to attach the spent bulb, 'I don't want to give you too much of this old man, you'll be off with the fairies if we're not careful so that is to remind me how many you've had!' The whole process had taken only a few minutes.

Number One had gritted his teeth as Jackson worked, but a short while after the injection, he felt slightly detached and the pain abated. Jackson told him that meant the medication was working. Number One nodded: the pain having subsided to an intense ache which he could cope with. Jackson looked at his watch and told him he'd administer more painkiller in around two hours if he needed it. Privately, Jackson knew he would need it because the round had smashed the bone: a compound fracture.

Jackson then helped Number One up and checked he could stand. He detailed the young lad, Thompson, to walk with Number One.

Jackson then looked around. His sergeant had told the lads to carry the two bodies over the track and arrange them on the grass above the beach with their rifles. Two men made some obvious scuffs on the roadside and threw a bully beef tin on to the beach. Finally, they checked the German rifles. One had not fired, so they closed the bolt and laid it next to the body. The other had fired, seemingly the round which hit Number One, so they ejected the empty cartridge next to the body, working the bolt to feed the next round into the chamber. They hoped the Nazis might conclude their enemy had fled by boat.

Leaving no signs of their presence on the woodland side of the track, they worked their way quickly back to their officer.

For the return journey, Jackson stayed on the lower slopes of Sønntopp away to their left, heading toward the denser pine forest between Sønntopp and Farrstopp. This had the advantage of screening them from anyone arriving from the lighthouse direction. Jackson doubted they heard the shots in Talga, because of the distance, but was worried the men had returned so quickly after they had apparently walked on past the wood. Perhaps their patrol ended at the wood, in which case there could be a patrol from the lighthouse which did the same thing.

They were slower because Number One wasn't as agile as he had been, but were making reasonable time toward the conifers. Jackson paused. 'An engine: a motorcycle, I think. Let's lay doggo for a few minutes.' It was around forty minutes since the shooting, so he wasn't sure if this was a response. Maybe the patrolling soldiers were overdue.

They lay in the grass and watched. The motorcycle came from the Talga direction, not the lighthouse. As it disappeared behind the slope of the hill, Sergeant Payne turned, 'It stopped, sir. I think the rider spotted the bodies.' As they watched, the motorcycle roared off back toward Talga, sliding and bouncing along the track at some speed.

Jackson spoke urgently, 'Right everyone, get a move on. We must be in that wood and have a perimeter set up before they get back.' turning toward Number One, helping him up, 'Come on, old man, not far to go now.'

They filed off, Jackson leading and Sergeant Payne bringing up the rear. They made sure that Bjarne, Tor and Number One were in the middle of their column as they snaked along the path, following the contour toward the forest.

As soon as they arrived, Jackson had his men out to establish the perimeter and scout along the slope of Farrstopp toward Friyatoft. The wood was in the steep-sided valley between Sønntopp and Farrstopp. Searchers approaching from the west would make a lot of noise, allowing them to stage an ambush or leave their hiding place. Sergeant Payne had picked a path going northeast toward Friyatoft inlet through the wood and was walking it with two men to remove all dry sticks, stones, anything that might make noise. Lieutenant Jackson sent Thompson and another soldier to keep a lookout from near the top of Sønntopp. He asked the remaining soldier to find a flat rock or similar to put the stove on, then to brew some tea for Number One.

Jackson was worried. His patient was pale, clammy and cold, so he was thinking of shock rather than infection. It was too soon for that, anyway. He checked the time, gave him another syrette to kill the pain and asked Bjarne to chat with him to keep him awake until he had drunk something warm. Number One nibbled some ship's biscuit, but he didn't feel hungry. When the tea was ready, Jackson supervised getting the hot, sweet liquid into Number One, after which he let him lay on the dry pine needles using his webbing pouches as a pillow.

Thompson came down and reported that some German sailors or marines had turned up in a lorry. They were searching the line of the track and the seaward side of it, so Jackson felt their ruse might have worked. He let the lad have some tea and a tin of cold rice pudding, then sent him to relieve the other lookout. He wanted them all to eat before evening came. It took until 16:00 to get everyone fed, at which point he let them catch some sleep if they could. Jackson himself pored over his map: Friyatoft inlet faced roughly north, with the bunch of crofts to the west side of the bay and the jetty to the east. He was considering defensive positions. Thompson had returned at around 17:45 to report that the Germans had withdrawn along the track toward Talga after searching the coastal strip. Jackson told him to rest too and took first watch.

Chapter 22

62° 52' 00" N, 06° 55' 12" E

(Slyngøya, Talga Harbour)

Wednesday 19th June 1940

Arthur and Archie made some last checks on White Nab. They repeatedly had to tell the lads to pipe down. The crew were dismantling the bunks in the fish room and the noise levels periodically rose.

Archie sounded the depth at the watertight bulkhead and it had gained only an inch while the shaft was still, so he was happy, but, as he told Svein, it would be very different if she went to sea.

Svein and Nils had been checking the stocks of lubricating oil on Arctic Flower. As they went up on deck to fetch a couple of drums from White Nab, they heard a motorcycle roar and the sound of its back wheel locking as it halted beside the minesweeper. Nothing else happened, so they carried on with their task, but as they came back, hauling a drum each, they heard shouting and running feet from the German ship. Svein put his drum down, walked across White Nab's well deck and leaned over the hatch to the fish-room, calling quietly, 'Get your rifles, lads, but don't come up unless I say.'

Nils stood staring at the minesweeper, as did an elderly couple who had walked from the opposite side of the harbour. Svein joined him as it seemed the natural thing to do.

Around twenty German sailors had formed up on the harbour-side with rifles sloped on their shoulders. They marched off, heading southeast, and Svein prayed this had nothing to do with their mission. They both went over to Arctic Flower and into the Skipper's cabin to report what they'd seen. Svein had hoped the activity might signal the minesweeper was sailing, but there was nothing on deck to suggest she intended to go. The Skipper looked sick with worry when they told him about the German shore party.

Svein went back to White Nab and stood the lads down. He told them the harbour would be quieter now, so if there was anything else that needed a lot of effort to dismantle, then they were to leave it. They had gathered the wooden components of the bunks and lashed them into manageable sized bundles which they lifted over to Arctic Flower using the boom on the foremast as a crane. Among the last things to come across was the 'Ganton Lass' nameplate, which the yard in Great Yarmouth had left in place but painted over.

Things were silent in the harbour by 18:00, so they went over to Arctic Flower in ones and twos to avoid large numbers being seen to transfer at one time. Nils went to the cafe, ostensibly to buy Johansen a meal, but in fact to sow the seed that Johansen had taken a drink or two with the captain of the newly arrived trawler, then gone ashore. Johansen's wife immediately said, 'The pig will be asleep at home. Once he takes one drink, he doesn't stop!' It was that statement which gave Nils an idea. He bought two bottles of akvavit to take back with him. As his parting shot, he grumbled that the ship upon which he had lavished so much care might leave as soon as that night, then paid his bill and left, clutching his bottles. On his way back, Nils called into a bar and asked to use their telephone.

Arthur and Fred had run a hawser from a towing bridle running across the stern of Arctic Flower, outside the rail on her starboard side, and shackled it to the anchor chain of White Nab. This would allow them to push White Nab away, then cast-off and go slowly ahead to tow, when the time came.

Once done, it was nearly 19:30, and the Skipper went back to White Nab with Svein and Archie. They set the scuttling charges in the engine room, slush wells and forepeak, with two smaller charges in the Skipper's cabin, around which they packed all the three-inch shells for the twelve-pounder, which were left onboard when they left Scotland. Finally, a detonator was placed against a depth charge which had remained in a locker on the after-deck. Svein wired everything back to a clockwork delay timer in the wheelhouse. Arthur had removed all White Nab's shorelines, so only the breast lines connected the two vessels. Arthur said the lads would pull the lines in on their side once they were ready. The Skipper was happy with the plan and sent them back to Arctic Flower while he kept lookout on a broken chair in the wheelhouse. The solitude allowed the Skipper to think. This was the point of no return. He would desperately like to save Ganton Lass, as he now thought of her again. But saving her would hugely increase the chance of failure. So, at the eleventh hour, he finally accepted that there was no real choice. If he was to honour his commitment to put the crew first, then this was the right plan, the only way to bottle up the Nazi ship long enough for them to disappear.

At 21:00, the transmission whine of a truck snapped him awake. In the still bright evening light, he saw men with rifles filing back onboard the minesweeper, then shortly afterward, raucously heading toward the street where the cafe was situated. This was good news, given they had heard no gunfire or seen any prisoners. Yet his thoughts were still with the shore party. Something had gone wrong, perhaps, but what?

Chapter 23

62° 53' 30" N, 06° 47' 12" E

(Slyngøya, skirting Farrstopp)

Wednesday 19th June 1940

Lieutenant Jackson had awoken, bleary-eyed, at 22:00. Number One was awake and sitting with his back against a tree opposite Jackson. The light, dimmed by the pine trees, revealed that he looked much better, and there was a can of peaches or something similar with a spoon stuck in the top right next to Number One. *Better and better*!

He sat up and stretched the creases from his spine, massaging a distinctly dead leg before venturing to his feet. He stood beside Number One. 'How's the arm, old man?'

Number One grimaced, 'Not too bad, so long as I'm still. When we move, I might need more of your fairy dust!'

Jackson smiled, acutely aware they had five hours to go, and he had only two more syrettes. He didn't want to think what might happen if the Skipper didn't show tonight. He called Sergeant Payne over. 'Chaps, I have the germ of a plan, but I'd like some input from you. Given the distance we have to go and the fact it's quiet at the moment, I think we should move toward Friyatoft. If we can follow the contour to the ridgeline where we had breakfast, we could make a slow descent with a short walk to the path between Friyatoft and Talga. That's the one that your Skipper mentioned Number One. That path descends slowly to the jetty itself so we could get to a defensible position above the jetty and overlooking the sea, well before the Skipper arrives.' he winked broadly, 'Can anyone see an issue with that?'

Sergeant Payne prodded a blunt finger at the path down from Dattertoppen. 'I'd suggest we halt before that point, sir, and reconnoitre ahead before we use it. As I recall from the path we took upward, it won't be possible to see anyone coming down from the hill before they're upon us, if you see what I mean?'

Jackson nodded. 'Absolutely, that's sensible. Anything else?'

Number One pursed his lips. 'Yes. If things get too bad, please leave me behind,' he raised a hand to stop their complaints, 'No. This isn't false heroics. If I were alone, I'd hide out and find the friendly in Friyatoft after things quieten down. I'm certain that they'd hide me and provide some food until the Skipper can get back over to collect me. Or I could steal a boat and head for Sweden once I'd healed. I hope it doesn't come to that, but please remember what I've said if the situation requires it?'

Jackson and Payne nodded, glancing at each other, then Jackson relayed the plan to his men, who were all now awake. He suggested they had a good feed and some tea before they left so they were fighting fit for the last stage.

After they ate, they made sure waste was buried and removed signs of their presence as far as possible. Despite his circumstances, they impressed number One with their discipline given that the chances of anyone coming here at night were probably zero; but that was their drill, so they followed it regardless.

At 23:40, they were on their way. Number One found the walking fairly easy. Sheep, or perhaps shepherds, seemed to follow contours, judging by the path worn into the hillside. Within half an hour, they could see the ridgeline and went off the path toward their original route. The uneven grass made things a little less comfortable for Number One, and the jarring caused by going downhill was even worse, but the medication helped and he gritted his teeth. Young Tor had volunteered to be Number One's gun-bearer and, after checking the weapon was safe they shortened the strap so that he could carry it across his back like a real partisan fighter, though their real concern was to leave his hands free in case he fell.

By 01:00 they were checking the path which came from Talga and realised there was little cover above the jetty to make a defensible position. They travelled, with great care, past the jetty, looking for somewhere they could use to wait for the Skipper. Around two hundred yards past the jetty, the roadway widened into a gravelled boat storage area which had a dry-stone wall around it made from rough rocks. The wall was four feet higher than the up-slope: probably built as a windbreak. They took up position behind it, with a clear view out to sea behind, and a view forward over the wall to the path, the jetty, and the crofts. Sergeant Payne removed a few stones to make firing slits of a kind, and they had found their position.

Number One felt dizzy with pain but held off asking for more medication. He had seen a strange look on Jackson's face as he gave the last dose, and wondered if there was a limit on the daily dosage or something like that. He decided that, while he was sitting still at least, he could endure the pain so he would try to manage without drugs. Glancing at his watch, he saw 01:45.

All they needed now was for the ship to turn up.

Chapter 24

62° 52’ 00” N, 06° 55’ 12” E

(Slyngøya, Talga Harbour)

Thursday 20th June 1940

The Skipper glared at his watch, the wheelhouse clock having transferred to Arctic Flower. He realised his wrist was shaking. He willed time to move faster. He had feared his plan was too wild. That this time his luck would fail, especially after he realised a warship was in harbour. Despite that, or perhaps because of it, he had lived in a bubble of unreality all day, hardly believing that they were unchallenged. Even Nils’ idea to pour most of a bottle of akvavit down Johansen’s throat and the rest over his clothes, then leave him in a doorway up in the town to sleep it all off hadn't given him pause. It was just one more move in a high-risk game which they were currently winning, or at least not losing. Now, when they might actually pull it off, when all that remained was to escape and get home, well, now he felt petrified they would fall at the last hurdle.

He walked around the well deck, memories forcing their way in. As he turned back he saw Arthur walking toward him, 'Skipper, I've just come to check whether you need anything,' he handed over a steaming mug and the Skipper smelled rum in the tea as he lifted it, 'aside from a Billy special that is?'

'No thanks, Arthur, I just want to get this done and go home. Evading the Kriegsmarine I can deal with, but the wait is getting on my nerves!'

Arthur looked at the deck. 'I know what you mean, Skipper. It's a grim way to fight a war. But this is the hand fate dealt us, so, as ever, we'll play it to the best of our ability and see what happens, eh?'

The Skipper smiled for the first time in many hours, 'That's right Arthur, we'll be home and downing a pint of Sturdy Mariner before you know it,' he lifted his mug, saying 'Slàinte Mhath - here's to Gerald.' He gulped the rest of the tea down.

Arthur clapped him on the back and took the mug. 'Right, I'll see if they're awake over there. By the way Skipper... We'll both miss the old lass, that I do know.'

'We will miss her Arthur, and thank you.' He glanced up at his old friend, emotions barely in control.

The Skipper could hear splashing as Svein moved Arctic Flower's shaft forward and astern, ready for Arthur to take over. The Skipper checked the hawser would run free, then headed for the wheelhouse. His watch said 02:15. It was time.

Fred and Len cast White Nab off and used boathooks to push her bow away. Arctic Flower went slowly ahead at less than walking pace, the lads easing the hawser from White Nab until it was astern, then making sure that the towing bridle was well clear of their rudder until the hawser picked up. Arthur nudged Arctic Flower away to starboard and forward until the hawser tightened and they were moving, only inches at a time, but moving at least.

The Skipper looked round the wheelhouse, his second home since childhood, and felt a great weight despite his resolve to go ahead. What would T'owd Skipper say? But he knew. Imagining his father standing in the wheelhouse, he knew what he would say: 'You do whatever you need to do to get our lads home safe, Reggie. Do you hear? Whatever it takes.' He looked at the timer dial and knew he could do it.

The hawser had pulled the ship's head to starboard, so he heaved the wheel to port, heavy without steam steering, and countered the swing. He judged that starboard rudder before the entrance would leave her straight as she entered. She was a lady to the end. Her head came round as planned and she slid between the walls of stone without so much as a scrape.

Arthur went dead slow astern and Len dangled a big rope fender over Arctic Flower's stern so that, as White Nab touched, she slowed and stopped.

As the Skipper turned toward the timer, he heard a shout from the harbour-side. Whatever it was, it would have to wait. He dialled three minutes on the clockwork mechanism, then headed for the door. He stopped. The small cupboard by the door was ajar, and he realised he hadn't seen his bat. Sure enough, there it was. He grabbed the bat and opened the door as a lance of blue seared his eyes. Someone was firing from Arctic Flower toward the harbour-side. He could see what looked like a Kriegsmarine Officer running back toward their old berth and a figure crumpled on the ground. *No time, just move!* The thought jarred him and he slid down the ladder to the deckhouse, then leaped on to the harbour wall. As he regained balance, the hut door opened and a man with a rifle came out. The Skipper went on instinct. He yelled 'Achtung, achtung!' and the man hesitated; fatally. The cricket bat slammed the side of his head and he went down instantly. Simultaneously, a figure came out of the guard hut and a burst of machine gun fire from the bridge deck of Arctic Flower cut him down. The Skipper turned and realised that Arthur was already going ahead. He'd wasted too much time and the wheelhouse of Arctic Flower was already past the end of the harbour arm! Then his childhood popped into his mind, a stupid 'dare' from an older boy. He ran down the harbour-side and, curving right, he threw his bat and flung himself into the air! Flopping like a high-jumper he landed hard in the port-side boat's canvas cover. He was gasping for air and winded, but he was off Norwegian soil!

He knew the machine guns were firing over his head, so he lay still on his back until they stopped.

He could feel the ship throb as she rapidly gathered way, and risked sitting up and turning round. As he did so, the dusk turned to black compared to the hellfire that split White Nab apart. The whole upper-works disintegrated, flattening the hut and guard post. Something slapped his face. It stung like a hundred bee stings; but still he stared. The twisted hell of metal and flame sat on top of what was, recognisably, his Ganton Lass. He put his hands to his face and sobbed like he hadn't since childhood.

After a few seconds, his father's imaginary voice came to his rescue again. 'Right, son, there are folks relying on you. Time to get on.' He nodded, turned and slid down the davit to the boat deck before running for the wheelhouse steps. As he entered the wheelhouse, Arthur turned and his jaw dropped.

Fred said, 'I'll get the towel and a first aid kit.'

The Skipper headed for the wheel, but Arthur set his jaw. 'No Skipper, you need stitching. You're going to have a grand duelling scar and it needs sorting.' The Skipper looked down and noticed blood on his hands and the deck.

Fred burst back in. 'Right Skipper, we're fishermen. We've all tried to fillet our own hands occasionally. It's not painful if it's done quickly, so, head under the light please!'

he told the Skipper to hold the towel over the wound while he opened the first aid box. Fred turned, holding some tweezers and a curved needle.

When Fred's work was done, the Skipper's eyes watered a little, but he had remained silent. That changed when Fred dabbed his face with iodine, however, and they lost count of the times he yelled, 'Bugger it!' and smacked his hand on the wireless room door.

Chapter 25

62° 55' 06" N, 06° 52' 37" E

(Slyngøya, Friyatoft Inlet)

Thursday 20th June 1940

Lieutenant Jackson jumped as he heard thunder from the east. No telling what it was, but it would affect their own future. That he knew.

The soldier on watch at the jetty ran back to their position, stooping low as he hurried to the safety of the wall. 'Patrol coming down, sir. They look like regular Wehrmacht to me, not sailors or marines. About ten men I'd say.'

Jackson inwardly cursed. 'Perfect timing. Right everybody, hold here. If they come toward us, we'll engage, but if they go the other way, we'll leave well alone. Totally still and quiet, please.'

The patrol came down the path cautiously. They turned toward the jetty and inspected it, but seemed to ignore the boat storage area. They headed off toward the crofts.

Bjarne sighed, 'My God, if they blame the people in the village for what we've done...'

Jackson looked at Payne, who nodded. 'Open fire chaps.' Payne took careful aim and fired. One of the Germans crumpled, and the others flipped round, going to ground just beyond the jetty. Two went off up the hill, clearly trying to outflank them, so Jackson said, 'Watch the hill, Number One. If they get far enough to get a shot, let me know.'

Number One rolled on his side and, rifle in his left hand, fore-stock on a rock and the butt on his good shoulder, he nodded to Tor, saying, 'Bolt.' The lad reached from behind the wall and worked the bolt. Number One aimed and fired; repeating, 'Bolt.' Sergeant Payne looked down at Number One. There was more to this lad than met the eye. The recoil was juddering his torso and his broken arm must have been agony, but he was slowing down the lads on the hill. They had dropped two more enemy soldiers, so the odds were better when suddenly the enemy ceased firing.

From behind their position, Number One heard a heavy machine gun and saw tracers tearing the ground around the now running soldiers. Another gun raked the hill, stopping when two limp bodies rolled downhill from behind a thorny bush. Sergeant Payne remained on the wall, his rifle pointed toward the running men, now disappearing behind the fold in the hillside which had covered their approach. The rest of the soldiers cheered as Arctic Flower slid up to the jetty. Jackson, jabbing his last syrette into Number One, squeezed the bulb, then frowned, 'Sergeant?' There was no response and Payne's head rested on the stome, so he rose and spun his sergeant and friend toward him. Payne was dead from a bullet wound in his throat: his body held against the wall by his webbing strap, hooked over the edge of a stone. Jackson nearly fell backward as the webbing slipped off and Payne's body slumped on to him. Two of his men grabbed him and they lowered Sergeant Payne to the ground. They held his webbing and began dragging him toward the jetty just as Lars arrived from his croft. He was deeply shocked as he looked up and recognised the Skipper.

Number One grabbed at Jackson. 'Would you rather have him buried here or at sea? We might be in hiding or even captured. It may be difficult to give him a sendoff.'

Lars' eyes flicked between Number One, Jackson and the Skipper. He decided.

'You can safely leave your comrade with us. We have a small plot uphill and it would honour us to give him a suitable burial in it. The choice is yours.'

Jackson placed his hand on the side of his sergeant's face. He said nothing, but they all looked away to give him privacy as his eyes misted. After a moment, he glanced over at Lars. 'Can you do this without the Germans thinking you were involved? I don't want to endanger your community.'

Lars smiled, 'The Skipper would do this, and more, for us, sir. It will be an honour. The enemy will know nothing.

Please let me have this man's details so we can mark his resting place at the proper time.'

As Jackson wrote in a tiny notebook, Lars ran to the jetty. The Skipper leaned over the bridge-deck rail.

'I'm sorry, old friend. We wanted to keep you uninvolved, to avoid reprisals. Unfortunately, circumstances were unpredictable, let's say.'

Lars nodded toward the hull, 'So I see! I think I recognise this ship?'

The Skipper gave a theatrical wink, saying, 'You do, Lars. She's called Ganton Lass and has been here many times.'

Lars roared with laughter, 'I wondered what that boom was about! I was hoping the Nazis had blown themselves up. You old pirate! With a wound to prove it too!'

The Skipper's face fell. 'I had to sacrifice her, Lars. We had to block the minesweeper in the harbour. She threw a piece of herself at my head to let me know she disapproved.' His voice trailed off. Lars nodded. He knew what doing that would have cost his friend.

Nils jumped off the ship and pressed some keys into Lars' hand, 'For my house. Use it as you see fit until the war is over when I'll return. I'm joining the King over in Britain.'

Lars shook his hand, nodding. 'Good luck my friend.'

Arthur yelled out of the wheelhouse, 'We're ready, everyone! We need to move quickly.'

The Skipper sent two lads to help the soldiers with the wounded, and they were soon onboard. The Skipper smiled and waved to Lars as Nils leaped back onboard. Lars waved as he headed for the crofts to organise moving the sergeant. He had already decided to make the coffin himself.

The Skipper went down on deck to help the soldiers. Number One was sitting, leaning against the bulwark with a cigarette in his mouth, wondering why things looked strange, when a piratical and blood-smeared figure came into view. 'I hope you weren't taking on the Luftwaffe again, Number One?'

Number One grinned as Jackson interjected, 'He wasn't sir, but he had a damned good pop at the Wehrmacht!'

The Skipper looked up, realising that Arthur was going astern. He watched Friyatoft fading away and prayed there would be no retribution from the enemy for their work that day. He saw three men running down from the crofts and was glad Lars wasn't alone. Shaking his head, he turned to Jackson, 'As you may notice, we've upgraded the ship a little, but we can talk later. For now, you look like you need sleep. My lads are reassembling some bunks below but at the moment I think it's mattresses on the floor. If your chaps go below, we'll dress her as a fishing vessel, as we did on the way in.'

Jackson went down with his men, saying he'd come aft to check on Number One as soon as he could. The Skipper told the lads to stop building bunks while everyone had a kip. He helped Fred and Len get Number One below and went up to see Arthur as the lads spread their fake net over the boom, hiding the deck cargo. As they headed off, the Skipper had his glasses trained on Svart Klippe lighthouse. Nearby was a new concrete block, but it looked only part-built. The man on the walkway around the lighthouse glasswork was waving a Norwegian flag, so they felt safe to turn as soon as they were clear of the rocks and shoals northwest of the island.

The Skipper stood out westward as they passed Bud, which was more likely to have an enemy presence because of its size. Forty-five minutes later they put into a place Nils had suggested, further southwest. There was a tiny inlet with fishermen's huts and a smokehouse. On the east side, they had built a breakwater using stone blocks and rubble. The Skipper hoped the enemy would expect them to head out to sea immediately and run for home. If they stayed for twenty-four hours, he hoped they would assume he'd given them the slip and relax their search.

Two trawlers were already in the tiny haven and as they pulled in, a group of fishermen standing on the rough stone-faced quay met them. Nils and Svein chatted with them for a couple of minutes and after they finished, the fishermen laughed and cheered, before taking their lines. They warped Arctic Flower in between the other two boats and set about laying lobster pots and other paraphernalia on the deck. From the air or seaward, their ship was practically invisible. The telephone call Nils had made from town had been worthwhile.

They installed Bjarne and Tor in the port aft cabin, Number One to starboard. Arthur, Nils, Jackson and Svein would sleep in the bunk berths. The Skipper and Arthur decided to postpone sending the success signal until they were ready to leave. If the enemy intercepted the transmission, it might reveal their location and they could not risk that. Especially when receiving help from locals.

The Skipper suddenly felt cold, shaky, and exhausted. He trudged down to his new cabin, hoping that their hiding place was unexpected enough to fool the Nazis. He didn't get to his bunk. A few hours later, when Arthur arrived with a mug of tea, he found the Skipper still fully clothed and snoring on his new settee. All was well, with nothing to report, so he gently closed the door and drank the tea himself.

Around three in the afternoon, a Heinkel seaplane flew past the entrance to the inlet. Everybody on deck froze, and Arthur called down for them not to look up. The aircraft carried straight on and they all breathed again.

A few minutes later, the Skipper clumped up the companionway.

'Now then, Arthur, what's the news?'

'Not much Skipper. I came down earlier, but you were still fast on, so I let you be. I'd have called you if anything untoward happened. One seaplane flew by, but showed no interest in us. We seem to blend in just fine. Nils' friends think they can get more morphine for Number One, but we'll see if they can pull it off. I'll get you a brew in a minute or two.'

'That's fine, thanks Arthur. I want to check on the lads in the aft cabin and speak with the crew while I can, so I'll grab a mug as I go. Have you rested yet?'

'I'm alright, thanks. Fred and I have been doing half-watches, so we've both had some sleep. Now you're up, I'll have a little longer if there's time.'

The Skipper rubbed his chin. 'Yes, I need to judge the best moment to make our move. I'll get back as quickly as I can.' With that, he strode off.

As the Skipper reached the galley and asked Billy for tea, he met Lieutenant Jackson, who appeared from the aft cabin companionway.

'Lieutenant Jackson, how are you and your men?'

'Alright sir, thank you. We'll miss Sergeant Payne, but one thing he taught us is that no single person is irreplaceable. The lads are fine. Actually, I'm really only worried about Number One. He's doing alright at the moment. I've cleaned his wound and re-dressed it and there's no sign of infection. My concerns are pain management if the fishermen can't get us extra morphine, but also the surgery. The bullet did not pass through and it appears to have smashed the humerus. I initially made a makeshift splint but it wouldn't have immobilised the arm enough during the march and subsequent skirmish. Sir, Number One must get surgery as quickly as we can manage, or he may lose the use of his arm.'

The Skipper stared into his mug. 'Thank you. I'm planning our next step now, so I'll get us away as soon as possible.'

Jackson beamed, 'That's a relief, sir.'

The Skipper took his leave and went down to the aft cabin. Bjarne and Tor were playing draughts at the table and Bjarne rose as he entered. 'Skipper, it's a pleasure to meet you properly,' his hand extended. 'I can't tell you how grateful we are, especially to that young man.' He nodded over the Skipper's shoulder.

As he turned, the Skipper realised that someone had wedged the starboard cabin door open, and Number One, his right arm supported by a pile of pillows, had been watching the game.

'My new role, sir. Strategic adviser to young Tor. Not that he needs me, I have to say!'

The Skipper grinned, 'Marvellous to see you in good spirits, Number One!' He turned to Bjarne.

'And you, sir, I hope my crew is looking after you?'

'Indeed, they are! They even gave us that game from their quarters, so Tor has something to do until he can go on deck.'

The Skipper listened while Bjarne and Number One sketched out their experiences. Bjarne was careful to mention Number One's heroics in the fire-fight, pinning down enemy soldiers despite his injury. The Skipper explained they had intended standing off as planned, but when they realised there was gunfire, they went for the jetty. Finally Bjarne repeated his request for his papers to be destroyed rather than reach the enemy and the Skipper said he had a weighted bag ready.

As the Skipper walked down the deck to check the fish room, he was frowning and rubbing his chin. Svein came out of the fish room hatch as the Skipper approached.

The Skipper smiled, saying, 'How are you doing, old friend?'

Svein nodded, 'I'm alright Skipper. They've strengthened the deck for a gun and I'm changing their adapter plate so we can bolt our Oerlikon mounting to it. Clamping it to the rail as I did with the machine guns earlier isn't really a solution.'

The Skipper examined the deck plate and nodded. 'Make sure you get some rest, Svein. I'm going to get everyone together in an hour to agree on the next step. We need to get Number One to a hospital as quickly as we can.'

'Yah, well, this won't take much longer, then I'll get Archie to bolt on the mount and lift the gun onto it.'

After checking in with the crew and soldiers, the Skipper went to his chartroom. As he walked aft, he saw the name-plate for Ganton Lass was bolted to the outer side of the bridge deck bulwark, forward of the wheelhouse. It was a moving gesture; but now he had to do some thinking.

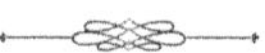

An hour later, The Skipper, Arthur, Nils, Svein, and Lieutenant Jackson stood in the wheelhouse. The Skipper looked around at their faces.

'Gents, we urgently need to get treatment for Number One so we can't lay alongside for long. Nils, did you get any feedback from the fishermen?'

Nils looked thoughtful. 'Some locals hauled lobster pots earlier and said there were a lot of those seaplanes buzzing around this morning when they shot the pots, but only one this afternoon. Maybe they think we're gone?'

'Could be; we can't be certain. Lieutenant Jackson, what sort of time do we have before we make things worse for Number One?' The Skipper's eyebrows lifted.

Jackson shook his head. 'In all honesty, sir, I don't know. All I can tell you is that, with that kind of injury, they would normally have evacuated him as soon as he was stabilised. There are no signs of infection, which is good, but he badly needs surgical help to get the round removed from his arm and repair the bone. The sooner the better, really, sir.'

Nils held up a finger. 'The fishermen say their friends are bringing morphine this evening, but not a large quantity. I suspect you'll find the packaging will be in German.'

Jackson smiled and said, 'Between the ship's medical box and that extra supply, we should be OK. We can support him with pillows and cushions while on passage, which will help.'

The Skipper sighed, 'So it's lack of knowledge about the enemy's movements, which is the difficulty. I have to balance Number One's welfare against the mission and the crew. At the moment, his life is not in danger. If I delay too long, we'll run out of morphine, and who knows how he'll fare. I don't feel that the risk to our mission justifies leaving immediately, but I'll review it at 20:00. I wonder if there's a vantage point from which we can observe Bud harbour entrance using glasses?'

Nils nodded, 'Why don't I walk to the tip of that little island? There's a bridge from the point over to the island. I should be able to see the sound outside the harbour at least.'

The Skipper thanked him and asked Arthur to find him the high-powered glasses that came across from his old cabin.

'Right, let's all meet here at 20:00 and see what we have.'

After watching the sound for two hours and seeing nothing, Nils walked back. Strolling around the inlet toward the trawlers, He watched a small faering type boat tying up. As he admired her lines, he half heard the crew talking. He called, 'Hei, sa du at det er tåke der ute?'

One fisherman looked up, 'Ja, den er veldig tykk.' Nils' eyes blazed as he waved and turned, running toward the Arctic Flower.

Onboard, Nils climbed, panting, to the wheelhouse. Arthur was alone, and he gasped out, 'We need the Skipper, quickly, Arthur. I think our opportunity has arrived!'

A few minutes later, he explained the conversation he'd had with the fishermen. 'I overheard them saying they couldn't shoot crab pots for tomorrow because of visibility. When I asked them if there was fog, they said it was very thick. This could be our chance Skipper!'

The Skipper's jaw set firm. 'Arthur, would you get Svein and Jackson, please?'

By 21:00 they had steam up and were ready to leave. The fishermen dropped over a German medical satchel and helped disentangle them from the other two boats. The Skipper and Arthur shook hands with the fishermen and passed over a few bottles of rum before leaving.

At 21:10, they slipped away dead slowly and headed southwest to clear Outer Harøya before turning west, then northwest, to find the passage to the open sea. They hoisted a white ensign at the stern and the red ensign which had covered Eddie's coffin flew from the starboard cross tree.

As they neared Kattskjaeret, the fog thickened, so the Skipper took bearings, plotted their position and rang dead slow ahead. He asked Arthur to take soundings as they went ahead, saying, 'I'll go to the west of the channel and stay in around twenty fathoms. If it shallows to ten, let me know straight away and I'll go off to starboard to stay in safe water.' Arthur headed down with his lead-line, saying he'd stream the patent log too.

The Skipper blew down the speaking tube to warn Svein they would go full ahead once in open water and he wanted to see what she could do. He posted some of the younger crew on the whaleback to carry out a listening watch, giving them his old trumpet fog horn and instructing they blow it if they heard anything, but not to call in English.

After ten minutes Arthur sent Bert Ryton up to say they now had 26 fathoms, so he turned due west and marked his estimated position on the chart. Visibility was down to half a cable, around a hundred yards, but he wanted to get clear of the coast before losing their cover, so he rang full ahead and timed his turn north-northeast. He sent Bert back down and told him to shout up if they heard a bell. He didn't want to get close to buoys marking shoal waters.

When his stopwatch showed him he was in open water, he turned west-northwest, asking Arthur to read the log as he marked the dead-reckoning position on his chart. About ten minutes later, Arthur stomped back into the wheelhouse, sporting a wide smile.

'Thirteen knots Skipper; we are doing thirteen knots. She really can move!'

The Skipper grinned, almost shouting, 'Good heavens! This is the fastest I've ever travelled in a trawler!' He blew down the speaking tube to let Svein know the good news.

Once he calmed a little, he realised that tearing into fog at this speed was crazy, but decided it was worth the risk to add sea miles between themselves and any searchers. The density of shipping was lower than home waters, yet he hoped he wouldn't live to regret this decision.

Chapter 26

57° 51’ 42” N, 05° 18’ 35” W

(‘Patrol Base 8’ near Badcaul)

Sunday 23rd June 1940

By 23:30, the fog thinned and quickly disappeared. Looking astern, a great milky grey band stretched from horizon to horizon, the dusk-blue sky above it lending a quality of strangeness to the view. The sea was calm, with an almost unnoticeable glassy swell, which changed the sound of the bow wave as they cut through it.

The Skipper shook himself, and asking Fred to take the wheel, he went to fetch tea. Arthur was also heading aft, having stood down the listening watch and sent two lads up to the flying bridge to keep a lookout. Arctic Flower had no dodgers or equipment atop the wheelhouse, just a slightly low railing which, the Skipper knew, Svein would rectify once they were safe in port.

At 02:15, the Skipper reduced speed to eleven knots, and at 06:50, set a course for Shetland. Their entire horizon remained miraculously empty, and the Skipper dared to hope that their plan had worked and the enemy had indeed believed they escaped on the first night. He decided he was now justified in sending the coded success signal, so he popped his head in the wireless room and asked Pickering to send it. Unlike the old ship, this one had the wireless room at the rear of the wheelhouse. Half an hour later, Pickering returned to report that Base 8 had acknowledged the signal.

At 08:00, the Skipper went off watch, leaving instructions for the wheelhouse to call him if any ship or aircraft approached. Waking at 11:30, he felt refreshed and took time to sluice himself down over the stern grating before heading for the wheelhouse. He called for tea and a slice of toast as he went.

The sun was bright and the sea calm. There was the usual summer haze in the distance, but the horizon was clear. He heard laughter from the foredeck and popped his head around to see Tor and two deckhands playing soccer with three soldiers using a sack stuffed with something or other to approximate a round shape. Looking up, he saw the watch keepers on the flying bridge, or rather the top of the wheelhouse. They were alert, undistracted, and he could feel the lighter atmosphere on board.

Arthur turned as he entered.

'Now then Skipper. Nothing to report, I'm glad to say. The lads saw an aircraft condensation trail astern about an hour ago, but it was far distant and didn't turn towards us. I doubt they'd have seen us at that range and height, so I let you be. Other than that, all's well. Svein and Archie have been busy and the machine-gun mounts are more permanent now, so we're not defenceless. Lieutenant Jackson has changed Number One's dressing again and is happy. Speaking of which, we need to change yours. It's hanging off at the top.'

The Skipper grinned. 'I bet Fred's been looking forward to round two!'

From the opposite bridge wing, Fred's voice boomed, 'I've found some triple strength iodine Skipper. You'll love it.' He gently eased off the dressing, cleaned it with a dilute solution and re-dressed the wound.

'You'll live Skipper.'

The Skipper dropped in to see Number One and found Bjarne reading to him. The patient was pale but comfortable. He seemed in good spirits. As he left, the Skipper turned, 'Keep it up, Number One. We'll be there tomorrow afternoon.'

Speaking to Jackson a little later, he learned they were only administering morphine when Number One was in extreme pain, which explained his paleness.

At 15:00, their heads snapped forward as they heard a powerful aero-engine dead ahead. From the flying bridge they heard yells of, 'It's a spitfire!' Jackson was on deck, making sure the Oerlikon crew knew the aircraft was friendly. The beautiful curve of the aircraft's wings was visible as it banked over and flew round them at low-level. The pilot was giving them a thumbs up through the cockpit canopy. After two circuits, the plane flew back toward Scotland, waggling its wings, the whistle of its supercharger audible over the roar of the engine as the pilot increased speed.

At 17:30, they were northwest of Shetland and turned slightly south to head for the Minch. The Skipper told Pickering to send another signal, announcing their arrival at 18:00 the following day. They were going home!

As they turned into Little Loch Broom, the Skipper smelled heather and sheep on the gentle early evening breeze. The rich yellow of gorse flowers seemed to light up Base 8 as they rounded the small headland, which hid the anchorage from seaward. They had parked a military ambulance above the jetty, so the Skipper went alongside the outside of the jetty rather than pick up a mooring straight away. They rigged a makeshift gangplank from the bulwark on the well deck to the jetty and, after they had helped Number One up the companionway, two medical orderlies laid him on a stretcher so they could take him ashore. The Skipper squeezed Number One's hand, saying, 'Hurry back Number One, we'll need you fit before our next job.'

Number One smiled. 'You can count on it, Skipper.' The orderlies, with help from Arthur, got him onto the jetty when a party of men rushed from Captain Stevenson's 'office'. The Skipper spotted an enormous amount of gold braid on the leader and guessed his identity immediately.

The Admiral looked down at the stretcher. 'My dear boy, you're injured!'

Lieutenant Jackson saluted crisply, saying, 'Sir, this officer distinguished himself in a land action during which I lost my sergeant. He is to be commended for his actions and courage.' The Admiral seemed taken aback.

The Skipper had gone to the jetty, and also saluted as the Admiral looked at him. 'He's also a valuable member of my crew, sir, and I'd appreciate him back in short order.' Behind the Admiral, McDonald stifled laughter and Captain Stevenson rolled his eyes and looked up at the sky.

The Admiral's bushy eyebrows lowered, 'Then I shall not stand in his way Skipper!'

The Skipper nodded and stepped back, saluting again. His chin jutted out as the Admiral stepped toward him and leaned in to whisper, 'Do you recall in 1917 you rescued a seaman from a destroyer which hit a mine?' The Skipper's eyes widened as the Admiral continued, 'I see you do. Well, we've both come a long way since that day, but I always wanted to thank you. Even now, I recall you looking over the side of the boat as you reached for me. It's also why I wanted my boy to serve with you.'

McDonald and Stevenson looked on, but could not hear the rest of the conversation, so they were flabbergasted when the two men shook hands.

'Right, my boy, let's get you sorted out!' with that, the Admiral turned and his retinue headed off toward the ambulance.

Stevenson looked along the length of Arctic Flower. 'Err, Skipper, do I detect a certain change in your ship?'

The Skipper looked him straight in the eyes, 'No sir, HMT White Nab, formerly Ganton lass, SH.423, same old workhorse.'

Stevenson's eyes narrowed. 'If you say so Skipper; if you say so!'

McDonald leaned in as Bjarne and Tor stepped ashore. 'I wouldn't be much of an intelligence officer if I couldn't change a few incorrect details regarding a requisitioned trawler Skipper. So don't worry about that. Oh, and we'll book you in for a refit to repair, erm, let's call it battle damage; and return the ship to pre-mission specification, shall we?'

The Skipper beamed, 'Thank you, sir. We shall assist in any way needed.'

McDonald shook hands with Bjarne and Tor, then led them away. They both turned to wave at the Skipper and crew as they reached the end of the jetty.

Stevenson shook his head again, 'Well, we'd better get you debriefed, Skipper. Let's pop up to my office, shall we?'

The Skipper looked up at Arthur and Svein, both leaning against the bulwark. He gave a mighty wink and turned, saying, 'Aye aye, sir!'

THE END

If you enjoyed this book

If you enjoyed this book then, first of all, thank you! I'd be hugely grateful if you could give me a review on Amazon so I can introduce more people to the world of The Skipper. The link is: https://www.amazon.com/review/create-review?asin=B0BQLX2FXS

If you'd like to know more about the series, writing, offers, and the world of The Skipper, then please subscribe to my monthly newsletter using the link below. You will receive a free ebook, exclusive to subscribers to my newsletter. I ask only for your first name and email address to add you to the mailing list. We do not collect data to pass on, and you can unsubscribe at any time; your details will then be completely removed from our server within thirty days.

For your exclusive free novella
'The Skipper's First War'
please go to:

https://subscribepage.io/zMC2Ri

The following pages are an introduction to the next book in The Skipper series: 'The Skipper Goes West' - I hope you enjoy reading the books in this series as much as I do writing them!

The Skipper Goes West - Chapter One

54° 16' 59" N, 00° 23' 25" W

(London and Scarborough)

Friday 14th August 1940

Euston Station smelled of cigarettes, coal and damp ashes. The iron grid work supporting the roof frequently disappeared in clouds of grey steam as locomotives moved or were raising steam. The noise of conversations, yelling and guard's whistles was a constant background.

Two men in trilby hats and dark suits leaned against a pillar, smoking. They watched a porter wheeling a black metal box on a barrow. The younger of the two tensed as two men ran up to the porter, laughing. The porter turned, looking shocked as they spoke to him. He then smiled and turned around, pushing his load toward the Liverpool train.

The dark suits glanced at each other and walked forward, then stopped. Four capable looking men had disembarked from the train and stood across their path. They had their hands inside their jackets and held their gaze on the dark suits.

A dark-haired man with a clipped moustache stepped between the four men and approached. He wore a grey suit and homburg hat and he was holding his jacket open to reveal a Webley service pistol on a lanyard.

'Gentlemen, we've cleared the area behind you in case we need to use violence, but I'd rather we didn't have to. Please put your weapons on the floor in front of you.'

He glanced left, then right as his men formed a half circle, two on each side.

The dark suits carefully placed a pistol and a nasty-looking dagger on the grimy floor. The man in the homburg smiled as one of his men scooped up the weapons and patted the clothing of the two prisoners.

'Good show. Now if you'll come this way, we'll find some privacy for a chat. Oh Lord! My manners. Please call me Captain McDonald.'

The Skipper and Arthur leaned against the settee back in the Mariner's Rest Inn. They had taken a table next to a window, which Gerald had left open to counter the sultry heat. Before each man was a pint of Sturdy Mariner: the best pint of bitter in Yorkshire, and therefore the world.

Arthur watched dust motes dancing in a bar of sunlight which lanced through the window. He gave a wry smile: it was like watching miniscule creatures going about their lives, being buffeted by tremendous forces beyond their control, a nice metaphor for wartime. A small gust of summer breeze or a passing person made them swirl and dance, tiny stars in the sunbeam. Looking over at his friend and employer, he remembered it was the Skipper who protected himself and the rest of the crew from at least some forces affecting their lives. His Majesty's Trawler White Nab, on which Arthur served as First Mate, was a happy and very effective ship. They were nominally part of the Royal Naval Patrol Service, escorting convoys and carrying out anti-Submarine patrols, but they also served as a support vessel for the Secret Intelligence Service, covertly dropping or collecting assets as required.

The Skipper took a long draught of his beer and smiled. 'This is the life, Arthur.'

'It is Skipper, it certainly is.'

As they spoke, two soldiers noisily arrived and leaned against the bar. The Skipper's eyes narrowed, but he said nothing. They resumed their chat, ignoring the extra volume until the words, 'This beer is like cat's pee!' rang out.

The Skipper slowly rose and strolled to the bar. Gerald, the landlord of the inn and the man who brewed the beer, reached behind him toward a cricket trophy board. He carefully removed the bat, which appeared solidly secured, but was in fact a secret weapon against loutish behaviour.

As the Skipper neared the two men, they looked up and, seeing the golden stripes on his RNR officer's jacket, fell silent.

'Gentlemen. The regulars here are enjoying a restful afternoon drinking what is an excellent pint of best bitter. So may I suggest you keep your voices down, your comments to yourself or simply bugger off?'

The two men stood at attention, apologising profusely with lots of 'sir' thrown in. The Skipper looked disappointed as they drained their glasses and left, still apologising. Gerald slid the cricket bat, 'Excalibur' to the locals, back onto its mount and grinned at the Skipper.

'There's no fun for you anymore Skipper, not since you got all that string on your arms!'

'I know, Gerald, I'll have to go into nets to practise at this rate.' The Skipper returned to his table.

A voice from the door made the Skipper and Arthur turn abruptly.

'A pint for me please Gerald and another for these two reprobates!'

Captain Horace McDonald paid for the drinks and strolled over to their table. The Skipper and Arthur both rose as he approached.

'I understand that many Yorkshire folk have Scandinavian blood in them. I suppose this explains your conquering spirit and predeliction for pillage?'

Arthur and the Skipper laughed, shaking his hand.

'What brings you to these parts, sir?' the Skipper asked.

'Well, I really wanted a quick chat with you chaps but I hear the enemy shot you up a little?'

'Nothing major sir, our very first convoy escort after refitting and a blessed e-boat peppered us in the dark. Usual tactic: sit inshore of the swept channel, wait until we pass, then start up and play havoc! The funnel and flying bridge suffered some damage and one boat got wrecked, but he only got one pass. We started responding with the twelve-pounder and an old V class destroyer got into him, so he fled. The yard couldn't get her in for a week, but the work will only take two or three days. Is that any use?'

'Definitely Skipper. If we can find somewhere quiet after our pint, I'll tell you what I can.'

Arthur stood. 'Gerald has a function room upstairs, sir. Should I ask if we can use it?'

'First rate, we'll sample the beer and speak at the same time.' McDonald smiled.

A few minutes later, they sat in the centre of the empty room, facing the door, which McDonald had left slightly ajar.

'Can't afford ears against doors, I'm afraid. Right chaps; first some background information. This is beyond top secret for all sorts of reasons, so we have to take incredible precautions during this job. A very senior scientist, Sir Henry Tizard, is currently in the United States on a mission to promote scientific collaboration between the US and ourselves during this war. It is sensitive, because as you know, the US is currently neutral. In fact, there are many over there who are against entering the war at all. Despite that, our Prime Minister believes, at least hopes, that they ultimately will ally themselves with Great Britain and declare war on the Nazis. The Tizard mission will offer mutual technology exchange and hopes to tap into the enormous manufacturing capacity which the Americans possess. Sir Henry flew ahead and his team followed a few days ago with some example technology. Questions?' His eyes flicked between them.

The Skipper and Arthur shook their heads.

McDonald nodded, 'Capital. Anyway, a few days ago, we captured two enemy agents in London. Someone in our sister organisation, the Security Service, got wind of a network of agents being established over here and we helped with surveillance. It turns out, from what we learned, this network was being built to either infiltrate the mission, or to steal the example technology which is being taken over there. We would never have discovered the network had more time been available for the enemy to prepare, but their haste led to errors and we caught them red-handed, trying to filch the box of goodies being sent to show the Americans. In reality, it was some machinery parts and radio valves in the box, the real one went by another route.'

The Skipper frowned. 'Do you know how the Nazis found out about the mission? They would keep it under wraps, I would have thought?'

'It was a low-level clerk at the Air Ministry with gambling debts. The Security Service tries to filter them out, but I'm afraid that every so often, someone gets hooked, one way or another. Anyway, we now know the Nazis are aware of Tizard's mission, but we don't believe they are aware of the technology under discussion. Either way, they want to throw a spanner in the works. Now here's the problem. There's an extra piece of equipment the team wants to take over. We're not keen on them taking it by train and ship this time, so we want to take it to them using a trusted party with the means to cross the Atlantic quietly. I expect you can see where this is going, but it's also why we're involved beyond our remit of assisting with surveillance. This mission involves getting goods into a neutral state's territory, which hostile agents would dearly love to intercept. Major scope for an international incident you might say. So who's up for a trip to the United States?'

The Skipper smiled, 'Of course, sir. They don't drink best bitter over there, so we shall suffer for the cause, but we'll get this thingummy delivered.'

McDonald grinned, 'Good show, oh and no piracy this time, Skipper!' The Skipper rolled his eyes and McDonald continued, 'Finally, gentlemen, this caper is code named "Operation Jasper."'

Acknowledgements

This book would not be here without these people:

My wife, Christina for, well, everything really; but mostly for having faith in me,

Joanna Penn for her amazing website and podcast,

Gary and Sarah Andrews for advice, and being amazing,

Helen Underdown for advice and making me smile (in a good way),

Jasper, Reuben and Bowie for lighting up my world,

Vicky Henderson for being herself, and for giving me moral support,

The rest of my family and friends who all supported me during the first part of my writing journey whether they realise it or not,

My Beta Readers, who provided really useful feedback; and

The members of Ranskill Book Club, advanced review readers.

THANK YOU ALL!

Printed in Great Britain
by Amazon

19996337R00210